HIS WAGES OF WAR

Laughing, Taber picked Raven up and tossed her over his shoulder like a sack of potatoes. "Come, lass, be a good sport. You can consider a roll in the hay part of the fringe benefits of the job."

He carried her up the ladder to the loft, ignoring her screams and kicks. Tossing her down on a bed of straw, he stood above her, a smug look on his face. The British were fools, he thought. It wasn't right sending a young, beautiful girl like this to do their dirty work.

"Do you want to remove your clothes, or shall I do it for you?"

Raven struggled to sit up, backing away as she did. "This has gone far enough. I don't know who you think I am, but I was not expected here. This is all a mistake . . ."

"A mistake? No, I dinna' think so, lass," he said as he began to unbutton her riding jacket. He meant to take his vengeance against the hated British, but somehow, the aroma of heather and grass tantalized his senses and made him forget why he had wanted to humiliate this gorgeous young woman. All he could think of as he stared into the blue eyes beneath black fringed lashes was that he was going to possess her—and take his time about it, too . . .

MORE BLAZING ROMANCES
From Zebra Books

FRONTIER FLAME (1965, $3.95)
by Rochelle Wayne

When her cousin deserted the army, spirited Suzanne Donovan knew that she had to go and get him back. But once the luscious blonde confronted towering Major Blade Landon, she wished she'd never left home. The lean, muscled officer seemed as wild as the land — and made her think only of the rapture his touch could bring!

ARIZONA TEMPTRESS (1785, $3.95)
by Bobbi Smith

Rick Peralta found the freedom he craved only in his disguise as El Cazador. Then he saw the alluring Jennie mcCaine among his compadres and swore she'd belong just to him. When he left his lawless life, he'd leave the enticing captive behind . . . but until then the hot-blooded Rick would have all of his needs fulfilled by his provocative ARIZONA TEMPTRESS.

PRAIRIE EMBRACE (2035, $3.95)
by F. Rosanne Bittner

Katie Russell was shocked by her passionate reaction to her bronze-skinned, jet-haired Indian captor. The gorgeous pioneer reminded herself that he was a savage heathen and beneath her regard, but deep inside she knew she longed to yield to the ecstasy of his PRAIRIE EMBRACE.

PIRATE'S CONQUEST (2036, $3.95)
by Mary Martin

Starlin Cambridge always scoffed that the ruthless pirate Scorpio would never capture her sleek, treasure-laden ship. But one day, the notorious outlaw overtook her vessel—and kidnapped its raven-haired owner. Furious that the muscular marauder has taken her freedom, Starlin is shocked when she longs for him to take her innocence as well!

VELVET DECEPTION
Casey Stuart

ZEBRA BOOKS
KENSINGTON PUBLISHING CORP.

ZEBRA BOOKS

are published by

Kensington Publishing Corp.
475 Park Avenue South
New York, NY 10016

First printing: July 1987

Printed in the United States of America

This book is dedicated to Leslie Gelbman for her belief in me, and for her patience;

For Adele Leone for the great things she is going to do for me in the future;

For Kathe Robins for always making me feel ten feet tall with her wonderful reviews;

For the readers who have been so kind and enthusiastic about my books;

And as always, for my wonderful family for their support and love, and especially for Kyle, the newest member of the family.

If I had never heard the name of thy sorrow and
    strength devine,
Or felt in my pulses the flame of fire they had
    caught from thine;
I would know by this rapture alone which
    sweeps through me now like a flood,
That the Irish skies were my own, and my
    blood was the Irish blood.

—Mary Blake

*When Eire first rose from the
dark-swelling flood,
God blessed the green island,
and saw it was good . . .*
William Drennan, "Eire"

Chapter One

Spring, 1811

The ship, *Inisfail*, sailed into Dangannon
Cove, an inlet known only to smugglers and
outlaws seeking sanctuary. Taber O'Flynn
stood on the deck, his dark eyes surveying the
deserted shoreline. The cove was lonely and
austere, the silence broken only by the cry of
gulls in search of food. An eerie mist rolled
over the water as the ship moved up the
twisting channel, adding to the enchantment
of the spot.

Ireland, he sighed. When he had been taken
away by the British seven months ago, he never
thought to see its beauty again. But he had

escaped their gallows and, like the proverbial cat, had landed on his feet again. From Newgate prison to the Courts of Napoleon, he smiled to himself smugly. It had taken most of the money his family had saved in a French bank to buy this ship, and then Napoleon, who had been promising for years to emancipate the Irish people from the British, had agreed to outfit him with a cargo of guns and ammunition for distribution to the Brotherhood. Now when the French forces came, the Irish people would be ready to fight for their freedom. He just wished he didn't have doubts that Napoleon would keep his word this time.

The creak of the capstan broke into Taber's thoughts. He stared up at the white sails as the seaman secured them. He had been lucky to find such a good crew. Most of them were Irishmen who were eager to return home to see their loved ones. A few of them had been soldiers in Napoleon's army, but had some experience at sea.

"Captain, will you be going ashore right away?" George Smythe, the first mate, asked.

"Aye, Patrick Casey and Fergus O'Brien are supposed to be waiting with some horses at O'Hara's cottage."

"I heard O'Hara took a wife," Smythe said, laughing.

"No," Taber said, disbelieving. "When did that happen?"

"A few months ago. I've heard tell she's more interested in his property than in O'Hara."

Taber laughed. "I'd believe that. O'Hara has been a grizzly old bachelor for too long."

Patrick Casey could have attested to that fact. He hadn't been at O'Hara's for more than an hour before the new wife was trying to seduce him. Patrick never hesitated enjoying a pretty woman, married or not, but he knew better than to cuckold the O'Hara. Dangannon Cove was part of his property and it was essential to have the use of the cove for getting guns to the Brotherhood. To Patrick's consternation, Fergus O'Brien found it humorous and even had the gall to ask O'Hara to show him around the place, leaving him to fend for himself against the amorous woman.

By the time Taber arrived, Patrick's nerves were drawn taut. After warmly greeting Taber, he insisted they immediately be on their way. As they rode away from the cottage, Patrick turned in his saddle and looked back to be sure the woman wasn't following them.

"What was that all about?" Taber asked.

"Jesus, man, I dinna' think you'd ever get here. Do you have any idea what I've been through? That woman was all over me, and her so beautiful. I tell you, the first thing I'm going to do when we reach O'Neill Street is to find me a stiff drink and a beautiful woman." He shot Taber a devilish smile. "Maybe not in that order, mind you."

"Ah, Patrick, nothing ever changes with you."

"It's a curse, I tell you. Women just canna' leave me alone."

Taber and Fergus laughed. "How about you, Fergus? Have you married Maureen Clancy yet?"

"No," Fergus answered, his face getting red. "I've got me sights on someone else. Soon as I make something of meself she says she'll marry me."

"I wish you luck, Fergus," Patrick said, laughing. "I feel damned lucky if I have enough money to buy a whiskey. Now if I could just find a woman who would take care of me . . ."

"You're not going to find one crazy enough to do that," Taber laughed. "Come on you two, let's ride. I want to get to Blackmoor House before dark."

Raven McClennon silently stared out of the coach window. The countryside seemed bathed in softness, awash in a lovely green blur as the dawn arrived. The air seemed different in Ireland, she thought. It was cleaner, fresher, but there was still the dampness. She pressed her chilled hands against the warmth of her body beneath her sable-lined cloak, wishing the journey would come to an end.

The sun had barely lit the sky before her uncle, Lord Charles Montgomery, and Lord Walter Denseley resumed their discussion about the Irish Rebels. She solemnly wished she had been able to stay with a cousin in England, but being without parents didn't give her any say in the matter.

Raven stifled a yawn and turned back to stare out over the Irish countryside. The ocean mist gave the atmosphere a soft, tranquil setting, yet according to her uncle, it was anything but tranquil. As a powerful leader of the British Tory administration, her uncle had been sent to Ireland to put down the Insurgents and break the spirit of Ireland so thoroughly that they would stop their resistance.

What was so terrible about wanting to be independent? she wondered silently. She had learned early in life that her own struggle for independence had been the cause of her being shifted from one relative to another after her parents had been killed. It had always been a puzzle to her why no one wanted to take in the daughter of Anne and Evan McClennon. Her mother had always told her she had relatives all over England, but she never stayed with one more than a few months. When she got older she learned that her beautiful mother had defied her family to marry the handsome Scotsman, Evan McClennon, Earl of Lamond.

Even though McClennon was rich with land, the Montgomerys never considered him good enough to marry into their family.

Raven stared at her aunt slumped asleep in the corner. For some reason, unknown to her, her aunt hated her and took great pleasure in making her life miserable. If it wasn't for a few kind words from her uncle, she would have gone crazy by now. And on top of everything else, her aunt insisted on introducing her as Lady Montgomery, knowing very well how proud she was of her Scottish title. Well, they could all go to the devil. She had been born into the world the daughter of a Scottish Lord and an English Lady and she wasn't going to let anyone take her heritage away.

At the mention of Taber O'Flynn, Raven's attention was drawn back to her uncle's conversation. Taber O'Flynn, the young Irish Rebel who preached treason—so her uncle said—had recently escaped the gallows at Newgate with a beautiful young English girl. Some thought he had fled to America with the girl, but others were sure he would return to Ireland to lead the United Irishmen. And the strange thing was, no one seemed to know what he looked like. Even the guards at Newgate couldn't put a face to the elusive Taber O'Flynn. All they were sure of was that he had been there.

Taber O'Flynn, she repeated to herself. The

man whose fame and renown were talked about through the provinces of Ireland. Now his escape from Newgate was the mystery everyone talked about. To her uncle's disbelief, O'Flynn was becoming a folk hero, even in some sections of England. Raven smiled as she remembered some of the stories she had heard about him. They say he could cast a spell on a pretty girl with a smile. Perhaps she would meet this Taber O'Flynn. That would certainly liven up her dull existence. She almost laughed aloud as she pictured herself having tea with the famous Irish Rebel while her uncle searched the countryside for him.

"If he's in Ireland he won't escape me," Lord Denseley said with assurance as he put a pinch of snuff to his nostril and inhaled. "This time he'll be hung, then drawn and quartered. He's an evil man and God Himself will see to his punishment."

Raven spoke for the first time, unable to contain herself any longer. "Are you sure God believes in hanging?"

Aunt Caroline stirred from her nap and rubbed her eyes. "Is something wrong?" she asked, staring into the red face of Lord Denseley.

"I'm afraid Raven has just shocked Walter," he laughed. "What you have to realize, Walter, is no one would be punished for their sins if Raven were to pass judgment. She is too kindhearted," he said, patting her hand.

"If she knew the crimes of this horrendous Insurrectionist, she wouldn't be so quick to defend the murderer." Lord Denseley leaned forward, his face only inches from Raven. "What your young niece needs is a husband with a firm hand."

"That is exactly what she needs," Aunt Caroline chimed in, now wide awake. "I've been telling Charles that all along. The girl will be eighteen in two months and should have been betrothed long before now."

"It has been a trifle difficult getting the girl settled when we have been traveling these past few months," Charles Montgomery answered irritably.

"There are many bachelors among the English gentry here in Ireland," Denseley explained. "I myself may be interested in offering for her."

Raven stared at the man she had come to despise, knowing his penchant for cruelty. He reminded her of a lean gray wolf waiting to pounce on its prey. She leaned forward, her blue eyes smoldering angrily. "When I am ready to take a husband, I will choose my own."

"Oh," her aunt swooned. "What are we to do with her, Charles? I can't take much more of this," she said, rapidly fanning herself. "She will be the death of me . . . just like her mother . . . stubborn and inconsiderate. Well, she's your responsibility. You must do something."

"The trip is wearing on all of us," Charles stated. "I suggest we save any further discussion on this matter until another time."

Raven was relieved when everyone fell silent and she was again allowed to watch the scenery in peace. The scent of salt air and fish became stronger as they approached the coast of the Iveragh Peninsula in County Cork. She rubbed her stiff neck, longing for a warm bath and a change of clothes.

Caroline stared at Raven with abhorrence in her eyes. It wasn't fair, she thought. She shouldn't have to be reminded of Anne Montgomery every time she looked at the girl with her pale blue eyes and raven black hair. Maybe it was fate, she smiled evilly. Anne Montgomery had ruined her life, but now her beloved daughter had been given over to her care.

Raven tried to ignore her aunt's hateful looks. Suddenly her attention was drawn to three riders galloping across the green hills to their right. She watched one of them, fascinated by the dark horseman and the beautiful black horse he rode. It was as if man and beast were one, moving in fluid motion, free as the wind that whipped his dark cape back from his shoulders.

"That's him," Lord Denseley suddenly shouted. "That arrogant bastard!"

Raven was shoved aside as her uncle and Lord Denseley strained to see the rider. She barely had a view as the riders topped the hill and stopped.

"How do you know it's him?" her uncle growled. "I thought no one knew exactly what he looked like."

"Well, they don't," Denseley answered nervously, "but I'm sure that's him. Who else would be so arrogant?"

"Who else indeed," Montgomery snorted. "Only half of Ireland."

"Well, maybe it isn't him, but I swear, if he's in this area I'll get him."

The rider Raven had been watching raised his hat in mock salute as his great black stallion pawed the air. What a magnificent sight, she thought breathlessly.

"If we can arrest this Taber O'Flynn and make an example of him by cutting his head off and placing it on a post for all to see, then maybe these Irish hooligans will know we mean business."

At the black look Montgomery sent him, Denseley knew he'd spoken improperly in front of the ladies. "Please forgive me. I forgot ladies were present."

What a disgusting excuse for a man, Raven thought silently. If Taber O'Flynn was all she'd heard, he'd make a fool of Lord Walter Denseley, and she'd love to be there to see it.

"So that's our latest adversary," Patrick said gravely. "I hear he's a clever one."

"Aye, his reputation preceded him for sure. We will have to be very careful with Lord Montgomery. I dinna' want to be returning to Newgate anytime soon," Taber said.

"I am going to be working for the man," Fergus announced. "He needed someone to handle correspondence, so Peter suggested me."

"That should be a help," Taber said. "Keep your eyes and ears open all the time."

"Aye, you can depend on me, Taber."

"Did you see the beautiful young lady watching out the window?" Patrick asked.

"Aye, I saw her. Looks like Lord Montgomery has a penchant for young ladies," Taber laughed. "Come on, I'm looking forward to some of cousin Edward's fine Irish whiskey," he said as he urged his horse to a full gallop.

The carriage slowly climbed the steep hill to a large stone dwelling that overlooked the city. The house was very impressive, Raven thought as she stared out the window.

"What do you think of Riverside House?" Lord Denseley asked, breaking into her thoughts. "It was once the home of the O'Flynn's."

Raven's head snapped around to look at him. "The O'Flynns? Do you mean Taber O'Flynn?"

"One and the same," Lord Denseley laughed. "It was confiscated from his family about fifteen years ago."

"Why?" Raven asked, ignoring her aunt's clucking tongue.

"It's quite simple, my dear. They were Insurgents. The O'Flynn family hasn't been loyal to the Crown for centuries."

"I can understand why," she mumbled to herself.

The carriage finally came to a halt in front of the steep stone stairs. Raven took the hand offered her and stiffly climbed from the carriage. Her legs felt like jelly as she stood holding the carriage door for support.

"Come along, Raven. If you stand about like a dolt the servants will know you're addle-brained," her aunt warned.

Raven bit back a reply and silently followed her aunt into the house, where the staff of Irish servants waited for instructions.

"We are exhausted," her aunt announced. "I hope you have food and rooms ready. Raven, I suggest you rest now. In two hours your uncle and I want to talk with you about your future."

"Caroline, I don't think that's necessary . . ."

"Please, Charles, not in front of the servants," Caroline admonished. "Go on, Raven. Get some rest," her aunt ordered.

"I have a meeting with Peter Muldane. I don't know when I'll be back," Lord Montgomery announced irritably.

Raven followed the pretty young red-haired maid, who said her name was Molly, to a second-floor bedroom. The windows had been opened and the smell of salt air perfumed the room. Raven leaned her head against the window casing and stared out over the city.

"Tis breathtaking, isn't it?" the maid asked as she unpacked Raven's bags.

"Aye, it is."

"When the fog lifts you can see forever."

"Can you see the future?" Raven asked sadly.

"The future?" the girl asked. "I've heard tell that you have to look into your heart to see the future. There, your clothes are all put away. Is there anything else I can be doing for you?"

"No, that will be all. Thank you, Molly," Raven said, turning back to the window as the girl left. There was something about the city below that seemed to draw her. The mists, ignited by the morning sun, rose above the city, exposing houses stacked on terraced hills. It was a beautiful sight and one she planned to explore as soon as possible.

Taber O'Flynn sat on the rocks and watched the sea lap against the shore. This was his favorite time of day, early morning, before the evils of the world had a chance to show themselves. The responsibilities on his shoulders sometimes closed in on him, but out here where the sea air was purifying, he could think. He ran a hand through his wavy black hair, a frown covering his handsome face. Right now he didn't know if he wanted to think. He was staying with Tomas Fitzgerald, a cousin and old family friend. At Tomas's suggestion, he was posing as Lord Devin Fitzgerald, a cousin who had lived most of his life in France until he had been lost at sea a few years ago. At least this cover gave him freedom to move about without anyone questioning him.

Taber uncurled his tall frame from the rock and sauntered toward the sea. He had been in Ireland only a week, and already he had received a message from Napoleon that he would have to postpone helping the Irish since his fight with the British was uppermost in his mind at the moment. To add to his troubles, Lord Charles Montgomery and his entourage were settled in at Riverside House, and he had no doubt that the man would be a thorn in his side. He knew only too well the Englishman's reputation. Well, at least Peter Muldane had already infiltrated the Montgomerys' residence with good people, so perhaps they could keep a step ahead of the Englishman.

Taber picked up a rock and skimmed it across the sea. It was the same old thing; the British sending men to keep the Irish in their place, and Napoleon making promises to help that he never kept. Tomorrow night he would have to meet with the other members of the Brotherhood and explain Napoleon's latest inaction. They would have to come up with a plan without Napoleon—a plan to free the Irish people. He stared out across the sea. Maybe it would be the plan that would finally free his people after hundreds of years of British tyranny.

Two days after they had arrived at Riverside House, Caroline Montgomery had taken to her bed, claiming the Irish weather was making her sick. Since Caroline insisted that her niece attend her, Raven spent every day sitting in the dark room, trying not to gag on the acrid scent of medicine and herbs that Caroline insisted upon using. It was difficult for Raven to understand how anything could help her aunt when she closed herself up in this airless room, but she kept her silence and did her aunt's bidding, agreeing that Charles should never have brought them to this godforsaken place.

A small ray of sunlight escaped the closed curtains and slipped along the floor toward Raven's feet. She stared at it, wishing that she could be outside exploring as she had planned. She stood up and went to the covered window. Barely touching the curtain, she peered out at the sun-dappled river below. She stood silently staring out the window at the blue sky with its fragments of white cotton clouds. Feeling as if she could no longer endure this dark room and her nagging aunt, she turned and stared at the velvet coverings around her aunt's bed. There was no sound from the bed. Perhaps just a walk in the garden, she thought. Raven moved silently across the room, pulled back the velvet hangings that covered the bed, and saw that her aunt was asleep. A moment of indecision ruined her plans. Caroline opened her eyes and stared back at Raven.

"What are you doing there, girl? Haven't you better things to do than stare at a sick person?"

Raven felt like telling her she did, but she bit back her words. "I was only checking on you, Aunt Caroline."

"Go get the girl Molly and tell her to prepare a bath for me. I am feeling much better and will take dinner downstairs with Charles this evening."

Raven's spirits lifted. She was going to be free again. "I'm glad you're feeling better," she said honestly. "I'll find Molly right away."

"Tell that girl the water better be hot," her aunt ordered. "I will not tolerate lukewarm water. And Raven, do not leave the house. I will want you to supervise cleaning and airing my room."

"But Aunt Caroline, we have servants to do that."

Caroline glared at Raven. "If it weren't for my generosity you'd be on the streets now, girl. You best remember, there isn't anyone else in the Montgomery family who will have you. It wouldn't take a second for me to decide to put you out on the streets so you can be a slut like your mother."

"My mother wasn't a slut," Raven said between gritted teeth.

"Get out of my sight, you worthless ingrate. Tell that girl to hurry with my water."

Raven practically ran down the hall. A few more months and she would have her inheritance, then she could do what she wanted and see whom she wanted. She would no longer be at the beck and call of her hateful aunt.

Raven spent the next day at her aunt's side, serving tea and trying to be polite to the friends that came upon hearing that Caroline Montgomery was accepting visitors. And still she hadn't been able to escape the confines of Riverside House.

One evening when Raven came down to dinner, she was relieved to see her uncle and aunt in such a jovial mood. She silently took a seat at the table, hoping to avoid her aunt's disapproving comments.

"If we could just get him, we'll quickly put an end to these Rebels," Charles Montgomery was telling his wife, "and then we could return to London."

"I pray that will be soon," Caroline said. "This weather could be the death of me."

Raven's curiosity got the better of her. "If you get who?" she asked, accepting the soup plate from Molly.

"Taber O'Flynn," her uncle answered. "One of my informants tells me that he thinks the Fitzgeralds of Blackmoor may have some knowledge of O'Flynn's whereabouts. Peter Muldane has assured me that the Fitzgeralds are loyal to the Crown, but he has promised to check out the rumor."

Raven stared at Molly as she poured the tea over the rim of her cup. "What is Blackmoor?" Raven asked, turning her attention back to her uncle.

"It's the residence of Lord Tomas Fitzgerald. I met the man the other day at Edgar Matthews's residence. He also introduced me to a cousin who is visiting for a few months. I believe Peter said the man's name was also Fitzgerald."

"Just think, you may be able to arrest this O'Flynn tonight and we could be on our way back to London by the end of the week."

"I'm sorry to disappoint you, my dear, but it won't be like that. No matter what Peter finds, I don't plan to make a move right away. I thought perhaps I'd place someone on Fitzgerald's staff just to be sure they are not involved."

"Oh, that's very clever, Charles," Caroline exclaimed.

"This Peter Muldane seems to be a good man. I believe he wants the riff-raff out of Ireland as much as we do. He's also done a very admirable job of getting us settled and staffing Riverside House."

"I do wish I had had a hand in selecting the staff," Caroline said. "They leave a lot to be desired."

"This is not London, my dear. We'll have to make do with what Ireland has to offer."

"Well, I'll just have to see that they are trained correctly." She sniffed. "I will not have them embarrassing me."

"I have no doubt that you will take care of that, my dear."

*　　*　　*

In the black of the night, lookouts stood at their posts at every approach to the abandoned stable on Mobry Road. Only when the sound of a whistle, imitating a bird, was heard did small groups of men begin to move forward. Heavy burlap had been hung over the windows to keep the lanterns from showing outside. Everyone spoke in low, controlled tones, waiting for Taber O'Flynn to start the meeting.

"Good evening, my friends," Taber began, his tallness all the more apparent in the closeness of the stable. His dark eyes surveyed the men gathered in the stable.

"Welcome home, Taber," a man in the back row greeted.

"Thank you, Robert. 'Tis good to be here in body, not just spirit."

This brought a round of laughter as everyone knew about Taber's narrow escape from the gallows in London.

"We heard you had a lass with you when you escaped, Taber."

"Aye, a lovely lass," Taber answered.

"What did you do with her?" another voice asked good-naturedly.

"She chose to go to America, though I canna' imagine why," Taber laughed. "Shall we get down to business, my friends?" Taber suggested, his voice reaching every corner of the stable. "Patrick Casey received a message while he was in Cobh that Napoleon canna' come to our aid at this time."

"We learned long ago not to depend on Bonaparte," an old gentleman stated. *"Sinn Fe'in,"* he said in a tired voice, and others repeated his words.

"Aye, *ourselves alone,"* Taber translated the Gaelic words. "Sean O'Sullivan is holding a meeting in Dublin tonight to set up a plan to help Seamus Murphy and Oliver Niels escape from their chains in the Provost's prison. God willing they are successful before those fine men feel the hangman's noose."

"Aye, God willing," all the voices echoed as one.

"'Tis time for the Hawk to reappear," someone shouted from the back. Everyone took up chorus agreeing.

"Aye, I agree," he said, holding up his hands to quiet the conversations that suddenly broke out all around the room. "'Tis the time to confuse the British with small matters. I have a cargo of guns and ammunition on my ship just waiting to be distributed to the men of the Brotherhood. I need several of you to travel to Tipperary, Limerick, and Kilkenny to inform the Brotherhood in those counties that the guns will be transported soon."

"What good will guns do us, Taber? You know if we're caught with them we'll be hung."

Taber snorted. "How long are we going to

be held in the bloody grip of arrogance? No crime a man commits in behalf of his freedom can be as great as the crimes committed by those who deny his freedom."

"Admirable words, Taber, but you know better than any of us the innocent are always the ones to suffer."

"Aye, but there is no way to end the suffering if we don't stand together," Taber shouted. "The Irish people are broken, shorn of the will to protest. The British are in control because of the apathy of our own people. They say we canna' bear weapons, so we don't; they say we canna' educate our children, so we don't; they say we canna' own land, so we don't! My God, people, think about it! We have been stripped of our manhood, our dreams have been destroyed, our fine young people emigrate to other countries. When are we going to put a stop to it? The British fear us as much as they hate us, and as long as a single Irishman continues to be restless, as long as a few men like us meet in a room like this, their Empire is never entirely secure. We may not see Ireland's freedom in our time, but we have to fight so a future generation will see it. Too many great men have died for this cause for us to give up. Think of Wolfe Tone, Sir Edward Fitzgerald, and my father, Sean O'Flynn. No, my friends, we can never give up! Not for their memory nor for ourselves, or the future generations of Ireland!"

Suddenly the crowd in the room came to life. "We are with you, Taber," was the shout around the room.

"We will run the British back to England," another shouted.

"I'm all for getting rid of the British," another said. "But where will we hide these guns?" he asked in a trembling voice.

"I have a plan I think may work, but I will discuss it with you at a later time."

Suddenly there was conversation at the stable door and Patrick entered, pulling Molly Devlin along behind him.

"I'm sorry to interrupt, Taber, but I think you should hear what Molly has to say."

"Good evening, Molly," Taber smiled. There was a buzz of curiosity as Molly moved toward Taber O'Flynn, her green eyes wide with the awe of being so near her idol. She quickly curtsied, unsure how to act.

"Good evening, sir. As you know, I'm working at Riverside House, sir. Mr. Muldane arranged for Colin and I to be on the staff."

"Get on with it, girl," Patrick urged.

"Well, sir, I overheard Lord Montgomery telling his wife that he suspected Taber O'Flynn may be staying at Blackmoor House. He is planning to place a spy among the household staff."

Taber ran a hand through his dark curly

hair. "I knew he was clever, but I dinna' think he'd be on to me this soon. He must have an informant."

"Aye, sir, I'm sure he does," Molly agreed, "but fortunately, he doesn't know Mr. Muldane is one of us. He's trusting him to check out the rumor."

"Ah, that's good to hear. Peter should be able to put him off my track."

"Aye, sir, I imagine he can, but Lord Montgomery still plans to put a spy on the staff, no matter what Mr. Muldane learns. He's a very cautious man, he is."

"Why would he do that if Muldane tells him the Fitzgeralds know nothing?" Patrick asked.

"He's a very clever man, Patrick, and clever men dinna' trust anyone. Our man is in no hurry. He hopes to place a spy in our midst, and haul in a big catch when he makes his move."

"There could be an informer here among us tonight," someone shouted.

"Aye, that is always a possibility. Informers are the bane of our existence. Trust no one," Taber advised. "We best adjourn now. We'll meet again next week."

As the group headed out a few at a time, Taber turned his attention back to Molly Devlin. "I appreciate your information, Molly. 'Tis good to know I have a friend in the Montgomery household."

Molly flushed to the roots of her red hair. "I

would do anything for you, sir. Just ask."

"Well, first you can start by calling me Taber." He smiled, showing even white teeth.

"Sure you be meaning it?"

"Aye, I'd be meaning it. Now go on with you before someone sees you," he said, affectionately hugging the girl.

Molly left the presence of her hero feeling as if she were walking on top of the world, but then she passed Brenna O'Neill and quickly came down to earth. She had heard rumors that Brenna was Taber's lady friend, but she had hoped it wasn't true. Brenna came from a family just like hers, but all the O'Neills put on airs, and Brenna was better at it than any of them. What makes a woman who sleeps with half the men in town think she's better than anyone else? Molly wondered bitterly. Taber deserves a saint, not someone like Miss high and mighty.

"Hello, Taber, or should I say Lord Devin Fitzgerald."

Taber turned around, surprised as the feminine voice spoke from behind him. "Brenna, tis good to see you, but be careful what you say, lass. The trees have ears."

"Why have you not sought me out?" she asked, her dark lashes dropping over her gold eyes.

"I had planned to."

"Fergus told me you have been over a week," she stated, giving him a cool look.

"Aye, 'tis true, but it's busy I've been. You know what's involved here."

"I haven't seen you in nearly a year, Taber, so dinna' make lame excuses."

A grin spread over Taber's handsome face. "Ye haven't changed, Brenna, still the same quick bite."

"I'm sorry, Taber. It's just that I've missed you and had hoped you felt the same."

Taber pulled her into his arms. "Aye, I've missed you, lass. I must admit, those gold cat eyes of yours have crept into my thoughts often."

"I wonder you had time to think of me," she pouted. "I hear you had a fine English lady with you in prison."

"You would be meaning Alaina Deering. A lovely thing she was, but there was no romance involved. She was an innocent and I protected her."

"Protected her? Now that doesn't sound like the Taber O'Flynn that I know."

"Ah, now you hurt me, Brenna. It's an honorable man I am. I've never taken anything that wasn't offered."

Brenna smiled up at him. "No, I dinna' suppose you have. I dinna' come here to argue with you, Taber. I thought perhaps we could take a walk. We have much catching up to do."

"I would like to, Brenna, but I have some important business to take care of tonight. I promise I'll come by tomorrow."

"If you don't, Taber O'Flynn, I'll find myself a nice settled young man to take your place."

"Ah, I dinna' know I had a place," he laughed. "Go on with you, lass. I'll see you tomorrow."

Brenna had only walked a short distance when a man stepped from the shadows and blocked her way.

"Who is it?" she asked, her voice trembling.

"It's your beloved," Fergus O'Brien answered in a sarcastic tone.

"Oh God, Fergus, dinna' do that to me," Brenna said, holding her hand on her heart. "I thought you meant me harm."

"Why are you here?" he asked. "You swore to me it was over between you and O'Flynn. You said we'd be married one day."

"I told you when you could give me the things I wanted, then I'd marry you. In the meantime, I canna' help it if Taber still desires me. I will not sit around waiting for you to make something of yourself, Fergus."

Fergus grabbed her and roughly kissed her. "Damn you, Brenna O'Neill. You know I'm mad for you. I want you to promise to be faithful to me. One day I'll have money to give you things."

"Oh Fergus, you're more of a dreamer than I am," she laughed. "Kiss me again like that, and I'll think about what you said," she teased.

I would go where the children play;
For a dreamer lives forever,
And a thinker dies in a day.
William B. McBurney

Chapter Two

Tomas Fitzgerald was hoping Molly Devlin's information was wrong, but the following morning the son of one of the housekeepers came to say his mother was sick and a friend would be arriving later that morning to take her place for a few days.

Tomas found his cousin having breakfast. "Well, Taber—excuse me, *Devin*—it looks like Molly was right. One of my servants sent a message that she was sick and sending a replacement. What do you want me to do about it?"

"Nothing," Taber answered. "We'll turn the tables on Lord Montgomery. Since we know about this spy, we can easily convince her that Taber O'Flynn never came back to Ireland."

Tomas laughed. "You're brilliant."

"Not really. I'm just used to being cautious. Waiting to swing from the gallows makes you so."

"Aye, I'm sure it does. Please be careful. From what you've told me about this Montgomery fellow, I'd say he's rather clever."

Taber laughed. "Now admit it, cousin, life wouldn't be nearly as exciting if they sent an imbecile to hunt us down. Besides, I'm going to enjoy making a fool of Montgomery."

"I dinna' like the idea that the man has already connected the Fitzgeralds with Taber O'Flynn."

"Aye, I have to admit that bothers me too. We must have an informer among our group, and they were all so carefully chosen."

"Perhaps it would be better if Taber O'Flynn dropped out of sight for a while."

"I was thinking the same. At least until we've convinced Montgomery that the Fitzgeralds dinna' know his whereabouts. I suppose the guns will be just as safe staying aboard the ship. As soon as we've convinced Montgomery of our loyalty to the Crown, we'll get back to the business at hand."

"Cousin, I know you're fond of Brenna, but do you think she can be trusted? She is one of the few who knows both of your identities."

"Aye, I think so, but I'll watch her carefully." Taber looked at his pocket watch.

"Speaking of Brenna, I promised to pay her a visit today, and I dinna' care to have her angry at me. I'm going to saddle Nighthawk."

"Be careful using that horse's name out loud, cousin. It could add to Montgomery's suspicions."

"Aye, I suppose you're right," Taber laughed. "If our spy shows up, give her my regards. I'll be back in a few hours."

Raven woke to the bright sun shining in her windows. She stretched like a cat, then slowly climbed from the bed to look out the window. The mist was drifting over the hillside, helped by a west wind. A breath of a breeze touched her cheek, bringing with it the faint scent of the sea. It was a beautiful day for exploring. Perhaps this morning she would meet Taber O'Flynn, she smiled to herself.

Molly's brother, Colin, was the groom at the Riverside House stables. The red-haired young man was only a few years older than his sister, yet it seemed to Raven that he was mature beyond his years. He talked to her with ease as he showed her the excellent stock of horses stabled there for the Montgomery family use, but he wasn't prepared to have Raven choose Devil Lady, the most spirited horse of the lot.

"She hasn't been ridden in a while, m'lady. She threw the mistress that lived here before. They were going to destroy her, but Lord Townsend decided just to leave her behind."

"Well I'm glad he did. She has beautiful lines," Raven said, stroking the powerful horse. "All she needs is a good workout."

Reluctantly, Colin lifted the sidesaddle from the hook, thinking the girl was daft to want to ride such a horse, and her not even being Irish.

"Not a sidesaddle, Colin. I want a regular saddle."

"But m'lady—"

"Don't worry, Colin, I've been riding all my life."

Colin smiled. "Sure and that's been a long time."

"I need some directions, Colin."

"Where would you be going, lass?"

"Blackmoor House."

Colin stared at Raven. "Now why would you be wanting to go to Blackmoor House. Nothing there to see."

Raven had gotten the same response from Molly, but she wasn't going to be dissuaded. "I hear it's a beautiful place sitting high above the river and I'd like to see it. I'm just going to look at it from a distance."

There was a contemplative silence as Colin tried to decide if he should give her directions.

"Well?" Raven asked as she mounted the

restless horse and straightened her crimson riding habit around her legs.

"Ride down this road to a crumbling chapel, then ride east along the quay. You canna' miss the house. It's made of black rock."

"Thank you, Colin. I won't be too long."

Raven rode through the gates and over the cobblestone path at breakneck speed. Colin watched them disappear in a cloud of dust.

"His Lordship is going to kill me," he said, shaking his head.

For the first few minutes the mare tried having her way, but Raven fought to keep her under control. She leaned over the mare's neck, digging her knees in to hold on. "I'm the boss here, my Devil Lady, and the sooner you learn that, the quicker we will enjoy each other." The horse finally seemed to tire of fighting the reins and the expert rider on her back, and slowed to a decent trot.

"Good girl," Raven praised. "I knew you and I were going to be friends."

Raven raised her face to the sun, delighting in being away from her aunt and uncle for a while. The ruins of the old chapel appeared just a few minutes along her way. Slowing the mare, she took the dirt path east on the quay along the river until she reached the beach, where she kicked the horse to a gallop, enjoying the feel of the salt air on her face. She came to an abrupt halt as she spied the house on the hillside. It looked like a fortress overlooking the River Lee. She rode a little closer before dismounting and tying her horse to a bush.

After climbing a path that led from the beach up the steep hill, Raven found herself in a beautiful garden of ferns and yews. She held her breath as she stared behind her at the view of the sea beyond the river. The view was much like that of Riverside House, but not as much of the city was in view here. The sight was spectacular. Reminding herself why she was there, Raven crept past the stables toward the glass doors on the garden side of the house. She peered in, but there didn't seem to be anyone around so she moved to the next set of doors. She was so involved in her snooping that she didn't see the man rubbing his horse down in front of the stables.

"What are you doing there?" a voice asked sharply.

Raven glanced at the man rubbing down his horse, then lifted her skirt and started running. Before she reached the path back to the beach she was tackled from behind.

"Not so fast," the voice warned, flipping her over on her back. "What have we here?" he asked, stunned as he stared into eyes the color of the sky. As she struggled against him, her beautiful blue-black hair tumbled from beneath her hat. He had given the British more credit then to send someone who looked like her. She was certainly not your everyday serving girl. But no matter, he would enjoy having a little fun at their expense.

Raven was also stunned as she stared at her captor. He was powerfully built with shoulders that stretched against his leather jerkin. His black curly hair tumbled above intense midnight blue eyes, and his skin was a warm golden brown as though he'd spent a lot of time in the sun. Her eyes fastened on the cleft in his strong chin, and she was tempted to touch it. Suddenly she came to her senses. "How dare you! Let me up this instant! I am not accustomed to being manhandled by . . . by stable hands!"

"Are you accustomed to sneaking around other people's houses?"

"I was not sneaking around. I was . . . I was admiring the architecture."

Taber laughed. "Whatever the reason, I'm glad you're here. We've been expecting you. And I must admit, I was needing a little feminine company."

Raven's eyes widened. "How dare you. Let me go this instant!"

Taber wasn't listening to her. He stared in fascination at the girl, caught up in his own mixed emotions. He was filled with a strange sense of wanting to know what was behind those sad, but defiant blue eyes. "God, but you are beautiful,'' he exclaimed, cutting off her protests with a hungry kiss.

She struck him a hard blow on the face. Taber grabbed her wrist in an iron grip that sent pain up her arm. His eyes had grown cold and his cheek showed the dull red imprint of her hand.

"Let me warn you, my lovely, the next time you try that, I'll return it in good measure."

"How dare you!" she finally managed to get out. "Let me up this instant."

As suddenly as his anger had come, it had disappeared. "Lord Fitzgerald said you were to share the loft over the stable with me," he said, his blue eyes dark with laughter. "What a delightful time I shall have taming you."

Raven struggled to get up. "I have no idea what you're talking about. No one was expecting me. I was just riding along the beach and saw the house."

"Whatever, lass," he said, pulling her to her feet. "Come inside out of the sun. It will be more private."

"No!" Raven protested, struggling to pull out of his grip. "I'm not going anywhere with you."

Laughing, Taber picked her up and tossed her over his shoulder like a sack of potatoes. "Come, lass, be a good sport. You can consider a roll in the hay part of the fringe benefits of your job."

He carried her up the ladder to the loft, ignoring her screams and kicks. Tossing her down on a bed of straw, he stood above her, a smug look on his face. The British were fools, he thought. It wasn't right sending a young, beautiful girl like this to do their dirty work.

"Do you want to remove your clothes, or shall I do it for you?"

Raven struggled to sit up, backing away as she did. "This has gone far enough. I don't know who you think I am, but I was not expected here. This is all a mistake . . ."

"A mistake? No, I dinna' think so, lass," he said as he began to unbutton her riding jacket. His gaze lingered on her mouth, appreciating the full underlip. This act was meant to be revenge against the British, but somehow, the aroma of heather and grass tantalized his senses and made him forget why he had wanted to humiliate this beautiful young woman. All he could think of as he stared into the blue eyes beneath black fringed lashes was that he wanted her—he wanted to possess her.

Raven was in shock. She stared into his dark eyes as he slipped her jacket off. Her pulse was throbbing with an unsteady, erratic beat and she found it difficult to speak or even breathe properly. She reached out and gently touched the dimple in his chin. It wasn't until she felt his warm hand against the softness of her breast that she began to fight.

45

"Please, you must stop."

"I've just begun, lass. Stop fighting me."

His mouth captured hers, gently putting enough pressure against it to part her lips. With a sense of disbelief she felt the softness of his tongue enter her mouth. She melted against him, returning the kiss while her hands caressed the curling black hair at the back of his neck.

Taber O'Flynn drew in his breath, shocked by the sensations he felt as he stared into the heavy-lidded eyes of this girl. What the hell was the matter with him. He was supposed to be punishing her for spying on him. Instead he ached with pain for the need of her. But did he dare carry it any further. Again he touched her lips with his tongue, then nibbled at her full bottom lip until she moaned.

"Please, you must not . . ."

Fighting his desire for the girl, Taber finally released her. Raven fell back on the straw and stared at him dazed. "What is your name, lass?" he asked, hoping to break this spell he was under.

"Lady Raven McClennon," she murmured.

He laughed. "Of course. A fine lady who has taken to sneaking around other peoples houses and peeking in windows," he said.

Quickly Raven sat up and straightened her clothes. "I was not sneaking around. I was just curious. I didn't realize you Irish people were so inhospitable."

"Now, lass, I'd say I've been anything but inhospitable. And if we were honest here, surely *you English* have little right to question our hospitality."

"I am not English. I'm Scottish," Raven answered defensively. Taber stared at the girl, beginning to wonder if he could be wrong about her identity. Was it possible she had stumbled onto the place, he wondered. He reluctantly moved away from where she lay, still looking very desirable to him. He was silent as he tried to bring his emotions under control.

"Do you finally believe me?" she asked, a note of sarcasm in her voice as she rose and straightened her clothes.

"I'm sorry, lass. It seems I've made a mistake. I was expecting a new girl to help out on Lord Fitzgerald's staff."

"My word, I feel sorry for Lord Fitzgerald's staff if this is the way they are all greeted."

"Do you now?" He smiled. "I rather thought you were enjoying yourself."

Raven's eyes widened. "You are conceited beyond words," she said, outraged.

"Aye, I guess I am, but it's the fair sex that has made me so."

Raven turned to face him, all ready to hit him with a withering rebuttal, when she saw he was teasing her. "If I am free to go now, I will be on my way."

"Of course, lass," he said, flashing her a beautiful smile. "I'll walk you back to the beach. I wouldn't want some rascal to bother you."

"That really isn't necessary. I think the only rascal I have to fear is right here in this stable."

He laughed good-naturedly. "You say your name is Raven. That's an unusual name."

Raven brushed the straw and grass from her riding habit. "My father named me. He said my hair was the color of a raven's wing."

"Aye," Taber agreed, reaching out to draw a piece of straw from her hair. "It's beautiful, but then everything about you is beautiful."

Raven stood mesmerized as his hand moved from her hair to her cheek, then suddenly she pushed it away. "I must be on my way now. I'm sure you must have chores to perform," she said, glancing over his shoulder at the magnificent black horse. "That horse needs to be rubbed down."

"Not to worry, Lord Fitzgerald knows I much prefer kissing a pretty lass to rubbing down his horses," he teased, a slow grin covering his face. "I hope you'll come back again."

"I do not think so. I was hoping to meet Taber O'Flynn. I had heard rumors that he was staying here."

It suddenly became terrifyingly quiet. Raven

saw the almost imperceptible change in his face, the brief narrowing of his eyes, but then he smiled, masking whatever he had thought.

"Taber O'Flynn sailed for America when he escaped Newgate," he stated flatly. "No one around here has seen him since the British took him away."

"If you don't mind me saying so," Raven stated, her hands on her hips, "it seems strange to me that a stable boy should know so much about the great Taber O'Flynn."

"You say the *great* Taber O'Flynn. And how is it a Scottish lass should know so much about Taber O'Flynn?"

"What I know would surprise you, Mr. . . . I don't believe you told me your name." She smiled.

"No, I dinna', did I. It's Devin, lass, but now tell me, just what do you know about Mr. O'Flynn?"

"That is not a subject I care to discuss with the stable boy," she answered pompously.

Taber grabbed her wrists. "I've no desire to hurt you, lass, but I wouldn't hesitate giving you a sound thrashing. Now tell me what you know about Taber O'Flynn."

Raven stared into his dark eyes defiantly. "Unhand me or I'll show you a thing or two," she warned.

Taber had to laugh. He released her wrists, but not before kissing her quickly on the lips.

"For your own good, lass, don't mention Taber O'Flynn's name around here. It makes people very anxious."

"I do not know why. From what I hear, most people think he's a saint," Raven stated. "And I plan to meet him."

"Perhaps you will, lass, but you'll have to go to America to do it."

"I don't think so. I think he's right here in County Cork. For all I know you could be him."

Again the scowl covered his handsome face. "Are you daft, girl? I told you Taber O'Flynn sailed for America. Now go on with you before I decide not to be so easy on a trespasser."

"It was interesting," Raven said over her shoulder as she headed down the path to her waiting horse.

"Aye, it was that, lass," Taber spoke softly.

Raven raced her horse back to Riverside House, hoping she hadn't been missed. She smiled to herself as she remembered the stable boy's kisses. It had been exciting, yet she had to admit, she was relieved he had had the willpower to end it. She felt a flush of heat cover her face as she thought of what would have happened if he hadn't stopped. She was amazed and puzzled at her feelings for the Irishman. My word, maybe Aunt Caroline was right, she thought, a slow blush spreading over her face. Perhaps I am a wanton woman.

As she rode into the courtyard, she saw Colin waiting for her at the stable door.

"Your aunt has been looking for you, m'lady. Seems you have a visitor."

"Do you have any idea who it is, Colin?"

"Can't be sure, but it looks like Lord Denseley's carriage."

"Oh . . . oh, damn!" Raven sputtered. "She's at it again," Raven hissed as she dismounted.

"Is there anything I can do?"

"I wish there were, Colin, but I think I'm going to have to handle this myself."

Colin smiled as he watched Raven storm toward the house. He didn't have any doubt that Raven McClennon could handle her aunt or Lord Denseley as well as she handled that wild devil horse.

"Where have you been?" Aunt Caroline met Raven at the door.

"I was riding."

"You were riding?" her aunt repeated. "Lord Denseley has come for tea and he has patiently waited for you."

"No one told me he was coming for tea," Raven answered, peeling her riding gloves off. *Not that it would have made a difference,* she thought silently.

Caroline's eyes moved from Raven's tossled hair to her soiled gown. "You look like you have been wallowing in the dirt. Go to your room immediately and get cleaned up. Mind you now, don't be more than five minutes. Lord Denseley won't remain patient much longer."

Raven slowly climbed the stairs, wishing she had stayed in the garden at Blackmoor House. She remembered with devastating clarity how it felt to be held in Devin's arms and how his kiss had made her blood race through her veins.

Molly curtsied as Raven entered the bedroom. "Is everything all right, m'lady?"

Raven pulled her velvet jacket off and threw it across the room. "I'm tired of people telling me what to do," she answered angrily.

"Aye, we all have someone who tells us what to do. My mother says if it isn't a father it's a husband."

"Well, I have no father, and I don't want a husband!" Raven said, stepping out of her skirt. "At least not one like Lord Denseley."

"What kind of a man would you be wanting?" Molly asked, making conversation while she picked up Raven's discarded garments.

"I want a man like Taber O'Flynn."

Molly froze as she leaned over to pick up Raven's skirt. She straightened slowly and stared at Raven, her green eyes wide with concern. "Whatever made you say that?"

"I want a man who has principles and compassion for people, and everything I've heard about Taber O'Flynn tells me that's the way he is."

"Aye, I suppose it is," she said, momentarily relieved.

"I went to Blackmoor House this morning hoping to meet him."

"Go on with you," Molly tried to make light of it.

"I did, Molly. I met Lord Fitzgerald's stable boy, or horse trainer. I'm not sure what he was, but he assured me Taber had sailed for America."

"Horse trainer?" Molly asked confused, knowing that Tomas Fitzgerald prided himself on training his own stock.

"He said his name was Devin. He was a handsome one, tall with black curly hair and dark, sapphire blue eyes. It gives me goosebumps just thinking about him." Suddenly Raven turned and faced Molly. "It's strange, the description I just gave you sounds like the description I've heard of Taber O'Flynn."

Molly turned her back to Raven, laying a beautiful blue silk dress across the bed. She was in a dilemma about Raven's discovery. Suppose the girl told her uncle.

"There are a lot of men in Ireland who fit

that description, m'lady."

"Are there now? Then the women of Ireland are very lucky," Raven retorted. "Can you help me with this dress, Molly. Really, I don't know why I'm bothering to put this lovely dress on for Lord Denseley. I have no intention of letting the man court me."

"I'm afraid your aunt has other plans, m'lady. She was the one who instructed me to lay this particular dress out."

Raven shrugged as she stood before the mirror. "She thinks to catch me a husband, but I have other plans."

Molly had a frown on her face as Raven left the room. Somehow she had to get to Taber.

Raven paused in the doorway, listening to her aunt's conversation with Lord Denseley. As usual it concerned the Irish Rebels, and a new Insurrectionist who called himself the *Hawk*. She forced herself to enter, plastering a smile on her face. "Good afternoon, Lord Denseley. I'm sorry to have kept you waiting, but no one informed me you would be coming for tea."

His colorless gray eyes took in her beauty from head to toe. "It was worth the wait, Lady Montgomery."

"Lady McClennon," Raven corrected.

Caroline's sniff of disdain was clearly audible. "My niece insists on claiming her Scottish name, but God knows why," her aunt sneered.

"My father's family was a proud Scottish family," Raven said. "His ancestors fought beside Bonnie Prince Charlie."

"They were on the wrong side, dear," Caroline said sarcastically. "Besides, Walter doesn't want to hear about your ancestors. He wants to know about you."

"Why should he want to know about me?" Raven asked, knowing only too well why the pompous fool was interested.

"My dear, I would like to discuss a possible marriage between you and I."

Denseley's face turned red as Raven laughed. "I am sorry, sir, but I'm not interested in marriage at this time."

"Raven," her aunt exclaimed, her face rigid with shock. "You have no say in the matter!"

"I will never marry a man I don't love," Raven stated emphatically.

Caroline gave Raven an outraged glare and turned her back on her disgraceful behavior. "Come, Walter, sit with me on the sofa while Raven pours us tea. I'm sure you have already noticed the girl is far too independent and needs a firm hand, but I don't believe that would be a problem for a man like yourself. Her father left her quite wealthy and she'll be receiving her trust in a few months, so she would come to you with a very nice dowry."

Raven could stand no more. "I will not

marry Lord Denseley or anyone else you choose. I suggest you speak with my uncle, because he is very much aware that my father left me his estate to guarantee that I could choose who I wished to marry. Now you'll excuse me, but I've lost my taste for tea and crumpets." Raven's skirts rustled as she left the room and ran up the stairs. When she reached her room she threw herself across the bed and cried. Damn them! Damn them all for treating her like property. How could her uncle be her mother's brother? Her mother was a kind, loving woman, with compassion for all living things. These people didn't care about anyone or anything.

"I beg you to forgive her, Walter. The girl is headstrong, but you should be able to handle her."

"I will have to give this a great deal of thought, Caroline. Even I don't want a wife who I have to constantly beat."

"Come now, Walter, you have to admit she is a beauty, and don't forget she has a considerable inheritance coming to her."

"You're very anxious to get rid of the girl," Denseley said suspiciously.

"Only because she reminds me of her mother, and I despised the woman."

"Why was that, Caroline?"

"That is none of your business, Walter. If

you're not interested in Raven, then tell me so I can make plans with someone else. There are others who are interested."

"I didn't say I wasn't interested, my dear, but I don't want to make a hasty decision and then be sorry for it. Besides, you yourself said Charles wasn't in favor of the match. Have you already changed his mind?"

"No, but I will."

"M'lady, can I do anything for you?" Molly Devlin asked from the doorway.

"Thank you for asking, Molly, but I have to handle this myself," Raven answered, forcing back tears. "Are your mother and father living, Molly?"

"Aye, m'lady."

"Love them, Molly. Tell them everyday how much you love them, because you cannot imagine what it's like to be without them."

"Aye, m'lady, I will," Molly promised, baffled as to what to do for Raven. "May I get you some tea, m'lady?"

"No, thank you, Molly. I think I'm just going to go to bed."

"But it isn't even dark yet, m'lady."

"I know, Molly, but if I can sleep I don't have to think about what my aunt is trying to do to me."

Molly paused at the door, wishing she knew some way to brighten Raven's spirits. She had always thought if you were rich you wouldn't have problems, but being rich certainly hadn't helped Lady Raven McClennon, she thought sadly.

O wind, O mighty melancholy wind
Blow through me, blow!
Thou blowest forgotten things into my mind,
From long ago.
John Todhunter

Chapter Three

For two days Raven was kept busy with duties. Her aunt had invited the wives of the British officers to tea one day and the next day she was forced to attend a ceremony honoring one of the officers. On the third morning, before the sun was up, Raven was in the stables having Devil Lady saddled so she could get away for just a little while before her aunt could give her something else to do.

Colin stared up at Raven as she mounted the restless horse. "Mind you, m'lady, be careful. I dinna' want your uncle's wrath to come down on either of us."

"I will, Colin. I'm just going to ride along the beach for a short distance. I'll be back before anyone knows I'm gone."

Taber O'Flynn was sitting on the cliffs looking out to sea, when movement on the beach caught his attention. He quickly moved back among the rocks and watched the approaching rider. As soon as the morning sun caught the black highlights of her hair, he knew it was the Lady Raven McClennon. Was she here to snoop for her uncle, he wondered bitterly. Maybe he wasn't being fair. Granted, he had been shocked when Molly informed him that her ladyship was Lord Montgomery's niece, but according to Molly, the girl was very unhappy with her situation. He smiled as he observed her expertly handling the spirited horse. There was nothing quite so pleasing as a comely lass riding a beautiful horse.

Slowing the horse to a trot, Raven stared up toward Blackmoor House, hoping to see someone, but the place looked deserted. Molly had tried to convince her that there wasn't any possibility Taber O'Flynn was at Blackmoor House, but still she couldn't help but wonder why Devin had been so adamant about his not being there. At the thought of Devin, the stable hand, she felt a warmth flush her skin. She had to stop this foolishness. It was one thing to insist on having the right to choose her own husband, but what would her uncle think if she told him she was enamored of a stable hand.

She turned Devil Lady back toward Riverside House and kicked her into a full gallop, oblivious to the beautiful scenery along the way.

Taber had seen her looking up toward the manor and for a moment he had considered showing himself until he remembered who she was. He couldn't take any chances—no matter how beautiful she was, or how much he desired her.

Molly felt sorry for Raven when she returned to her room. It was obvious she was disappointed about something. She slowly changed her clothes, preparing to join her aunt and the officers' wives for tea and needlepoint.

"Tell me about your family, Molly," Raven said as she dressed. "Have you any brothers or sisters other than Colin?"

"Aye, a brother older than Colin and I, and a wee sister."

"Oh, that must be wonderful," Raven exclaimed. "I imagine your house is always full of love and laughter."

Molly laughed. "Anyone who has observed the Irish close know about their love for their children. When my brother Brandon left for Australia I thought me poor mother's heart would break."

"It must be terrible when your children leave home. I don't know if I could bear it. Why do you think so many young people leave Ireland, Molly?"

"They don't stand a chance here because of the English," Molly answered before thinking. She looked at Raven sheepishly. "Please forget I said that."

"Molly, I wish you would stop thinking of me as the enemy."

"I'm sorry, m'lady."

"I have no friends in Ireland, or anyplace else for that matter," Raven said sadly. "I had very much hoped you and I could be friends."

Molly looked embarrassed. "I'm just a serving girl, m'lady."

"Poppycock. You and I are about the same age. I'm sure we have many things in common."

Molly smiled. "Like men?"

"Exactly!" Raven laughed. "I love your country and I want to know more about it and its people."

Raven tried to concentrate on her needle-point while her aunt and friends discussed the Irish Rebels. We are guests in this country, she thought bitterly, yet all we do is criticize the Irish people for wanting their freedom.

"The Hawk struck again last night," Mrs. Forrester announced, never looking up from her sewing. "My husband says at least thirty horses were stolen and driven across country."

"Who is the Hawk?" Raven asked.

"No one knows for sure if it's one man or a group of men who are stealing our horses," Mrs. Lane answered. "Whoever it is, they always leave a feather behind to irritate us. My husband says when they catch whoever it is, they're going to tar and feather him with those feathers before they hang him."

"It sounds to me like someone playing games," Raven commented, trying to concentrate on the needle in her hand.

"Believe me, the people whose horses have been stolen don't consider it funny or a game," Caroline said.

"Most people believe it is Taber O'Flynn returned to Ireland, but my husband doesn't believe it's just one person," Mrs. Forrester offered. "He thinks it's an organization of people, and each one leaves a feather behind after doing his dirty work."

"He's probably correct," Aunt Caroline agreed. "There are so many of the Insurrectionists around."

"Ireland is their country," Raven couldn't help pointing out. "I think we would all react the same way."

"Oh, but you're wrong, my dear. Ireland belongs to England, and that is why we are here. These poor ignorant people have to be reminded all the time that they owe their allegiance to the Crown."

Yes, reminded by having their homes and possessions confiscated, Raven thought bitterly.

"Is it true this Taber O'Flynn had family who were knighted," Mary Sims, the youngest wife of the group, asked.

"That's a ridiculous rumor," Caroline hissed. "How could a man like that be from anything but peasant stock?"

"I'm afraid it's true, dear Caroline. How do you think his family acquired the very house we're sitting in?"

"Well, no matter," Caroline said, continuing her sewing. "That was many, many years ago, and he certainly wouldn't be considered a gentleman now."

"I'm told somewhere in his family tree he claims to be related to Gerald Fitzgerald, Earl of Desmond, who was one of Queen Elizabeth's favorites for a short while," Mrs. Blackney said.

"Yes, that's true," Mrs. Forrester answered. "The Queen confiscated all his property when he angered her, but in the end returned some of his holdings, including Riverside House."

"Has Taber O'Flynn ever lived in this

house?" Raven asked.

"Yes, I'm told he lived here until he was twelve or thirteen. That was just before his father was killed after joining Wolfe Tone and Napoleon Bonaparte in an uprising at Bantry Bay. They would probably have been successful, except for a storm that came up. It blew near hurricane force, sending most of the French ships back to France. The ships' crews that were captured were hung, including Taber O'Flynn's father, Sean O'Flynn."

There was a mumble of conversation as everyone talked at once about this latest revelation. Raven was wondering which room Taber O'Flynn had used, and was anxious to leave the group and ask questions of the Irish servants.

"I must say, to hear stories of this sinful man you'd never know he was from a family who had ever been loyal to the Crown," Mary Sims exclaimed.

"The Earl must not have been loyal to the Crown if the Queen found it necessary to confiscate his property," Raven said tartly. She could feel all eyes in the room on her, but she continued pushing the needle back and forth in her tapestry.

"Perhaps you're right, Raven," her aunt agreed sharply. "All the more reason this Taber O'Flynn should go to the gallows. If he has no children, the line of Desmonds will come to an end."

"Oh, I doubt that, Caroline." Mrs. Forrester leaned forward to tell her secret. "I understand he has slept with half the women in Ireland, married and unmarried, so he probably has bastards in every county."

Raven pricked her finger with the needle. The dark stain of her blood seeped onto the white cloth she held. She was growing weary of the malicious gossip.

"They say he's devilishly handsome," one of the women giggled. "Pamela swears she saw him one day, and described him as tall, with wide shoulders, and a shock of beautiful black curly hair."

"I didn't think anyone knew what he looked like," Raven commented. "Uncle Charles said if he passed him on the street he wouldn't know him."

"I suppose that's true, but everyone knows he is dark and handsome."

"Half of the men in Ireland are dark and handsome," Raven pointed out.

The discussion continued, but Raven was suddenly lost in a daydream as she stared up at the afternoon rays of sunshine coming through the window. She tried to imagine riding Devil Lady along the beach with Taber O'Flynn at her side—yet for some strange reason, in her daydreams Taber was always in the form of Devin, the stable boy. It had to be because he was tall and dark, she thought, frustrated that she should be daydreaming over a conceited, arrogant stable boy. Yet she had to admit she had never met anyone who had the effect on her that he had. Every night since they'd met she'd wake up in a sweat, remembering the feel of his hands and mouth on her. It was only because he was the first man who had ever kissed her that way, she told herself, forcing her attention back to the gossiping women.

Taber sat across the table from Peter Muldane, drumming his fingers on the polished wood as Peter scrutinized the list of names before him. His head was engulfed in a cloud of smoke as he puffed at the clay pipe held between his teeth.

"I dinna' see it," he said, shaking his head. "I would stake my life that every man and woman on this list are as honest as the day is long."

"Aye, I would have too, but someone had to tip Montgomery or Denseley off. We've been careful to keep the connection between the Fitzgeralds and the O'Flynns quiet."

Peter shrugged. "I believe Montgomery is convinced that his informant was wrong. Thank God for Molly Devlin's warning, or we would never have had the opportunity to throw his spy off our tracks."

"What do you make of the man, Peter?"

"He's a tough one, he is. Loyal to the Crown down to his toenails. But he is an honorable man. Now that fellow Denseley is another story. He'd slit his mother's throat if it served his purpose."

"Molly mentioned that Lady Montgomery was pushing for a marriage between Denseley and her niece," Taber mentioned casually.

Peter folded the paper and stuffed it in his pocket. "Perhaps she has. I know Lady Montgomery would do anything to get rid of the girl. Seems a shame. The young lady is lovely. I dinna' know why she hates her so, unless it's because Lord Montgomery has a soft spot in his heart for her." Peter tamped the tobacco in his pipe, then relit it. "Unfortunately, he hasn't been able to do much about softening the aunt's harsh treatment of the girl. Still, I can't believe he would favor a marriage with Denseley . . ."

"I hope not for the girl's sake," Taber said, trying not to think of the pain in Raven McClennon's blue eyes.

"I just remembered something about this Denseley," Peter said, concentrating on a cloud of smoke above his head. "He was engaged to the daughter of another English Lord in Dublin. As much as I can remember, the girl met her death in a very suspicious accident. I can't recall anything being proved though.

Perhaps I'll look into it. I wouldn't want to see any harm come to that lovely lass." Suddenly Peter looked at his friend, a twinkle in his gray eyes. "Have you met the young lady?" he asked, knowing very well that Taber had.

"I'm sure you already know I have," Taber answered, knowing there wasn't much that went on in County Cork that Peter Muldane didn't know about. "She thinks I'm Tomas's stable hand."

Peter laughed. "Now how would she get a notion like that?"

"I was rubbing down one of the horses when she appeared out of nowhere."

"And you didn't bother to correct her assumption?"

"I thought she was the spy we were expecting, and I must admit I acted like a stable hand."

"My God, you didn't?" Peter said, nearly dropping his pipe.

"No, but I would have liked to. God, but she is beautiful."

"Be careful, my friend. You're playing with fire with that one."

"I dinna' expect to see her again, Peter. I'm sure Lord Denseley will be keeping the young lady busy."

Molly accompanied Raven into the city the

next day. It was a beautiful morning and everyone seemed in high spirit, all talking of the fair that was to take place in two days.

"Are you planning to attend?" Raven asked Molly.

"Aye, Colin competes in many of the events, so I will be there to cheer him on."

"It sounds wonderful," Raven said sadly, wishing she could go. It seemed every place she went she was an outsider. In London they treated her as if she were a bumpkin from Scotland. Here they treated her as if she were the enemy. She was beginning to wonder if she would ever find a place where she fitted in.

Cork was a city of twisted lanes and steep stone steps, arched stone bridges, and lofty spires. It seemed to Raven that the city and the river were one. The city itself had been built at the mouth of the River Lee, and even when you thought you were putting it behind you, you would suddenly take a turn and have to cross it again.

"What is that?" Raven asked, pointing to a little drinking trough that was labeled *madrai*.

"It's a drinking trough for dogs," she explained.

The area seemed to have a little of everything—seascapes, mountains, and fertile river valleys, Raven thought as they passed the bow-fronted houses heading for the market. First she was looking up, then turning around to take something else in. "I love it," she exclaimed, examining a plaque that announced someone's marriage vow in the year 1606. "Look at this, Molly. It's just incredible that it's still here after all that time."

"It's a wonder the city is still here with all that has taken place," Molly said as they walked.

"What do you mean?" Raven asked.

"Cork was established in the seventh century by Fionn Bair, a holy man who established a monastic center at the mouth of the river. Since then it has been occupied by Vikings, Normans, and of course the English. When Oliver Cromwell was here in 1659, he ordered all the city's bells to be melted down to make guns and ammunition for his conquest of Ireland. In 1690, during the Siege of Cork for William of Orange in his battle with James the Second, much of the city was burned."

"It's little wonder the Irish hate the English," Raven said. "I'm beginning to hate them myself."

They were crossing the street heading toward the marketplace when Raven saw Devin, the stable boy. Their eyes met without warning, and she felt a lump in her throat. He was standing next to a beautiful auburn-haired woman, his shoulders leaning against the baker's shop wall, with one boot on the cobbled street and the other propped against the stone step. He seemed to exude masculinity, sending Raven's pulse racing.

Molly, unaware of Raven's inner turmoil, fought to control her own emotions when she saw the tall, dark vision of her dreams. She hoped to be able to enter the shop without acknowledging his presence, but she should have known better.

Taber stepped in her path, a beautiful smile lighting up his face. "Ah, Molly me love, were you not going to speak to an old friend?"

"Hello . . . Devin," she murmured, trying not to notice Brenna O'Neill.

"And Lady McClennon, how nice to see you again," Taber said, taking her hand in his. "Are you still studying the architecture of our homes?" he asked, a mischievous grin in his dark eyes.

"Not recently," Raven answered. "I kept running into interference from nosy people."

"Ah, that's too bad. You were so accomplished at it," he said, a twinkle in his dark eyes. "Have you met Miss O'Neill?" he asked as Brenna possessively wrapped her arm in his.

He presented them, his poise giving credit to the most polished courtier. Raven smiled politely in the face of the woman's slow appraisal. She admitted reluctantly that Miss O'Neill was beautiful with deep auburn hair and topaz-colored eyes.

"We must go," she said, dismissing Raven

and Molly. "I still have shopping to do."

Taber's eyes held Raven's for a long moment before he said good-bye. "I hope to see you again soon, Lady McClennon."

"Her rudeness has no bounds," Molly spat. "I canna' imagine why Ta—why Devin bothers with her."

"I was wondering why she would bother with him. She looked rather grand for the likes of a stable boy," Raven said as they entered the shop.

"She just thinks she's grand," Molly answered. "I want you to try one of those sticky buns," she said, changing the subject.

But Raven wasn't ready to drop the subject. "Is she his sweetheart?"

"She thinks she is," Molly answered.

"Do I detect a note of jealousy, Molly Devlin?" Raven asked, studying her friend.

"Of course not," Molly laughed.

Her voice was light, but the look in her eyes told Raven otherwise. The man is a womanizer, she thought. Imagine a stable boy breaking the hearts of all the females in Ireland.

The red rose whispers of passion,
And the white rose breathes of love;
Oh, the red rose is a falcon,
And the white rose is a dove.
Author Unknown

Chapter Four

Molly was positive the Brotherhood wouldn't look kindly on her inviting Lord Montgomery's niece to the fair, so she had decided to mention it to Taber beforehand. She had been surprised and a little puzzled when he quickly agreed that the Lady Raven McClennon should be invited. Suddenly Molly began to question the wisdom of her decision.

"Suppose someone should slip and call you Taber O'Flynn in front of her?" she asked.

"You said yourself that she wasn't interested in her uncle's work. Besides, our friends know better than to mention Taber O'Flynn's name."

"What about Brenna?" Molly asked.

"What about her?"

"Will she be at the fair?"

"I suppose she will," Taber answered. "I dinna' see what that has to do with Lady McClennon."

"Perhaps you should ask Brenna what she thinks," Molly said, storming from the room.

"Men! They're all such fools," she mumbled to herself.

Raven was delighted for the opportunity to attend the fair with Molly and her brother Colin. She waited wisely for her uncle to be busy before mentioning her invitation, and as she had hoped, he was too preoccupied to argue with her.

On Tuesday morning Raven woke with the dawn and dressed in a bright plaid skirt and a white ruffled blouse embroidered with red roses. Around her hair she tied a bright red scarf. Quietly she crept from the house and headed for the stables, where she was to meet the others. It was a beautiful morning with a clear blue sky dotted by white puffy clouds. Raven breathed deeply of the clean, fresh air, feeling like a caged bird about to be set free.

"So you're going to the fair," Connor, the gardener, called as Raven ran through the rose garden.

"Aye, how did you know?"

"I told him," Molly giggled as she ran to

greet Raven. "What took you so long?"

"Faith, girl, you must have slept out here. The sun is barely up," Raven laughed.

"We dinna' want to waste any time. The fair is an hour away and the roads are already filled with people."

Colin led out a beautiful mare hooked up to a two-wheel jaunting cart. Gay red ribbons were tied to the horse's tail and mane, for luck, he explained to Raven.

"You must be careful on the way to the fair," the gardener instructed. "The road is often beset by dangers. If you meet a funeral, be sure to take three steps backwards with it. And be careful at the crossroads. That's where the devil may be waiting for you."

"We'll be careful, Connor," Molly promised, pulling Raven toward the horse before she had a chance to question the gardener's superstitions. "We're stopping at our house for some tea and Bothy bread before we go on."

Raven waved to Connor as Colin touched the whip to the mare's flank. "Whatever was he talking about?" she asked as they pulled away from Riverside House.

Molly laughed. "The Irish people are very superstitious. Just wait until you hear the warnings my mother will give us when we leave home."

Molly and Colin lived in a quaint white

cottage with a thatched roof and windowboxes filled with bright flowers. It was plain, yet it had an inviting look of welcome.

Raven was warmly greeted by the Devlin family as they gathered around the hearth to eat oatmeal and Bothy bread. Molly explained that the bread was made from potatoes when Raven exclaimed how good it was.

It was nearly an hour before they started off again. As Molly had predicted, her mother insisted they carry salt in their pockets and pin a sprig of hazel to their blouses to keep away evil spirits. To Raven, the traditions only added to her excitement.

The road to Cobh was filled with people heading for the fair; ladies in bright-colored dresses, men in bright-colored shirts. The atmosphere was one of gaiety as they passed tents pitched in fields where some had stayed the night. There were wagons loaded with wares to sell, cattle being driven to the fair for bargaining, women loaded down with baskets of food. The closer they got, the more excited Raven became. She listened with interest as Colin bragged about his skill at the ancient game of hurling and how he was going to do his best to beat last year's champion.

"Last year's champion was . . . was Devin Fitzgerald," Molly added. "I believe you met him."

Raven's attention snapped to Molly's face.

"Do you mean the stable boy?"

"Here we are," Colin announced, quickly changing the subject. "You ladies go on while I see to the horse. I'll meet you at the races later."

"This is wonderful," Raven exclaimed, turning around in circles, trying to see everything as they walked. "Look over there. It's a magic man," Raven said, pointing. For a few minutes they stood watching and laughed as he pulled a rabbit from his hat and handed it to Molly.

"Come on, let's look at the wares," Molly urged. "There is too much to see to stay in one place too long."

Canvas-covered stalls with white sheets spread over the counters lined the lanes. Some offered apples, gooseberries, plums, meatpies, and oysters, while others sold laces, gloves, and trinkets.

At the sound of the fox horn, the crowd began to move toward the center of the fair. "We must hurry, Raven, if we are to have a good place to see."

"What is it we're going to see?" Raven asked, running behind Molly.

"A horse race."

A collection of the most beautiful horses Raven had ever seen were lined up ready for the race. Raven had her eye on a beautiful black stallion when she happened to look up and see its rider. Across the distance his eyes met hers, glittering with a challenge. He nodded his head toward her before giving his full attention back to the spirited horse beneath him. "Molly, it's Devin," she whispered.

"Aye, I know. He's a great show of a man he is," Molly answered, watching the expression on Raven's face.

"He is very handsome," she agreed, studying the wide set of his shoulders and the proud arrogance of his dark head. He was dressed in a saffron-colored pleated shirt, and black pants tucked into shiny black boots. Quite a dashing figure, she thought. He looked more like a pirate than a stable hand.

"His arrogance knows no bounds," Raven exclaimed as he winked at her from atop his horse.

The other horses lined up alongside him, the riders wearing bright-colored shirts as well, but Raven couldn't take her eyes off Devin Fitzgerald. He sat easily in the saddle, his hands careless on the reins, while the other riders struggled to keep their mounts under control. Then the signal was given and they were off, thundering across the field toward a rock wall. Raven was quickly caught up in the excitement of the race, and cheered enthusiastically as all the riders made it over the first obstacle. The crowd ran down the field and she ran along with them, watching Devin and his magnificent black stallion take one obstacle after another. He rode low in the saddle, leaning over the neck of the horse as together they easily took the jumps. The only other rider close to him was Colin, and he was still a jump behind.

While Molly cheered Colin on, Raven watched in awe as Devin took the last rock wall to the cheers of the spectators. Then she lost sight of him as he was quickly surrounded by the excited crowd.

"Come on, let's get some refreshment," Molly said, pulling Raven along. "Colin and Devin will be a while before they can get away from the well-wishers."

"Have you known Devin long?" Raven asked as they walked.

"Aye, all me life. Colin and Devin always seem to be competing in one event or the other."

"Has he ever been married?" Raven asked, trying to keep her voice steady.

"No, his business makes it too dangerous," Molly answered before thinking.

"His business?" Raven asked incredulously. "Being a stable boy makes it too dangerous for him to marry?"

"Oh, I'm only teasing you," Molly laughed, the red of her face matching her red hair. "I've a terrible thirst. Let's have a cup of apple juice before we move on to the next event."

Raven and Molly sat quietly under a striped canopy and sipped their juice. Molly was wishing she didn't have to deceive her friend about Taber O'Flynn, but too much was at stake not to be cautious. If Raven was ever to know who Taber was, he would have to tell her himself, she decided.

"Are you ready for the next event?" Molly asked. "It will be the turf-cutting contest."

"How does Colin fare in that event?" Raven asked, laughter in her voice.

"Usually second to Devin."

"The poor lad. Maybe if we cheer him on, he will win."

They paid for their fruit drink and joined the milling crowd heading for the next event. Everyone gathered at a bog bank where four men, including Devin and Colin, waited for the word to start. "That's Patrick Casey." Molly pointed to a large, golden-haired man. "He is Devin's best friend. Doesn't he look like a Greek god?" she giggled.

"Yes, he is quite handsome." *But not as handsome as Devin*, she thought as she watched him.

When the signal was given, they began to cut the bog, stripping and cleaning it before cutting it into bricklike shapes. Devin and Colin were way ahead of the other two men while the sound of laughter and friendly cheers hailed them on.

"Hurry, Colin," Raven and Molly cheered. For a split second Taber looked up, his eyes meeting Raven's, and at that moment Colin cut the last piece of turf and was declared the new turf-cutting champion.

Molly and Raven were congratulating Colin when Devin joined them. "That was foul play, you know," he said, a serious look on his handsome face.

"Foul play?" Colin exclaimed. "How can you say that? I won fair and square."

"How could any man concentrate when you had the two most beautiful women at the fair cheering for you."

Colin laughed. "Of course, you're right. Have you met Raven McClennon?"

"Aye, tis a pleasure to see you again, m'lady." Taber found he couldn't take his eyes off her face. Her cheeks had the tint of roses and her eyes were bright with laughter.

"I was very impressed with the horse that you raced earlier," Raven said. "He was very beautiful."

"A week ago he was as wild as the wind," Colin bragged. "Devin has the gift of *cogar i gcluais an chapaill*," he said in Gaelic.

"That means having the ability to gentle the fiercest of wild horses," Molly explained.

"And of wild women," Colin laughed,

punching his friend in playful gesture.

"Just how do you tame a wild horse?" Raven asked, skeptical.

"Ah, lass, I'd like to tell you, but then it wouldn't be a secret. But I'd gladly introduce you to the horse if you'd care to walk back to the stables."

Taber offered Raven his hand and pulled her along, while Molly and Colin followed.

The stables smelled warmly of horses, hay, and oiled leather, a combination Raven loved. When she was a little girl, she had spent many hours in the stables with her father while he saw to his fine stock of horses.

"There he is," Taber pointed out.

"Oh, he's so beautiful," she exclaimed in a whisper.

The black horse was standing quietly, but at the sound of Raven's voice, he lifted his head and moved uneasily.

"Lady Raven McClennon, meet Nighthawk," Taber said, rubbing the velvet nose of the horse while he whispered something to the beautiful beast in Gaelic.

"He's even more magnificent up close," Raven said softly, gently touching the great horse. There was no doubt of his fine ancestry, she thought, noting the proud head.

"Perhaps one morning I'll let you ride him on the beach," Taber suggested.

Raven stared up at him. His eyes held the

slightest hint of a smile. So he had been watching her ride on the beach, she thought with an odd pleasure. Colin and Molly moved off, admiring other horses in the stable.

"That is a magnificent animal you've been riding," he commented.

"Aye, Devil Lady is a fine horse. She hadn't been ridden very much because everyone is afraid of her."

"But you're not," Taber laughed.

Raven smiled mischievously. "Perhaps I, too, have a gift for taming fierce animals."

"Perhaps you do." He smiled warmly. "There is a dance this evening after the games are over. Would you be my partner?" he asked.

"I came with Molly and Colin, but if they are staying, I'd like to be your partner."

"We wouldn't miss the dance," Colin announced as he rejoined them. "Isn't that right, Molly?"

"Aye," Molly answered, but the look on her face told Raven something was wrong.

"I must have a word with Molly alone," Raven said, drawing her friend outside. "Molly, is there something between you and Devin?"

"Nay."

"Are you sure you aren't in love with him?"

Molly looked back over her shoulder at Taber O'Flynn and her brother. All of Ireland is in love with him, she thought silently. "Stop worrying about me and enjoy yourself," Molly smiled.

"I want to be sure, Molly. I don't want to do anything to hurt you. Our friendship is too important to me."

"Devin and I are just good friends," Molly assured her, knowing that was the way it had to be. "Besides, I've got me sights set on Patrick Casey."

"Wonderful," Raven laughed. "I wish you luck."

As they headed back to the stables, Molly put her hand on Raven's arm and stopped her. "Just be careful, m'lady. Don't lose your heart."

Raven and Taber walked hand in hand, taking in everything. At the games of chance he won her a beautiful silk scarf, which he tied around her neck, then they watched for a while as the cattle and horses were being sold. Each time she looked at him he was staring at her, his eyes dark with an emotion she didn't understand.

"Would you like your fortune told?" he asked as they stood before the fortune-teller's tent.

"I'm not sure I want to know what my future holds," Raven admitted.

Taber stared down at her. "Aye, my beautiful Raven McClennon, let us think only of the present. Come away, and let's find us a spot on the hillside where I can admire your beauty."

Her heart was beating erratically, but she forced a laugh. "What luck, I've found myself an Irish bard."

"No, lass, just a man bewildered by your beauty."

"You do have the gift of blarney," she laughed as he pulled her toward the green deserted hills.

"And what do you know about blarney?" he laughed.

"Molly said it's the truth as any Irishman can tell it."

Taber laughed as he pulled her along. When they reached the green hillside, he bowed and offered her a seat on the grassy slope.

"The best seat for m'lady," he teased.

"Thank you, kind sir." Raven spread her skirt and settled down on the grass.

"How long will you be in Ireland?" he asked as they both sat looking down on the activities of the fair.

Frowning, Raven picked at a blade of grass. "I don't really know. As you are aware, my uncle is here to subdue the Insurrectionists."

"Aye, so I've heard." Taber lay back on the soft grass and stared up at the blue sky, and Raven did the same.

"Are you an Insurrectionist, Devin?" she asked as she turned on her side and studied him.

"We're all Insurrectionists, love. Some of us against England while others are against Ireland. The British people are supreme masters at manipulating Irish against Irish, you know."

"I remember my father telling me stories about his ancestors fighting the British. His grandfather and great-grandfather were killed by the British while they tried to protect their rights in Scotland."

"Then you understand what we feel. But come, let's not talk of the English on such a beautiful day. Tell me a little about yourself, Raven McClennon."

Raven laughed. "There isn't much to tell. I love horses, poetry, and music. I want to be independent of others and be able to live my life as I want to live it."

Taber rolled over, leaning on one elbow as he smiled down into her somber eyes. "We have much in common, lass. I've been trapped all my life by responsibilities, and now it seems I'm to be trapped by a pair of haunting blue eyes. We are kindred spirits, Raven McClennon," he whispered before his mouth came down over hers.

Her hands clung to him as if she were drowning. She could feel his muscles tense beneath the linen of his shirt, feel the hard length of his body against hers. He suddenly ended the kiss, staring down into her blue eyes.

She was the most desirable woman he'd ever been with. The shape of her mouth invited his kisses, and the curve of her breasts was irresistible. He wanted her as he had never wanted anyone or anything in his entire life.

"Ah, Raven, Raven, what am I going to do with you? I have this strange feeling that somehow you are going to be my undoing."

Raven gently touched his face. "I would never willingly bring harm to you."

"No, I dinna' believe you would, but there are always circumstances we canna' control. You know very little about me."

"Nor you about me."

"I know you're a beautiful Scots lass with sky-blue eyes and raven black hair." He touched the side of her face. "There is no need to know anymore at this moment."

"Have you always lived in Ireland?" Raven asked.

He was silent for a moment before he spoke. "I lived in France for a few years, and I've visited Australia."

"You are very well educated and traveled for someone in your profession."

"My profession?" he asked, puzzled. "Oh, you mean a stable boy," he laughed. "I suppose I am. What about you? Why are you living with your uncle?"

"My parents were killed in a freak carriage accident several years ago. Uncle Charles is the last of my family to take me in," Raven said with a bitter laugh. "I've been through them all."

Taber pushed back a strand of her dark hair. "I canna' imagine you being a problem to anyone."

"You must tell my aunt that. I'm afraid she wouldn't agree with you."

"Is your life very difficult, Raven?" he asked sympathetically.

"It could be worse. My uncle is kind to me. Besides"—she forced a bright smile—"it won't be long before I'm on my own."

"And what will Lady Raven McClennon do when she's on her own?"

"I may go back to Scotland to see what became of my father's estate. I have very little memory of it. Or I may go to America."

"America, is it?" He laughed. "My, aren't we the adventurous one."

"There isn't anything wrong with a woman being adventurous," she stated adamantly. "Why do you men think you're the only ones who can do anything?"

Taber's expression softened. "Ah, you're right, lass, there is nothing wrong with it. I'm sure you'll have a glorious life with whatever you do. I must admit, one day I'd like to see America myself. 'Tis a strange thing, isn't it? A man longs for foreign places, yet when he's away from his homeland he yearns for it."

Raven studied Devin's strong profile as he stared off toward the sea. "I find the sea draws me more than foreign places," he said quietly.

"Have you also been a sailor?" she asked in awe.

"I've tried my hand at many things, lass."

"It sounds like you've led a very exciting life."

"There have been times I wished it weren't so." He smiled, moving his thumb along her jawline as he stared into her eyes. "But I wouldn't trade this moment for anything."

His look was unnerving Raven. "I hear the music," she said, hoping to draw his attention away from her.

"Aye, I suppose it is time for us to return." Taber took Raven's hand and pulled her to her feet. "Come along, Lady Raven McClennon. I'll show you how the Irish dance."

As they neared the tented pavillion, Raven glanced across the crowd of people and met Brenna O'Neill's stare. There was a look of hatred in the girl's eyes that startled Raven. She pulled her hand from Devin's and stopped.

Taber stared at her, a surprised expression on his face. "What is wrong, lass?"

"I don't want to cause trouble. Perhaps you should be dancing with Miss O'Neill."

"Now why would I be wanting to do that when I have the loveliest girl at the fair standing beside me?"

"Don't be teasing me, Devin. I can see that Miss O'Neill is upset that we are together."

He gently touched the side of Raven's face. "I belong to no woman, lass. Put it out of your mind."

Raven glanced back toward Brenna. "I would wager there is at least one who would say different."

The fiddles were playing a wild tune as Taber led Raven toward the circle of people. When she held back, hesitant to try her skill at the wanton beat, he pulled her on.

"Come, lass. Let me show you how it's done." His eyes sparkled mischievously. "Of course, if you dinna' think you're up to it . . . ."

"Lead the way, my Irish friend, and I'll show you how we dance in Scotland," she laughed.

The fiddlers increased the tempo and Raven found herself spun off her feet, whirling faster and faster. Her head was spinning, but she was thoroughly enjoying herself for the first time in ages. Taber lifted her high over his head as the music came to a final wild crescendo, and everyone applauded.

His eyes were warm with laughter as he set her on her feet. "I think I've met my match, girl."

Raven's breath caught in her throat. She forced a nonchalant smile. "Aye, Irishman, you've met your match. Never doubt the ability of a Scotswoman."

"I'll remember that," he laughed. "Come, I've a terrible thirst after that dance."

The sound of the music suddenly faded, replaced by the thundering sound of horses' hooves and screams of women and children.

"Get to the hills," he ordered, pushing her before she could make her feet move.

"What is it, Devin? Who are they?" Raven asked as she watched in horror while the horsemen swept through the crowd wielding swords and clubs. When she looked back at Devin, she hardly recognized him. The man who only moments ago had been laughing and dancing now had the cold hard look of hate blazing in his eyes.

"Don't you recognize your friends, Lady Raven McClennon," he asked in a mocking tone. "The man leading the butchers is Lord Denseley, but you are safe, Lady McClennon. Your friends wouldn't hurt you."

Raven couldn't make her feet move as Devin left her to lead women and children to safety. She watched in disbelief as a shot felled the young man who had been laughing and dancing beside them only moments ago. Suddenly a small child ran toward the body.

"Stop!" Raven screamed, but her voice fell on deaf ears. She ran through the crowd, dodging horses and men fighting hand to hand. When she finally reached the sobbing child, she grabbed him in her arms and began to make her way through the crowd. Suddenly a man blocked her way, a sword in hand and the look of stark hatred on his face.

"Get out of my way," she ordered, trying to keep her voice from quivering. "Your fight is not with women and children."

"Ah, but you're wrong, my Irish slut. If we rid the country of the women and children, eventually the breed will die off."

Raven stood frozen, the child still clasped in her arms. This man meant to run her through. Clammy coldness gripped her as she stared at the wicked point. As he lunged toward her, she instinctively sidestepped. The cold silver blade left a stinging sensation as it sliced through the flesh on her upper arm.

He will finish me now, Raven thought as the stinging sensation on her arm turned to red hot pain. She tried to pray, but all she could do was remember the words Devin had said: *They will not hurt you.* Little did he know . . .

The web of our life is of a
mingled yarn, good and ill together.
Shakespeare

Chapter Five

Raven opened her eyes and met Devin's concerned look. He was kneeling above her, blood dripping from a nasty gash on the side of his temple.

Suddenly she remembered what had happened. "The child," she exclaimed as she tried to sit up.

"The boy is fine. He's with his mother now."

Raven fell back. "What happened?" she asked, still groggy.

"The British sent their butchers to kill us."

"Yes, I saw that," she said, closing her eyes and taking a deep breath. "I meant . . . I thought that man was going to kill me."

"He would have if I hadn't killed him first. It seems I owe you an apology."

"An apology? I don't understand."

"I left you unprotected assuming they wouldn't harm you."

"Because you thought I was one of them?"

"Aye, you are one of them. I was a fool to think otherwise."

"That's ridiculous. Do you think I would come here knowing that the British planned to attack your people?"

"It doesn't matter what I think, Lady McClennon. It is obvious it would be best if you stayed with your own people."

"My people?" Raven exclaimed, gasping in pain as she moved her arm.

"This isn't the time to argue," he said abruptly. "You're going to have to remove your blouse so I can see to your arm."

Raven stared into his dark shadowed eyes. She could see the pain and hurt of a lifetime reflected in their depths. He, like all the Irish people, had seen too much death and destruction. She wanted to reach out and comfort him, but she didn't dare.

"There are others worse than I," she said. "My arm will be fine."

"The others are being treated. Take the blouse off, Raven," he ordered. "I dinna' have a lot of time."

Raven removed her blouse, exposing herself to the cool night air.

"Good, 'tis a clean cut," he said, removing a

bottle from his pocket. "This is going to hurt. Take a deep breath and close your eyes."

Raven bit into her bottom lip as the whiskey burned the cut like liquid fire. She closed her eyes as the world began to spin about her, not opening them again until she felt Devin ripping a strip from her petticoat.

"This will have to do for now, but when you get home have someone clean and bandage it properly," he instructed.

"I have the count you wanted," a man said from behind her.

"Is it as bad as we feared?" Taber asked.

"Seven dead, including Peggy O'Hara," the man answered.

"Damn," Taber swore, running his hand through his dark hair in frustration.

"Does he mean Peggy who worked at Riverside House?" Raven asked, her voice trembling.

"Aye," he answered in a cold voice.

"But Peggy wouldn't hurt anyone," Raven whispered, still finding it hard to understand any of what happened.

"Tell your uncle that, Raven McClennon."

"My uncle wouldn't do this," Raven insisted, but in truth she was having doubts. She had seen Walter Denseley leading the men.

"I'm not going to argue with you," Taber said impatiently. "This is Patrick Casey," he said, nodding toward the man standing in the shadows. "He's going to take you home."

"But I came with Molly and Colin . . ."

"Colin was injured. He's already been taken home."

"Oh, no. Will he be all right?" Raven asked.

"Only God knows," he said, holding his hand out to her. "Can you stand?"

"I'll take her," Patrick said as he grasped her arm. "I have a horse saddled over there. I hope you dinna' mind riding with me?" he asked.

Raven was too weak and confused to argue.

"Patrick, try not to be seen," Devin instructed. "Take her to the servants' quarters."

Raven turned to tell him that she would like to stay and help with the injured, but he had already disappeared in the darkness.

"Come along, lass. Tis going to be a long night for all of us."

By the time they reached Riverside House, Raven's anger was out of control. She was so anxious to face her uncle with her accusations that she forgot the pain in her arm. She had seen Walter Denseley leading the group of murderers, so she was sure her uncle must have known about it.

"How is the arm, lass?" Patrick Casey asked as he helped her from the horse.

"It's not so painful now," she answered.

"Thank you for bringing me here."

Patrick placed a hand on her shoulder as she started to move away. "If you dinna' mind a little advice, lass, I would suggest that you stay with your own people."

Raven's eyes widened in disbelief. "Do you also think I had something to do with what happened tonight?"

"I dinna' say that, lass. I just think it would be better if you stayed away from us," he said, quickly mounting his horse. "Particularly Devin," he said over his shoulder as he rode away.

Instead of silently creeping into the house, Raven slammed doors with all her strength. As she had hoped, the door of her uncle's study opened and he stared in puzzlement at her.

"Where have you been, Raven? I've been worried about you."

"Where have I been?" she asked with a bitter laugh. "Did you forget, Uncle Charles? I was at the fair where you sent your men to raid and kill!" Raven lifted her sleeve to expose the bloody bandage. "I'm one of the fortunate ones. I was only wounded."

"My God, child, what are you saying? I had no knowledge of a raid on the fair. Do you think I would have let you attend if I had?"

"I saw Walter Denseley leading the ruffians, and I know he takes orders from you," Raven shouted.

Charles rang the bell for a servant, then turned back to Raven. "Calm down, child. We'll get someone in here to take care of you, then we will get to the bottom of this."

Raven silently watched her uncle pace, while May, one of the Irish servants, dressed her wound. She wondered if it was possible he didn't know about the raid. She couldn't imagine her uncle purposely putting her in danger, but she could imagine Walter Denseley taking matters into his own hands, and hoping to come out a hero.

"Are you going to be much longer, May?" he asked impatiently.

"No, sir, but it's a deep gash, and I dinna' want it to become infected."

"What is going on down here?" Caroline asked from the doorway.

"Go back to bed, Caroline. Everything is under control."

Caroline's eyes took in Raven with disgust. She clutched her wool robe around her and moved into the room. "What has she been involved in now? I told you, Charles, you had better do something about that girl before she ruins us," she said without waiting for an explanation. "We're already the laughing stock of society."

"Raven is my problem, Caroline. I'll handle her the way I see fit. Now return to bed!"

"She's just like her mother. Wild and uncontrollable," she said, ignoring her husband. "I tried to tell you we should have put her in a private school when she didn't last a month with your brother, but you wouldn't listen. I tell you, if you don't marry her off soon, I'm returning to London. I will not be ruined by this wanton tramp."

"Caroline, I'm not going to tell you again . . ." Charles moved menacingly toward his wife.

Caroline pulled her robe even tighter, then lifted her haughty nose in the air. "I shall return to my bed now. If you will take my advice, you'll arrange her marriage with Walter Denseley immediately before he finds out what she is like."

"Denseley!" Raven exclaimed, coming to her feet. "You must be crazy if you think I'd ever . . ." Her uncle put a hand on her shoulder to stay her.

"Good night, Caroline," he said, turning his back to his wife. "May, are you finished?"

"Yes, sir." The woman curtsied, anxious to be out of the line of fire.

"If you think I would marry that butcher . . ." Raven fumed.

"Sit down, Raven. We have other things to discuss. Now tell me exactly what happened tonight."

Alone on the fairgrounds, Taber scanned the area. All the wounded had been tended, and the dead had been carried to their homes. Only a few men remained, discussing what had happened. He touched the gash at his temple and flinched. His grandfather and father had died trying to free Ireland from British rule, and now he was fighting the same battle. Was it hopeless, as so many thought? he wondered. He loathed the injustices he saw every day, yet his efforts to change things were thwarted at every turn.

His thoughts turned to Raven, to the look of fear and pain in her beautiful eyes. He had wanted to hold her, to comfort her, yet the question of whether he could trust her stood between them like a wall. He was sure she had never experienced anything like the events of tonight, yet he was certain her uncle had caused it.

He ran his hand through his dark hair, wishing he had never met Lady Raven McClennon. Why was he drawn to her? he wondered. Granted, she was beautiful, but there was something else—she seemed vulnerable, yet at the same time there was a hidden strength deep within. He had had many women, but none that made him wish he wasn't involved in such dangerous activities. It didn't matter, he told himself silently. He had no choice but to put her out of his mind. His life was tied to the Irish cause.

Raven lay in the dark of her room, staring at the space above her. She was afraid to close her eyes for fear the events of the evening would invade her dreams. It was bad enough she couldn't put the horror out of her mind while awake. She touched her bandaged arm, remembering the fierce look of hatred in the man's eyes as he'd lunged at her. He had meant to kill her. To kill her like they had killed Peggy O'Hara and the others. Poor Peggy. Why would anyone want to kill such a kind lady? She lived with a brother and sister and never caused harm to anyone.

Her uncle had promised to help the family, and she was determined to see that he followed through with his promise. It was strange, but by the time she'd left her uncle in the study, she had been convinced that he didn't know anything about the raid. He had promised to deal with Denseley, but Raven wondered if the only reason her uncle was upset was because she had been there and had been wounded. Did he really care that innocent people had been killed and injured? She finally fell asleep after deciding that she would check on Colin in the morning and then pay her respects to Peggy's family.

Taber O'Flynn stood with his back to the window, studying the young man lying unconscious on the bed. He had known Colin since the lad was born. Now, as he had done with so many others, he waited to see if his friend was going to live. He was so absorbed in his thoughts that he hadn't noticed Brenna O'Neill's presence.

"Have you been here all night?" she asked.

"Most of it," he stated tiredly.

"You look terrible. Have you had anyone look at that gash on your temple?"

"It's nothing," he shrugged. "What happened to you last night? I didn't see you after the fight."

"You know Fergus, he's so protective," she said, hoping to make Taber jealous. "He insisted on taking me home before I got hurt."

"You should have stayed and helped the wounded."

"I know. I wanted to, but Fergus wouldn't hear of it. I think he realized how frightened and upset I was."

Patrick Casey, who had been dozing in a chair next to the bed, spoke. "I thought I saw you dragging Fergus away as the trouble started."

"You don't know what you're talking about," Brenna snapped, then quickly turned her attention to Molly. "Molly dear, why don't you fix Taber some breakfast."

"*Devin* has already had breakfast, Brenna O'Neill," Molly spat. "We dinna' neglect our friends."

"You know better than to call me Taber," he warned.

"There isn't anyone here who doesn't know," Brenna said defensively.

"That's beside the point. My life depends on my anonymity."

"Everyone knows that," Molly said in exasperation. "At least anyone with a brain knows it."

"How dare you," Brenna retorted.

"It's time for you to go, Brenna," Taber said. "Colin needs peace and quiet right now."

"I can see I'm not wanted. I shouldn't have come in the first place, but I was concerned about Colin."

"That's refreshing," Molly said sarcastically, "since you've never been concerned about anyone but yourself before."

Before Brenna had a chance to retort, the room fell very silent as everyone stared at the doorway where Raven McClennon stood with a bouquet of wildflowers in her hand.

Her eyes met Devin's and held for a moment before she spoke. "I'm sorry if I've interrupted something, but I wanted to see how Colin was."

"You haven't interrupted anything, m'lady," Molly curtsied. "Miss O'Neill was just leaving."

Brenna turned on Molly, her eyes flashing angrily. "By all the saints in heaven, Molly Devlin, I will not forgive you for this. You treat one of your own like dirt and welcome our enemy into your home."

"She is not our enemy, Brenna O'Neill," Molly stated.

"Really? Well, we shall see about that," Brenna said, storming from the room.

"Did I miss something?" Raven asked.

"M'lady, you shouldn't be here," Molly said. "When there is trouble like last night, the people become . . . well, let's just say irrational."

"I had to come, Molly. Is Colin going to be all right?"

"We dinna' know yet, but he is resting well."

Raven noticed that Devin had turned back to stare out the window. Dry blood was caked on his temple, and he was wearing the same clothes he had had on at the fair. She was sure he hadn't had any sleep.

"Can I get you a cup of tea, m'lady?" Molly asked.

106

"No, thank you, Molly, and please stop calling me m'lady. We are friends, remember?"

Molly looked away, fidgeting with the flowers Raven had handed her.

"Molly, surely you don't think I had anything to do with what happened last night . . ." Raven pleaded. "Even my uncle didn't know anything about it."

Taber spun around and faced Raven. "Did he tell you that?"

"Yes. Last night when I got home we had a long talk. I told him I saw Denseley there and he was furious."

"Of course he was." Taber laughed sarcastically.

"My uncle is a fair man. He wouldn't kill innocent women and children," Raven insisted.

"Then he's the first Englishman who wouldn't," he snarled.

"Maybe he is. I know he wants to bring your people under British control, but he wouldn't have ordered a raid that would kill innocent women and children."

"Go home, Lady McClennon," he said, turning back to stare out the window.

Tears filled Raven's eyes. "Why are you all treating me this way? I had nothing to do with what happened last night. I was injured too, if you remember."

Taber turned around and faced her, his blue

eyes dark with an emotion she didn't understand. "I remember only too well, Raven," he
said in a soft voice. "That's what I'm trying to
prevent again. You are in the middle of
something that canna' be controlled."

"Well, far be it from me to cause you any
worry, Devin Fitzgerald. I'll go and you'll
never see me again," she exclaimed, rushing
from the cottage.

"Aren't you going to stop her?" Molly asked,
her heart going out to Raven.

"No, it's better this way. I was a fool to think
I could bring her into our circle. The very fact
that her uncle is Lord Montgomery makes her
our enemy."

"If you think that, then you're as daft as
Brenna O'Neill. Well let me tell you, Taber
O'Flynn, if you'd rather sleep with a tramp
who whores with every man in town,
including some you call your enemies, then
you dinna' deserve someone like Lady Raven
McClennon!" Molly stormed from the room,
leaving Taber with his mouth hanging open.

"That's quite a spirited young lady," Patrick
said, with a new appreciation in his eyes for
Molly Devlin. "I never realized how lovely
Molly is."

"You've never seen her mad before," Colin
said from the bed.

"Thank God," Taber said, rushing to his
friend. "My God, but you gave us quite a scare,

my friend. How are you feeling?''

"I'm starved," Colin replied.

Taber laughed, clasping Colin's hand. "That's a good sign, lad. I'll get Molly and your mother. You just lie still and take it easy."

"I feel fine, Taber."

"You've been unconscious for eighteen hours, my friend, so dinna' tell me you're fine. Since you're finally awake, I'm going home to wash up and get some sleep. I'll be back this evening to see you. And I better find you in this bed taking it easy."

"I'll be here," Colin smiled. "To be honest, I do feel a trifle weak."

Taber was looking forward to a bath and some sleep now that his friend was conscious. He had gone only a short way when he came upon Raven leading her horse. He hesitated only a moment before riding alongside her.

"Do you need help?"

"Not from you."

He continued to ride beside her. "It's dangerous for you to be on the road alone."

"I'll take my chances."

Taber dismounted, then had to hurry to keep up with Raven. "If you'll stop for a moment I'll take a look at your horse."

"I don't need your help," she persisted, walking swiftly on.

"Will you stop for a moment before you ruin this beautiful animal?" he said, grabbing her by the arm.

Raven's blue eyes blazed with anger. "Take your hands off me."

"Be reasonable, Raven. This poor animal shouldn't be made to suffer because we have a problem."

Raven stared at him for a long moment, realizing what he had said was true. She nodded her head. "You have my permission to look at her."

"Thank you, m'lady," he said with a flourished bow. "You are too kind."

Taber knelt down on one knee and felt along the horse's fore cannon and fetlock. "It looked like she was favoring her lower leg, but everything feels all right."

"It happened very quickly," Raven offered. "She was trotting without a problem, then suddenly started limping."

Taber lifted the horse's right hoof and closely examined it. "Here is the culprit."

"I looked at her hooves, but I didn't see anything," Raven said, staring over his shoulder.

"You can barely see it, but it's enough to cripple a horse."

Taber took his knife from its sheath and carefully dug out a small sharp rock. "Here is the offender, m'lady," he said, handing it to Raven.

"Thank you. I'll have my uncle give you something for your trouble," she said coolly.

Taber grabbed her by the wrist. "Dinna' push me, Raven McClennon," he warned. "I'm not one of your lackeys."

Raven stared at him. He looked tired and the wound on his head still had not been tended to. She would have offered to take care of it, but he had spurned her attempt at friendship and she would not give him the chance to hurt her again.

"If you will kindly move away from my horse I'll be on my way."

Raven's haughty demeanor irked Taber, pushing him to do something he knew he shouldn't. "Surely you dinna' plan to leave until you reward me for coming to your aid."

"I told you my uncle will reward you," she snapped, pushing past him.

"I dinna' want anything from your uncle."

"What do you want?" she asked angrily.

"This," he said, pulling her into his arms. He captured her mouth in a consuming kiss. Raven struggled against him for a moment, but when his tongue touched her own, her knees went weak and she leaned helplessly against him.

When he finally ended the kiss, he stared down into her smoldering eyes, wondering why of all the women in Ireland, he was drawn to her. He was about to apologize for his actions at the Devlin's house when she abruptly pulled away from him.

She swung up on Devil Lady, then turned, and smiled coolly at him. "Go home to *your* people, Devin Fitzgerald. I don't need the likes of you and your troubles."

"Raven, wait!" Taber shouted, trying without success to grab the reins as she urged the horse to a gallop. "What am I going to do about you, Raven McClennon?" he said, watching her disappear down the road in a cloud of dust.

Love bade me welcome,
yet my soul drew back.
George Herbert

Chapter Six

Raven opened her eyes as the morning sun crept through the opening where the heavy drapes met. A wave of drowsiness swept over her and she closed her eyes again, wishing she could sleep until the day was over. This was the morning of the big party her aunt and uncle were giving. She dreaded it and wished there were some way to avoid going. Her aunt had threatened to announce her engagement to Walter Denseley if Raven didn't choose one of the eligible bachelors invited.

Sitting up, Raven stacked the pillows behind her. They could invite the King of England and she wouldn't marry him—unless she wanted to. She smiled to herself, imagining King George asking her to marry him. Or better yet, the Irish rebel, Taber O'Flynn, she

113

giggled to herself. Wouldn't that unhinge Aunt Caroline. Her mother had married a rebel Scotsman, she thought smugly, and everyone was always telling her she was just like her mother. Why not a rebel Irishman?

She clutched a pillow to her chest, remembering how her mother and father loved each other. Her life had been perfect with the love of two such wonderful people. They hadn't needed her mother's English relatives, they had each other—until their tragic death.

Raven closed her eyes and took a deep breath. Her mother and father were together for eternity, she told herself. Mourning only gave her pain, and it wouldn't bring them back.

It was odd, she thought back. Aunt Caroline and Uncle Charles had visited them in Scotland for the first time just before her mother and father were killed. Everyone had gotten along famously, then all of a sudden they cut short their visit and hurried off to London. When they returned for the funeral, her aunt had treated her like a leper, and to this day she didn't know why her aunt hated her. Even though she had gone to live with one of her mother's sisters, Uncle Charles had always been in charge of her inheritance. He had always been kind to her, making her wonder all the more why Caroline hated her so, and why before she had even gone to stay with her relatives, her aunt had filled their heads with stories about how wild and uncontrollable a highlander brat she was. She had never stood a chance with any of them.

"Oh, m'lady, are you still abed?" Molly exclaimed as she hurried into the room. "You're going to need a good breakfast to get you through this day," she clucked. "Knowing your aunt, if you're not downstairs in the next few minutes, she'll send everything back to the kitchen."

"Then I'll eat in the kitchen," Raven laughed, delighted to have her Irish friend back.

"But that wouldn't be proper, m'lady," Molly said, pulling the quilt back.

"In all honesty, I'd much prefer the company of the cook to my aunt," Raven pointed out. "At least Maureen doesn't bite my head off."

"Aye, but your aunt will have my head if I dinna' have you downstairs quickly."

Realizing what Molly said was probably true, Raven climbed from the bed. "If you will lay out my blue morning dress, I'll comb my hair."

"Thank you, m'lady."

"Molly, if you don't stop calling me that when we're alone, I'm going to have your head."

"I'm sorry, Raven, but if your aunt or uncle heard me call you that, they would dismiss me, and with Colin unable to work, my family is depending on me."

Raven stared at her young friend. "I'm the one who is sorry, Molly. I should have thought about my request putting you in danger." Raven stepped into the dress Molly held out. "How is Colin?"

"He's improving every day, but he is still quite weak. Everyday he gets up and announces he is going to work, but after he's up for an hour he's as weak as a baby. The doctor says it is just going to take time."

"I'll talk to my uncle and see if he won't help your family."

"Oh, no, m'lady, please dinna' do that. We are fine. Our friends are helping us."

Raven snorted, unladylike. "Friends like Devin Fitzgerald?"

"Aye, m'lady. Devin has been a good friend. Now please, we dinna' have time to talk about this," she said, urging Raven to hurry.

"I think you're making a grave mistake, my friend," Patrick Casey said as he sat across the table from Taber.

116

"It would look strange if I dinna' accept Lord Montgomery's invitation, and Peter agrees," Taber explained.

"And what about Lady Raven McClennon? What's to stop her from exposing you? After your last parting I'm sure she'd take great delight in doing you in."

"Expose me for what? A stable boy? They can't put me in prison for that," Taber laughed.

Patrick shook his head. "By God, I have to admit, I'd like to see Montgomery's face when he learns Taber O'Flynn was a guest in his house."

"You better hope neither of us is around if he ever learns that, my friend. Now let's get back to our plan. Is everyone straight about what they are to do?"

"Aye, we went over it last night. The Hawk will strike at nine o'clock. Sean Gilmartin volunteered to help since Fergus is going to be involved here."

"Good. And is the distribution point for the horses set?"

"Aye, Finnegan is handling that."

"Be sure that mine and Tomas's horses are taken too."

"Nighthawk?" Patrick asked in astonishment.

"Do you think I'm a fool, man?" Taber laughed. "We'll be using two of Tomas's riding horses.''

"Ah, very wise," Patrick said as he stood to leave. "Well, I better be on my way. I'll see you at the party." Patrick turned back to face Taber when he reached the door. "And Taber, be prepared to walk home," he laughed.

Taber stared after Patrick, his lighthearted mood quickly disappearing. His friend was right—he was concerned about Lady Raven McClennon. Her reaction to his presence at her uncle's party could seriously jeopardize his cover. Yet come hell or high water, he couldn't pass up the chance to see her again, and that really worried him. He had never let a woman cloud his judgment before. It had been two weeks since she had ridden away from him— two miserable weeks of wanting to see her, yet knowing how dangerous it was.

Taber shook his head. How was it that a sensible man could so quickly turn into a fool when his heart was involved?

The gold thread in Raven's white satin gown glimmered in the candlelight as she descended the stairs on the arm of her uncle. The daring, low-cut gown had been a last-minute surprise from her aunt and uncle. Part of the plan to parade her like a peacock before the eligible bachelors, she was sure.

"Just relax, Raven," her uncle whispered.

"You're as stiff as a board."

"I don't like being put on display."

"Enjoy the evening, my dear. I've already told you your aunt will have no say in who you marry. But I must be honest, it is time for you to be picking out a husband, Raven."

Before she had a chance to protest, a half-dozen men swarmed around them as they reached the foot of the stairs.

"Gentlemen, I know you are all anxious to meet my niece, but please, give her room to breathe," Lord Montgomery said good-naturedly.

After introductions were made, Raven was continually surrounded by men. In thirty minutes time she was bored with all of them. She found herself comparing each one to Devin Fitzgerald; to the deep, melodious voice that sent shivers down her spine, or to the dark eyes that haunted her days and nights.

She was trying to pretend to be interested in her dance partner's constant conversation, but she was finding it extremely difficult. He had introduced himself as Oliver Lane, from London, who had taken over one of the Irish estates to the west. She found him pompous and boring, and even though she tried to be attentive, it was impossible. She found herself glancing around the room at the other guests as he talked—and talked. She spotted Brenna O'Neill on the arm of Peter Muldane. The girl must have changed her mind about who was the enemy, Raven thought disgustedly. She certainly looked as if she was enjoying herself.

Suddenly Raven stiffened, drawing in a deep breath as her eyes locked with those of Devin Fitzgerald. She couldn't believe it. Her stable boy was dressed in a black velvet suit with a shirt of white silk. He looked the fashionable cavalier, making all others in the room seem absurdly vulgar in their bright colors.

"Oh," she exclaimed when he had the audacity to smile at her. "Oliver, you must forgive me, but I see someone I must speak to immediately." Without waiting for a reply, Raven headed toward Devin.

"Are you out of your mind?" she asked, glancing around to see if anyone was watching them. "I cannot believe you would come here masquerading as a gentleman. This could get you into serious trouble."

He took her hand and kissed the inside of her palm. "I'm touched by your concern, m'lady, but I assure you I was invited."

"Invited? By whom, the cook?" she asked sarcastically.

"Ah, Raven, I see you have already met Lord Fitzgerald," her uncle said as he joined them.

"Lord Fitzgerald?" Raven repeated faintly, staring at him as if he had sprouted horns.

"Yes, m'lady," Devin smiled, "and this is my cousin, Tomas Fitzgerald, Lord of Blackmoor."

"Lord Fitzgerald," Raven repeated again, oblivious to the introductions just made. "But that's impossible . . ."

"M'lady, may I have the honor of this dance?" Devin asked. Before she could reply, he was pulling her along to the center of the room where other couples were dancing.

"I don't want to dance," Raven spat, pulling her hand out of his. "I want some answers."

"And I will give them to you, but not if you make a scene."

"A scene?" she exclaimed. "Does scratching your eyes out constitute a scene?"

"Calm down, Raven," he said, pulling her back into his arms. "If you will shut up, I'll explain."

But before he had a chance, Oliver Lane was suddenly there, tapping on Devin's shoulder. "I've been waiting to finish our dance, Lady Montgomery. You don't mind, do you, old chap?"

"Yes, I mind. The lady is dancing with me," Devin warned, his voice a low growl.

"I'm so sorry, *Lord* Fitzgerald, but I did promise Oliver I'd be right back to finish our dance. You must excuse me," she said, moving into the Englishman's arms.

By God, I'll break her beautiful neck, he thought as he stood alone in the middle of the floor.

"Are you having trouble keeping a dance partner?" Brenna asked at his side.

"Something like that," he answered, his eyes still on Raven.

"Peter is only interested in talking politics. I was hoping you might dance with me."

Taber stared down into Brenna's topaz eyes, then took her into his arms. As they moved around the floor, he wondered why he couldn't have been content to stay with Brenna and enjoy her when he felt like it. Instead he had to long for the infuriating, obstinate niece of his enemy. God, what possessed him, he wondered in frustration.

"I haven't seen much of you lately," Brenna said, touching the curling hair at the back of his neck. "Not since that unfortunate day at the Devlins'."

"You have a way of rubbing people the wrong way, Brenna," he answered indifferently.

"I dinna' use to rub you the wrong way, if you know what I'm talking about," she said seductively.

Taber stared down at her, a cruel smile touched his lips. "Why Brenna, I had heard you were Peter's constant escort of late. Do you think he'd approve of you seeing Fergus and me at the same time?"

"Dinna' be cruel, Taber."

Devin's hand clutched hers in a deathlike grip. "I've warned you before . . ."

"I'm sorry, *Devin*. I was going to say that

you know I wouldn't see anyone else if you'd make some commitment to me."

"I'm afraid the time for commitments is past, Brenna. There was a day when I might have asked you to be my wife, but that was before I learned you slept with most of my friends."

"I dinna' think it's that at all. You came to me when you first returned. I think it's the Lady Raven McClennon."

Devin stared over Brenna's shoulder toward Raven. "Perhaps you're right, Brenna," he admitted.

"I've never known you to be a fool before," she said bitterly.

"I guess there's always a first time."

Lord Fitzgerald, Raven fumed. How dare he pretend to be a stable boy . . . and Molly . . . wait until she faced her. They had all lied to her, but why? Why would he pretend to be a stable hand and have everyone go along with him? Even Colin had. Damn the man! He'd had every opportunity that day at the fair to tell her the truth. They had talked for hours. And damn him for bringing his mistress here. Look at him dancing and smiling at her. How dare he! He was beneath contempt. Before the night was over, everyone in the room would probably know about his little joke, and be laughing at her for a foolish woman.

When the music stopped, Raven quickly made her way to her uncle's side. "I suddenly have a terrible headache, Uncle Charles. If you don't mind, I'm going to lie down for a while."

"Of course, my dear. Is there anything I can do for you?"

Yes, get rid of Lord Devin Fitzgerald, she thought silently. "No, I'll be fine."

Taber joined Tomas and Peter Muldane in conversation, but he couldn't take his eyes off Raven. He had expected her to be surprised— maybe shocked—to see him there, but he hadn't planned on her not giving him a chance to explain.

He watched her speak with her uncle then leave the room. He looked around, considering going after her.

"Careful, cousin. You are very easy to read tonight."

"Am I, Tomas?"

"That lady could be very dangerous to you and the Brotherhood."

Taber knew what he said was true, yet he had a physical desire for Raven McClennon which he could no longer master. As he watched her dance with another man, he had been rudely jolted from thinking he had control over everything about himself. He had endured physical and emotional pain, and had always survived because he was strong. But now he felt totally devastated by this new weakness—a weakness for a mere girl.

"Lord Fitzgerald," Charles Montgomery called, stopping Taber from his intention. "Lord Denseley tells me he hasn't been introduced to you this evening, but that you looked very familiar to him."

"How do you do," Taber said, turning on the charm. "I've been anxious to meet you after hearing so many tales of your exploits."

Walter Denseley forgot his suspicions, thinking he had an admirer among the Irish gentry. To Taber's frustration, he found himself trapped in conversation. As they talked, he overheard Charles Montgomery tell his wife that Raven had retired to her room with a headache.

Taber glanced at Tomas as the clock chimed on the quarter hour. In a few minutes his men would arrive and when they did, he needed to be a visible, outraged guest. That meant he didn't have time to pursue Raven until the raid started. When Walter Denseley became involved in conversation with another guest, Taber excused himself and made his way toward Molly.

"Good evening, Molly."

"Good evening, sir," Molly answered, her face turning a bright pink. "Would you like something to drink, sir?"

"No, not right now. I want to know where

Lady McClennon's quarters are."

Molly's eyes widened. "Ye dinna' mean to go there . . ."

"I'm afraid I do, Molly," he smiled.

Molly glanced around cautiously. "She is in your old wing, sir."

Taber smiled. "How kind of the Montgomerys to accommodate me. Does Raven know about the tunnel?"

"Oh, no sir. No one knows about it except Colin and me."

"Good. When the raid begins, I'm going to disappear for a while. If you hear anyone ask about me, tell them you saw me dash out the door after the freebooters."

"Please be careful, sir."

"I will, Molly. Right now I think I should ask Lady Caroline Montgomery to dance."

With her mouth hanging open, Molly watched as Taber and Lady Montgomery danced around the floor. Then as the commotion broke out from outside, she realized why.

A shot rang out, and then another. Raven strained to see in the darkness. A woman's shrill scream came from below. She could hear horses whinnying and stomping below her window. Then the air seemed filled with thunder as a great number of horses were stampeded out of the stables onto the cobblestone yard. When the horses had disappeared and the night was silent again, she could still hear shouts and running feet in the lower part of the house.

Frustrated that she couldn't see well enough, Raven pulled a chair over to the window and leaned out. She could see the whole incredible scene quite easily now. Mounted horsemen cantered around in the dark as the last of the horses were herded past. Guests from the party were running around trying to catch horses in vain, while shouting obscenities at the raiders.

She giggled, putting her hand over her mouth to keep from being heard as she watched Walter Denseley running around in circles, shouting for someone to find him a horse.

"You dinna' look ill to me," said a voice from behind her. "I'm glad. I was afraid I wouldn't get that dance we started."

Raven spun around to face Devin Fitzgerald standing only a few feet from her. "How did you get in here? The door was locked from the inside."

"So it was."

Raven realized how foolish she must look standing up on the chair. She closed the window behind her and climbed down. "I suggest you find your way out before I call my uncle."

"Not until we talk."

"I have no intention of listening to more of your lies."

"Are you referring to the fact that you thought I was a stable hand?"

"Of course I am," Raven snapped.

"You were the one who assumed I was a stable hand."

"And you never bothered to tell me you weren't, and you've had many opportunities since then to tell me the truth. What I can't understand is why everyone has gone along with your lie."

"I was wrong not to have told you the truth, but I was afraid our relationship would be different if you knew who I really was."

"Our relationship?" Raven laughed cruelly. "We never met that you didn't end up telling me to go home, or your friends would tell me to stay away from you. I don't call that a relationship. And while I'm on the subject, what is a gentleman like yourself doing involved in your clandestine meetings?"

Raven suddenly fell silent. "I wouldn't be surprised if you didn't have something to do with what happened downstairs a few minutes ago."

Taber let her ramble, thinking how beautiful she was with her blue eyes blazing and her pert chin tilted defiantly.

"Perhaps I did, little one, but that has

nothing to do with us. You and I have another matter to settle."

Raven should have sensed Devin's mood had suddenly changed, but she knew little about what went on in the minds of men. He moved toward her, and before Raven realized what he meant to do, he pulled her into his arms. His lips nuzzled along the curve of her jaw before pressing a flurry of kisses in the hollow of her throat.

"No," she moaned in a husky voice, yet her body responded as his tongue touched her own, sending shock waves through her.

"Are you aware that you drive me crazy," he whispered against her mouth. "You're the most irritating, yet desirable woman I've ever met."

Somehow Raven found the willpower to break away. She took several deep breaths, trying to still the erratic pounding in her chest and temples.

"I will not be distracted from the issue here," she said breathlessly. "I want some answers."

Taber smiled. "Ask away, love. I'm at your service."

It took a moment for Raven to clear her head and remember what questions she wanted answered. "First tell me how you got in here."

"Ah, Raven, my sweet, have you never heard of secret passages that lovers use?"

Raven stared at him suspiciously. "Or that a

young boy who lived in this house used?"

"I prefer to think of it being used by lovers," he said undaunted.

"You're not a stable boy," Raven said as if the fact had just sunk in.

"I told you that."

"I don't believe you're this Lord Fitzgerald either. I think you're Taber O'Flynn."

Taber laughed uneasily. "My word, lass, what an imagination you have."

Raven's eyes sparkled with discovery. "It all fits. The night at the fair . . . you were in charge . . . the others looked to you." Raven threw her hands up. "My God, how could I have not realized it. Molly told me you were helping her family. How could a stable boy have helped them financially?"

Taber leaned casually against the bedpost and let Raven go on. "I've had this feeling about you ever since that day we met at Blackmoor House . . ." she mused.

"Aye, I've had it too," he agreed amiably, "but if you believe I'm Taber O'Flynn, why haven't you called for your uncle?"

Raven's eyes suddenly took on a wary look. "I've stumbled on something I shouldn't have," she said, a tinge of fear in her voice, as she moved toward the door.

"Come here, Raven," he ordered softly.

Raven went still, as if held by his soft command.

"Come here," he repeated. Something in his voice sent a quiver along her nerves. She turned and faced him, meeting his dark gaze with a questioning look.

"My God, you really are Taber O'Flynn," she whispered in disbelief.

"What difference does it make what names we use. We are drawn together, you and I, and neither of us has any control over it."

"No," she protested feebly, as he pulled her into his arms. "I could never feel anything for a man who doesn't trust me enough to be honest with me."

Taber held her angry gaze for a moment before trying to explain. "My caution comes from a life of not trusting people, Raven. My existence has depended on it. And to make matters worse, you are the niece of my enemy."

"But *I'm* not your enemy."

Taber smiled at her. "Aye, I have to admit, I have a hard time thinking of you as my enemy." Holding her gaze, he touched the skin exposed at the neckline of her low-cut gown. "In honesty, all I can think about is making love to you."

Raven pulled away and walked across the room toward the fireplace. She needed to widen the distance between them before she did something she'd surely live to regret.

"Is that what you tell all the young women who flock to your side?"

"Ah, lass, you cut me deep. There are no flocks of women at my side. I practically live the life of a monk."

Raven turned and studied the dark head and powerful shoulders. No man who looked as he did could live the life of a monk. "I've heard that Taber O'Flynn has bairns across the breadth of Ireland."

Taber laughed. "God's love, but someone has a high opinion of my virility." When Raven turned back to the fire, he moved to stand behind her. "Those are the words of my enemies, Raven."

"Aye, I know, but can you deny them?"

He forced her to turn around and look into his eyes. "Do I need to? You talked of trust . . ."

"This is ridiculous," she said, moving away again. "What are you doing here? Why would you be interested in me? Did you think to entertain yourself by having a lark with your enemy's niece?"

Her word angered him, yet he understood her fear. Patience, he told himself. "If I recall correctly, you came looking for me that morning at Blackmoor House. Did you mean to have a lark with me to spite your uncle?"

"Touché," Raven said softly.

They were silent for a few moments. "Isn't it very dangerous for you to be here?"

"Aye. But I was afraid you might be frightened by the thieves and reivers below your window. I had in mind to soothe the lovely lady if she was distressed."

Raven couldn't help but smile. "I'm not so timid to let a bunch of horse thieves frighten me."

"Aye, I could see that when I entered. What were you laughing at as you hung so precariously out the window?"

"Walter Denseley was running around like a chicken with his head cut off, shouting for someone to find him a horse."

Taber laughed. "It must have been a glorious sight. You should have shared it with me."

"Aye, I should have." She smiled.

Taber moved around the room, touching the four-poster bed, then the large chest against the wall. He moved with such grace that Raven was reminded of a very dangerous cat who was setting a trap—a trap to snare his prey—and she was the prey.

"I understand you grew up in this house."

"Aye. These were my rooms."

She understood now how he had got into her room. "I am sorry it no longer belongs to you. I know it must bring back painful memories."

He moved toward the window and gave a cursory glance at the stables below. "My sister and I used to stay up half the night reading books to each other or playing games."

"Where is your sister now?"

Taber's expression showed nothing, but his voice was cold and hard. "She is dead, as well as my mother and father."

"I am sorry," she said quietly. "I had no right to ask personal questions."

"You had every right. Do you want to know how they died?"

"Not if it pains you to speak of it."

"The pain has passed. Only the need for vengeance remains."

Raven winced at the bitterness in his voice. She sat on the edge of the bed and stared at the man who had suffered so much in his young lifetime.

"My sister, Katy, was a beauty—auburn hair and emerald green eyes. She had a sprinkling of freckles across her nose and cheeks that I used to love to tease her about . . ."

The love in his eyes as he spoke of his sister tore at Raven's heart. She wanted to hold him, comfort him, but she stayed where she was and let him talk, knowing that it had probably taken him years to be able to speak of his pain.

"On a beautiful morning her intention to marry Allan Donnally was announced at mass. We were going to have a celebration." Taber took a deep breath. "Instead we prepared a funeral for two people. Katy was trampled to death beneath the hooves of a horse ridden by a drunken British soldier, and Allan was shot in the back and killed by another British officer when he dragged the drunken soldier from his horse."

"Oh, Taber," Raven gasped. "I'm so sorry . . ."

"My father was hung," he went on relentlessly as if Raven hadn't spoken. "With the help of the French, he led a group against the English at Bantry Bay. A storm came up and most of the ships were blown off course. The ones that made it into the harbor were captured. Some of them escaped, but the ones who were captured were hung. My mother and I were forced to watch, and then when we returned here, we found the British had confiscated our home and everything in it. My mother's health plummeted. I took her to France to visit her sister, hoping it would help, but in less than three months after the hanging, my mother died."

"Why did you come back here? You could have started a new life away from the horrors of what this land has done to you and your family."

"It's not Ireland. It's the English," he spat.

"Hatred is a waste of time, Taber. It's not going to bring your family back."

"No, I suppose not, but it's the only life I know. My father was the leader of the Brotherhood, and it came to me when he died."

Suddenly the sound of the music resuming

interrupted their conversation.

"You should go now before someone misses you," she said.

"Aye, I should," he agreed, but didn't move. "Come back to the party so we can finish our dance."

"I think not," she said soberly. "My indiscretion has gone far enough for one night. Besides, don't you think it would look suspicious if you and I showed up together?"

"If you'll wait a few minutes before going back down, I'll make my entrance through the front door. No one will ever guess we were together."

"The front door? But how?"

"Never question me, lass." He smiled warmly. "Just believe."

He moved closer, and reached out to touch a lock of her hair. Raven lost any inclination to move away at his touch, yet still she trembled.

"Dinna' be afraid, lass."

"I think I have good reason to be afraid," she answered breathlessly.

"Are you sure?"

No, she was sure of nothing at that moment as his mouth descended on hers. Time hung suspended, and then he released her. Raven's eyes were still closed against the devastating effect of his kiss.

"You are becoming an expert at the art of kissing," he said with a smile on his handsome face. "Are you sure you haven't been practicing on Walter Denseley?"

Raven's eyes flew to his face and met his teasing grin. She had to laugh, easing the tension of the moment.

"The time never seems right for us, Lady Raven McClennon, but mark my word, you will be mine, and soon."

He moved away from her to the oversized chest. She watched in amazement as he touched something on the chest and a panel of the wall slid open just enough for him to step through.

"I'll meet you downstairs," he said. "And Raven, if you're not there in fifteen minutes, I'll come back for you."

"I'll be there," she whispered.

She stood frozen to the spot as the panel closed, leaving her alone in the room. She touched her lips where only moments before Taber O'Flynn's mouth had been warm and enticing against hers. Her heart was still beating an erratic rhythm. He said she would be his. Is this what love feels like? she wondered.

Taber entered by way of the front door, making a great commotion about finding the feather of a bird on the front steps.

"And of course we all know the Hawk and Taber O'Flynn are one and the same. Damn the bastard," Denseley swore.

"Watch your mouth, Walter," Charles Montgomery warned. "There are ladies present."

"I'm sorry, Charles, but it just infuriates me that we can't catch the man when he's right under our noses."

Taber had to smile. "What makes you think Taber O'Flynn and the Hawk are the same person?" Taber asked. "I heard O'Flynn sailed to America when he escaped Newgate."

"That's what he would like us to believe," Denseley snorted.

"I think some of us would hear something about him being in Cork if he was," Peter Muldane commented. "I really believe this is a bunch of hoodlums commiting these crimes and hoping people will blame O'Flynn."

"You could be right," Montgomery said, noticing that his party was falling apart. "Please, everyone continue to enjoy yourselves. The tables are loaded with food and drink. Don't worry about transportation. James Blakeney has already sent his groom to fetch horses for those of you who rode. Those of you who came in carriages have no problem, since they were not bothered."

Lord Montgomery noticed his daughter coming down the steps. "Ah, here's my niece. Maestro, please play something happy," he ordered. "My niece and I will get the dancing started again."

Taber watched Charles Montgomery lead his niece to the dance floor, unaware that Walter Denseley followed his gaze.

"She's a lovely thing, isn't she?" Denseley asked.

"I'm sorry. What did you say?"

"Lady McClennon. I said she was lovely."

"Aye, that she is."

"I have been considering asking for her hand," Denseley said smugly.

Taber wanted to strangle the pompous fool at his side, but he forced a cool tone. "How nice for you."

"My only hesitation has been that she has a rebellious streak in her."

"A rebellious streak?" Taber pretended shock. "My word, I can understand why you're hesitating. By all means, I would stay away from a woman like that. She would only cause you great distress and embarrassment."

Denseley was surprised by Fitzgerald's opinion. "But surely you can see my dilemma. She is very desirable. If only she could be brought under control."

Taber clenched his fist at his sides. "I doubt it would be worth the effort. There are too many willing women around."

"Ah, but not with a fortune coming to them in a month," Denseley whispered conspiratorially.

"But is it enough to make your life with a nagging, rebellious woman worthwhile?"

An evil smile lit Denseley's face. "Sometimes taming a woman like that can be very worthwhile, if you know what I mean?"

"Has her uncle given you reason to think he'd agree to a marriage between you?" Taber asked, trying to keep his voice calm.

"Her aunt has, and I think her uncle will come around soon enough. If I can catch this damned Taber O'Flynn, Montgomery would be proud to have me for a son-in-law."

If that's what it depends on, you can forget it, Taber thought angrily. He returned his attention to Raven. She had changed partners and was now dancing with a handsome young man from Dublin whom he had met earlier. "You may have some competition," he pointed out to Denseley. "The lady seems to be enjoying herself."

Without answering, Denseley made his way through the crowd to Raven. The young man looked amazed when his dance was interrupted, but he reluctantly turned Raven over to Denseley.

Taber smiled when he saw the look of disgust on Raven's face as Denseley took her into his arms. *The lady looks as if she needs saving,* he thought smugly.

Walter Denseley hesitated, a black scowl on his face when Taber cut in on his dance with Raven.

"He's a dangerous man," Raven whispered as Denseley walked away. "You of all people shouldn't cross him."

"You mean he doesn't like stable boys?" Taber asked with a mischievous grin on his handsome face.

"Be serious," Raven snapped. "You know very well what I mean."

"I do, beautiful lady, and I appreciate your concern, but Walter Denseley doesn't bother me."

"Well, he bothers me," Raven exclaimed.

"I can understand why with your aunt trying to force you into marriage with him."

Raven looked up in surprise. "How did you know that?"

"Denseley just told me his life story."

"I'll see him in hell before I marry him," she said bluntly.

"You dinna' think there's any chance your uncle would ever agree to this match?"

Raven lowered her lashes. "That is something that has also bothered me of late. I don't think he would, but my aunt has been putting a great deal of pressure on him."

"I would speak for you myself, but if I did, I'm sure your uncle would check into my background, and that could be disastrous."

Raven stared up at him. "Why would you even consider offering to marry me?"

"I thought that was obvious. I've been drawn to you since that day in the garden at Riverside House. I thought you felt it too."

"Aye, I feel it," Raven admitted quietly.

As the music came to an end, Taber saw Raven's aunt bearing down on them. He smiled down into Raven's face. "We are about to be interrupted by your aunt. If I dinna' have a chance to speak to you again this evening, I want you to know that if you need anything, you can send a message to me through Molly."

"How do you know you can trust me?"

"I feel it," he said, squeezing her hand.

Her aunt and Walter Denseley never gave Raven another chance to talk with Taber. She suffered in silence as she listened to Walter boast about how he was going to capture Taber O'Flynn soon. The man was an idiot, Raven thought. Taber was right under his nose and he didn't even know it.

Raven turned to leave Denseley and saw Taber at the door preparing to leave. He was talking to her uncle and Peter Muldane. Again she thought how his tall, good looks made every other man in the room seem insignificant. He laughed at something her uncle had said, and that delightful sound touched her nerves like a flicker of fire.

Suddenly he turned, his dark eyes meeting

hers. She didn't move or take her eyes from his. The room seemed to spin about her, as he smiled, and she found it hard to breathe.

Tomas Fitzgerald placed a hand on Taber's shoulder, drawing his attention from her. She felt very alone as she watched him disappear through the door. She suddenly wanted to escape the noise and crowd and retire to her room, where she could think about what they had said and done. What he said was true, she thought as she made her way through the crowd. She was drawn to him—drawn like a moth to a flame.

I am tired of planning and toiling
In the crowded hives of men;
Heart-weary of building and spoiling
And spoiling and building again . . .
        William B. McBurney

Chapter Seven

Coffins coming into Ireland were not un-common. Many people returned family or loved ones to the Old Country for burial—and that was what Taber was depending on. The night of Montgomery's party, the guns had been moved from the ship to a warehouse on the docks during that eerie time between dusk and darkness when the fog rolled off the sea. And for the past two weeks, each day two coffins had been loaded onto flat-bed wagons and headed for various points around Ireland. The only thing that made these coffins different was that each one was loaded with guns instead of a body.

The minutes ticked off agonizingly slowly

for Taber as he paced in the shadows. This was the time he hated—the waiting when there was nothing he could do but pray everything went as planned.

The Brotherhood knew there was no way to match the British on a battlefield, so instead they had to wait for the right moment to do damage a little at a time. Their hope was if they hit and picked at them long enough, maybe they'd go back to England and leave them in peace. Peace, Taber thought bitterly. What a foreign word that was to an Irishman. They talked about it, prayed for it, but had never known it. They had tried fighting with weapons, with the aid of the French, and with words. Oh yes, the Irish were never at a loss for words, he thought, remembering all the martyred patriot speeches he had heard since he was born.

Taber thought about what his life could be like if things were different and he could be with Raven McClennon. They'd live in a cottage by the sea and raise a dozen little raven-haired children.

He ran his hand through his hair, trying to bring his mind back to the business at hand, but it was no good. She haunted him day and night. He'd tasted her sweet lips and it only made him want more. He wanted her naked on his bed so he could explore her lovely body, learn how she felt and how she tasted. He closed his eyes and tried to imagine how her breasts would feel in his hands, and how they would respond to his kisses.

Taber slammed his fist against the rough planking of the wall. Why was he torturing himself? It wasn't bloody likely he'd ever have Lady Raven McClennon. His life belonged to the Irish people—and her uncle was his enemy.

Hell, he'd just find himself a warm and willing woman tonight, he decided. That must be what he needed. He'd had plenty of women, but none that ever meant anything to him. There was never an affair he hadn't controlled or walked away from without a second thought. Why now? Why at this time did he have to fall in love ... yes, it was love, he admitted to himself. Raven McClennon had obliterated his defenses and exposed his weakness, his own human frailty—he was alone and needed someone. With a deep breath he admitted to himself that he didn't want any other woman. He wanted Raven. Something had happened to him that day at Blackmoor House when he had nearly seduced her. And he had felt it each time he saw her since, until it was excruciatingly painful even to think about her, knowing how futile it was to love her.

"Are they on the way yet?" Peter Muldane asked, breaking into Taber's thoughts.

"They're ready to leave now. The *Donegal* is in port unloading so I thought to have our wagons blend in with theirs."

"Aye, good thinking. We might as well use any opportunity for cover we can get."

Peter studied Taber, knowing there was something on his mind, and he was afraid he knew what it was. "I heard from O'Hara. The rifles arrived at Wickslow without any problems."

"Good. Now if the rest will go as smoothly."

Silence fell between them. Taber stared out the window, but Peter knew he wasn't looking at anything in particular.

"What's bothering you, lad?" Taber shoved his hands in his pockets and continued to stare out the window. "Is it a woman?" When Taber didn't answer, Peter laughed. "Of course it's a woman, but it's not just any woman. It's Lady Raven McClennon, isn't it?"

Taber turned and faced his long-time friend. "Aye, rotten luck, isn't it? I've fallen in love with my enemy's niece."

"Jesus," Peter hissed through clenched teeth. This had gone farther than he had thought. "When did you sleep with her?"

Taber stared at Peter. "I dinna' have to sleep with her to know how I feel."

"I've never known you to be a fool, Taber. Think about it. You're infatuated with the girl. Lie with her and get it over with, then you can get your mind back on business."

"It's not like that," Taber growled.

148

"Hell, what are you doing, man, thinking about rose-covered cottages and wee babes about? Give her up. Your ass belongs to us. You don't have the right to inflict your life on a woman. Think of the suffering you'd put her through. Her life would be hell with every tick of the clock. And don't forget, when we get caught, they dinna' just settle for punishing us—they go for our loved ones too. Can you see that pretty little thing being used by them bastards, then left to starve or rot in prison. All because you *wanted* her."

Taber reeled under his words. "I'm thirty-four," he said defeated. "I gave up ever finding someone I loved, but now . . ."

"You'll have to settle for loving your country, lad. It was your father's destiny and it's yours."

"My father married," Taber retorted.

"Aye, and look what your family suffered."

Turning back to the window, Taber stared into space. "Listen to me, lad, if anything happens to me, you're the number one man in Ireland, and by God, I haven't worked with you for all these years to have you throw that away for a fancy piece."

Taber spun around and grabbed Peter by the shirtfront. The look in his eyes was a mixture of anger and confusion. Then he shoved Peter away from him without a word.

Peter straightened his clothes. "I know what

you're feeling, Taber."

"How the hell would you know?"

"I was in love once. May was her name. She was from London visiting a relative in Sligo. Her lovely face and the memory of the one night we shared kept me from going insane when I was in prison. Every night for six years I'd remember every word, every move we made. I'd remember how her skin felt and how her eyes looked when I made love to her."

Tears filled Peter's eyes, but he cleared his throat and continued in a choked voice. "I dinna' know until I escaped that two days after I had been captured, they'd stripped her naked, shaved her head, and then stoned her to death in the Court Square—all because I had been a rutting animal and had wanted her in my bed."

"You said you loved her . . ."

"Aye, I loved her, but not enough to give up my work with the Brotherhood. That's the only way, man. You either have to walk away from the girl or from your country. And I dinna' think after all these years that you can walk away from what you've been taught from the cradle."

"What has the love of Ireland done for me," Taber asked angrily. "It's taken my family, my home, and now I'm supposed to walk away from the only woman I've ever loved. It's a damn high price to pay."

"Aye, that it is, lad, but thousands have paid

it before you."

"And thousands will pay it after me. That's the hell of it. Is what we're doing going to make any difference?"

"Would you rather roll over and play dead?"

Taber stared at Peter, then laughed bitterly. "'Tis funny, man. I thought that was exactly what you were asking me to do."

Before he could answer, Taber turned and left the room. Peter didn't follow him. There wasn't any need to. He had known the boy since the day he'd been born. He'd seen him through his father's death, and his sister's and mother's deaths. No matter what he felt for this girl, Taber wouldn't abandon his people or the cause.

He was living in limbo, Taber thought as he watched the last wagon disappear out of sight. What kind of life was it when you lived from one day to the next trying to figure a way to destroy your enemy before he destroyed you. This was the only way he had known since the day he was born. Damnit, he'd like to have someone to go home to, someone to welcome him with open arms and a word of comfort when things didn't go right.

He started up toward the cliffs overlooking the city. Raven didn't have anyone either. They were alike, the two of them, kindred souls, for all the good it was going to do them.

His feet moved in the direction of Riverside House, but Peter's words kept echoing in his brain: *they'd stripped her naked, shaved her head, and then stoned her to death.* He was standing at the pathway staring up at the house. It had been almost two weeks since he'd seen Raven. Two weeks, and he had lived through it. More importantly, if he stayed away, she would be safe. She would find a nice, suitable Englishman and settle down. Taber clenched his fist and stormed down the hill toward the pub.

If Molly knew Taber had taken her into his confidence, she certainly wasn't acting like it, Raven thought irritably. Two weeks had gone by and when she hadn't heard from Taber she asked Molly if she knew where he was. Her friend had replied that she was a lowly servant girl, not privy to the whereabouts of Taber O'Flynn.

What Raven didn't know was that the Brotherhood had already talked to Molly and strongly suggested that she do everything in her power to discourage any relationship between Taber and Raven.

Molly was in a quandry. Taber himself had asked her to let him know if Raven ever needed him. He was her friend, her idol, yet if she helped them get together, Taber would be lost to the Brotherhood, and that would hurt all the Irish people. She knew she couldn't let her personal feelings for Raven interfere in this case. Taber was too important to the Irish cause.

Raven tried to throw herself into the social activities her aunt was constantly involved in. But nothing seemed to help. Her friendship with Molly had deteriorated to the point where Molly actually tried to avoid even talking to her. And when she did finally mention Taber, it was to tell her that she had heard Brenna O'Neill and Taber had gone on a holiday to the Aram Islands. Then to Raven's amazement, Molly had broken down in tears and begged Raven to forgive her. Before Raven could ask what she was apologizing for, Molly had rushed from the room.

Was she sorry Taber was with Brenna, or sorry that she was the one to tell her? Raven wondered. What did it matter, she asked herself. In a few months she would be on her way to America. Then she would put Taber O'Flynn out of her mind—and she hoped out of her heart.

Under the watchful eye of her aunt, Raven

had little chance to ride or even leave Riverside House. Each time she tried to escape, her aunt came up with something for her to do, or someone for her to entertain. To add to her problems, Walter Denseley persisted in courting her. Nothing she said or did seemed to dissuade him.

The only bright spot in her life came in the surprise of her uncle's clerk, Fergus O'Brien. The Irishman was from Cork and delighted her with stories of the area and its people. Raven was sure her uncle wouldn't have employed the man if he had any connection with the Brotherhood, so she didn't bother to question him about Taber O'Flynn. Then to her surprise, many of Fergus's stories were about Taber O'Flynn and his exploits.

Raven silently enjoyed the stories, not mentioning to Fergus that she knew who Taber was. She found herself admiring Taber even more for his love of country, but at the same time it infuriated her that he could ignore her completely after . . . after what? she asked herself. The man did little more than kiss her. Good heavens, what did she expect. He probably considered her a trollop for the way she had acted, and deservedly so. It still amazed her that she had responded to the man the way she had—yet even at that moment, just thinking about him made her pulse race.

*　　*　　*

Bored with her daily existence, Raven decided to explore the tunnel Taber had disappeared through. She announced that she wasn't feeling well and was going to stay in her room for the day. Then, locking her door from the inside, she felt along the chest where she had seen Taber do the same, but nothing happened.

"I was sure it had something to do with the chest," she mused aloud.

Pulling a chair over to the chest, she stood on it and searched the top. She turned each ornate dowel, one way and then the other, but nothing happened. Could it have been something on the paneled wall, she wondered in frustration. She slid her hand over the smooth wood, about to give up when she felt it. A small crack along one of the framed panels. It moved when she pushed up on it, and a section of the wall slid back.

"Very clever." The paneling could be dusted and waxed, but unless you knew to move the trim, nothing would happen. She quickly reached for the lamp so she could find out how the secret door opened from the other side.

She passed indentations in the stone wall that she was sure were the entrances to other rooms. Suddenly she could see a bit of daylight at the end of the tunnel. When she came out in daylight, she was amazed to find herself in a private garden. The tunnel entrance was overhung with trees, hiding it from the world.

From beneath the trees she could see a high stone wall ten or fifteen feet away.

Raven wandered through the overgrown garden, wondering how it had come to be isolated from everything else. Was it to protect the O'Flynn children, she wondered, imagining Taber and his sister playing safely here.

Coming upon a large wooden gate on rusty hinges, Raven pushed at it and was amazed when it opened easily. On the other side of the wall was a well-worn path that passed the side of the house. One way looked as if it went down to the village, while the other climbed the steep hill to the land above. Deciding on the latter, Raven whistled a tune as she happily climbed the path. It was grand to be outside the walls of Riverside House with no one to answer to. It was likely she would pay for her indiscretion later, but she wouldn't think about that now.

Suddenly the path flattened out before her. There seemed to be a hundred different shades of green in the beautiful landscape. She was drawn to the ruins of an old chapel in the distance. It was a lonely and silent place with headstones dotting the unkept grounds.

Raven was sure the ancient chapel and its small cemetery must have been used by the nearby families. Perhaps even the O'Flynns, she thought. Pulling weeds and briars away from a leaning headstone, she read what was still decipherable: *Mary Margaret Fitzgerald, born 1682, died 1699.* The rest she couldn't make out. She didn't live very long, Raven thought sadly. Mary Margaret had been barely a year older than Raven when she died. On her next visit up here, she would have to bring some tools to clear away the weeds, and perhaps some flowers to lay on the forgotten grave.

Pulling at the weeds on another stone that wasn't quite so overgrown, Raven froze as she exposed the writing: *Katherine Brigit O'Flynn, born 1790, died 1807. Beloved daughter and sister of Ireland. May you finally rest in peace in God's hands.*

Tears streamed down Raven's face. She wasn't sure why finding Taber's sister's grave should affect her this way. Perhaps she was crying for him—for the pain she knew he had suffered. He was alone just like her, and loneliness was certainly an emotion she could relate to.

As Raven cut across the field of wildflowers, she took the combs from her hair, letting it fall loose around her shoulders. She felt wonderful and free, as a soft breeze caressed her skin. Suddenly she spotted what looked like a cabin in a grove of trees. Her curiosity got the best of her, and she peeked inside. There was no sign of life, yet the cabin looked as if it had been recently used. A bed large enough for two people took up a good part of the room. In front of a stone fireplace sat a table and two chairs, and on the floor an empty dish that she assumed must be for a cat or a dog. Cozy, she thought as she closed the door.

Raven jumped as something furry touched her leg. "Oh, kitty cat, you gave me a scare," she laughed, picking up the furry animal. "I guess that's what I get for snooping. Do you live here?" she asked, scratching the cat between the ears. "I bet that bowl on the floor belongs to you. Well, I must leave you now. I have some more exploring to do. You be a good kitty and stay here."

Through a larch of trees Raven picked up a trail. Without knowing where she was going, nor caring, she followed it, and to her delight she came upon a beautiful, quiet part of the River Lee. The green hills rose behind it in majestic beauty against the blue sky. It was so beautiful, it took her breath away.

This place must belong to the little people, she thought, seeing a ring of mushrooms. Leprechauns, Molly had called them. Raven dropped to the ground and removed her shoes and stockings. If it did belong to the little people, she was sure they wouldn't mind her enjoying it for a little while.

Barefoot, Raven wandered along the edge of the river, humming a tune to herself, and occasionally holding out her skirt and dancing. The exciting sense of being alone and able to do whatever she pleased made her giddy. The sun was hot and the dress she had worn was not one that she would normally wear for an outing such as this. The clear green water lapped at the shore, inviting her to enjoy its cool pleasure.

"Why not?" she said aloud. "It's just me and the leprechauns, and I don't think they'd mind."

She laughed aloud as she shed her last garment and slowly slipped into the water. It was icy cold, coming from the mountain streams, and Raven gave a whoop as she dived into the clear water.

The guns safely delivered, Taber had decided to get away for a few days to the little cabin he and his father had built when he was a boy. Very few people knew about it, and he felt peace here when he could find it no place else. And now with a couple of quail for his meal . . .

Taber froze in his tracks as he heard a feminine scream. He dropped the quail slung over his shoulder and took off running in the direction of the river. When he reached the water's edge, he realized the sound he'd heard had not been one of panic, since now a sweet lilting tune floated over the water toward him.

If he believed in fairies . . . He moved nearer, scarcely able to believe his eyes. The fates had chosen to take the decision out of his hands. Raven was here, in all her glory, at his secret place.

He moved nearer, careful to make no sound that would betray his presence, wanting to savor the moment. Just staring at her pink nipples made prominent by the cold water made his breathing quicken. He ran his tongue across his lips, imagining how each bud would feel in his mouth.

Gracefully she dived under the water, and moments later appeared, raising her arms to the sun. His first impression had been correct, he thought. She was the most exquisite woman he'd ever seen. His eyes traveled over her full breast, narrow waist, and then lingered lower on the dark triangle of hair that covered the beautiful mystery of her womanhood.

With a deep breath, Taber struggled to bring his emotions under control. Exercising every ounce of willpower he possessed, he concentrated on Raven's beautiful face. The only decent thing to do would be to let her know he was there, he decided.

He moved closer, but before he had a chance to speak, she dove under the clear water again. Taber knelt down on one knee at the water's edge and waited.

She came up slowly, her eyes closed, and her black hair clinging to her face and shoulders. She reminded him of a story he'd heard as a boy.

"Lady of the lake," he said, "will you give me the sword you gave to Arthur so I may slay my enemies?"

Raven stared at him, unable to believe her eyes. Then suddenly she realized he could see every inch of her in the clear water. "Please have the decency to turn around while I get out."

"Dinna' do that." He smiled. "I plan to join you."

"Don't you dare, Taber O'Flynn. Turn around this instant. I am freezing."

"I'll warm you," Taber said as he removed his shirt.

"Taber, this isn't right. Please go away."

"This is my land, little one. Or it was at one time, and you're trespassing."

"Well, if you'll turn around I'll dress and be on my way."

"Not in a million years," he laughed.

His muscles rippled beneath tanned skin as he leaned over to remove his boots. She had never thought about a man's body being

161

beautiful, but his certainly was.

"Oh," Raven exclaimed, diving under the water as Taber began to remove his pants.

When he dove into the water, Raven came up gasping for air. She screamed as he grabbed her ankles, pulling her back beneath the surface. Her dark hair floated about them as his hand moved from her ankles to her waist. She fought to gain the surface. Bubbles rose as he laughed before deeply kissing her.

When they finally broke the surface, Raven was gasping for breath. "Are . . . you trying . . . to drown me?"

"Maybe it would be better for both of us."

Raven stared into his brooding eyes. "Why would you say that?" she asked, oblivious to the fact that he held her naked body against his own.

"It's been hell trying to stay away from you, and now that I see you again, I know I'd rather stop breathing than not be with you."

Raven could feel his heart beating against her own. "Why have you stayed away?"

He gently pushed a strand of wet hair off her face. "It's a long story, little one."

"Tell me, Taber. I've all the time in the world."

"Do you now?" he laughed, making an effort to brighten the mood. "Do you mind telling me how you happened on my secret place?"

"Your place? And just what gives you the right to call this beautiful fairyland your place?"

"It has belonged to my family for two hundred years. The British claim it now, but they'd have to kill me before I'd give it up."

"I didn't know. I just happened on it."

"You were sent to me," he whispered, lowering his lips to hers. His arms were warm around her chilled body. The sensation, combined with the lean hardness of his body, sapped her will to argue. She was consumed with feelings she didn't understand as his mouth left feather-light kisses on her breasts. He slipped his hands behind her knees and lifted her from the water, carrying her to the soft grass along the shore.

"Taber . . ." she pleaded in a breathless voice.

"It's too late for protests, little one. You and I both know that."

Raven ran her hands up and down his muscular arms. "Aye, that's true," she sighed, unable to deny the fiery thrill of his touch. As he knelt above her like an animal, muscles rippling beneath his skin, her breathing became rapid. She felt a strange sense of fatalism, as if she had been waiting for this man and this moment, all her life.

She inhaled sharply as his hand moved to caress between her thighs. His slow and tantalizing arousal continued, driving her to the brink of pain. Her eyes were wide and reflected the sky as she stared up at him.

He touched her cheek, then ran his finger along her jawline. "It will hurt for a moment," he gently warned.

Her breasts rose and fell in anticipation, but she couldn't find the words to tell him she knew and it would be all right.

He gathered her close, entering her tender flesh with but the barest resistance.

A strangled cry caught in her throat and she pushed violently against him. Capturing her wrists, he held them above her head. "Lie still for a moment, love. The pain will ease."

Time hung suspended, and then again he moved within her. She realized that the pain had given way to waves of sensation, warming her entire body.

Brushing his lips against her temple, he whispered, "I've lived for this moment, my Raven."

His movement began to grow stronger, and her urgency matched his. The hands that had held him off now clung to him, and she raised her hips to meet his thrust as the sensations became exquisite. At the same moment she cried out, Taber's release came.

For a long time they lay with their bodies entwined, neither wanting to return to reality. Finally he leaned up on one elbow and stared down into her beautiful face.

Her pale blue eyes met his with a warm smile. Reaching up, she touched a lock of his hair, curling it around her finger.

"You are beautiful, Raven McClennon."

"So are you, Taber O'Flynn."

"I was hoping it wouldn't be anything special so that when it was over I could walk away and never see you again."

Raven's blue eyes widened in disbelief. "Why would you wish such a thing?"

"Because I love you, Raven, but I'm afraid that love won't do anything but cause you pain."

"I don't understand," she said, touching his face.

"We will never be able to have a normal relationship. We'd have to meet in secret, catching a moment together whenever we could. You deserve a man who can offer for your hand in marriage. A man who can give you a home and children."

"But it is my choice what relationship I choose, Taber O'Flynn. And if it has to be meeting you in secret, then so be it."

"It is foolhardy to seek pain, sweet Raven."

"No pain is unbearable, except that of regret," she whispered.

"I fear you will come to grief before you're done with me, but I promise I shall do everything in my power to see that you'll not know regret on my account.''

"I'll hold you to that, Irishman," Raven said through chattering teeth as suddenly the sun went behind a cloud. The cool air against her fevered skin started her shaking all over.

Taber wrapped his shirt around her shoulders. "Come on, I have a place not far from here where you can dry before the fire while I fix you some hot tea braced with blackberry brandy.''

"I shouldn't. I didn't want anyone to know I'm gone.''

"How are you going to manage that?" Taber asked as he quickly dressed.

"I . . . I used your tunnel," she admitted hesitantly.

"Wonderful," he laughed. "I had hoped you would. Come on before you catch cold," he said, holding out his hand to her. "I'll take you back to Riverside House later.''

He put his arm around her shoulders and held her close as they walked. "You didn't tell me how you came to be here.''

"I just happened on it. I also found an ancient chapel and its graveyard.'' Raven studied Taber's face to see his reaction, but there was none. "Is it your family's plot?''

"Aye. My father and sister and most of my ancestors are buried there.''

"Someday I plan to return to Scotland and find the graves of my ancestors.''

"Sometimes delving into the past can only cause you pain," he warned.

"That's a strange thing for you to say. Isn't your fight with England because of things that have happened in the past?"

"Aye, and that is how I know about pain."

They say that Hope is happiness;
But genuine love must prize the past;
And memory wakes the thoughts that bless;
They rose the first—they set the last.
Byron

Chapter Eight

The place Taber had invited Raven to turned out to be the cottage she had come upon while exploring.

"I was here earlier visiting the cat," she laughed.

"Ah, so you've already met Emmet. He takes care of the place when I'm not here," Taber said as he started the fire in the rustic fireplace.

"Emmet is a strange name for a cat," Raven commented.

"Aye, I suppose it is. He's named after Robert Emmet, a patriot of the Irish people."

"I believe I've heard of him," Raven said. "Wasn't he the one who gave a stirring speech about his epitaph as he was about to be hung?"

"Aye. He said, 'When my country takes her place among the nations of the earth, then and not till then, let my epitaph be written.' His epitaph still has not been written," Taber said bitterly.

"It seems Ireland has a great many patriots."

"A country that is suppressed usually does. Unfortunately most of Ireland's patriots have become martyrs, leaving only their words and deeds for us to remember."

"Do you sometimes get tired of never living at peace?"

"It's the only life I've known." He shrugged. "Here, sit next to the fire now. It should warm you quickly. Would you like a brush for your hair?"

"That would be wonderful. I was wondering how I was going to get these tangles out," she said, running her hand through her matted hair.

Taber handed her the brush, then set about to fix them a pot of tea. He couldn't take his eyes off her as she pulled the brush through her hair, bringing it to life with blue-black highlights. He would never forget the sight of her swimming nude in the lake, her beautiful body exposed for his enjoyment, he thought.

Remembering what he was supposed to be doing, he took the pot to the fire, then placed two crude cups on a small table beside Raven.

"You'll have to forgive everything being so plain. I dinna' usually entertain here."

"Everything is fine," Raven assured. "Do you come here often?"

"Whenever I need to get away and think," he answered as he stared into the fire. "Lately I seem to need the isolation of the cabin more and more." He didn't mention that in three days a British ship loaded with gunpowder was supposed to anchor in Cobh harbor, and he and his men meant to capture it, or that a dream had haunted him for the past few nights that something was going to go wrong with their plan. Taber forced all thoughts of his mission from his mind and turned back to watch Raven brush her long hair.

"Do you get lonely here?" she asked.

"Sometimes," he admitted. "Particularly when I think of you."

Raven stopped in midstroke and stared up at him. "You think of me?" she asked in disbelief.

Laughing at her expression, Taber stooped down in front of her. "Why should that surprise you? I told you at the party how I felt about you."

Raven stared down at the brush in her hand. "Yes, but then I didn't see or hear from you . . ."

"I know and I'm sorry." He stood up and leaned once again on the mantlepiece. "My work takes much of my time," he said, staring into the fire.

"I wasn't questioning you, Taber," she said, resuming her brushing.

Taber turned and smiled at her. "I know you weren't. Here, let me finish brushing your hair," he volunteered as he knelt behind her.

"Thank you. It's very difficult getting to the back."

Threading her raven strands through his fingers, he was amazed at its vibrancy as it curled around his fingers. "You should always wear it like this," he whispered in a seductive tone.

"'Tis not practical," she answered in a husky murmur.

"I suppose not, but still I prefer it this way." Raven's eyes met his and they both fell silent. Suddenly the water in the teapot sputtered over, hissing in the fire.

"The water is boiling," she whispered.

"So am I," Taber admitted. "Ah, sweet Raven, I canna' seem to keep my hands off you." He lowered his head and found her soft mouth. Raven wrapped her arms around his neck as he lifted her in his arms.

"You should have left your clothes off," he growled.

"Why?" she asked breathlessly.

"Because this is a damned waste of time," he answered, laying her on the featherbed. Gently he undressed her, his eyes dark with passion, as he removed each piece of her clothing. Then quickly he shed his own.

"You are so beautiful," he whispered, capturing a firm nipple in his mouth. "I want to devour you." He left a burning trail across her breasts and shoulders, then along the slim line of her throat. His mouth found hers, plundering the sweetness inside.

Raven's hand explored the contours of his flat stomach and muscular chest. Her body was on fire. She was desperate for him to be inside her—desperate for release from the fires that were building inside of her.

"Taber, love me," she pleaded.

"Not yet, my love," he whispered. "Our lovemaking at the lake was over too quickly. This time we must take our time."

"Must we?" Raven sighed.

Taber had to laugh. "Trust me. It will be better this way." He knelt above her, running his hands down the outside of her legs, then slowly up the insides.

Her whole body quivered in anticipation. She moaned his name as the hot intimacy of his fingers aroused and tormented her to a painful pleasure. She wanted to touch him back, but he moved from her reach.

"That would end this sweet torment, my love. Just lie back and let me pleasure you."

Raven fell back, too weak to argue as he continued his slow and tantalizing arousal, until every nerve ending felt as if it were exposed.

He lay half on top of her while his warm hand cupped one breast, gently rubbing the nipple until it stood rigid against his thumb. She arched her body toward him as she could feel his manhood pulsating against her thigh. Her emotions were spiraling out of control as his mouth moved lower along her stomach.

"I need you, Taber," she whispered hoarsely. "I cannot stand this torment any longer."

When he finally moved on top and entered her, she cried out her pleasure almost instantly. Taber went rigid as he poured his seed into her. Afterward they clung together, both trying to calm their breathing.

"You are magnificent, Raven McClennon," he whispered against her hair.

Raven turned to face him, cozy in his loving arms. "I was thinking the same about you, but I didn't know if I should say it."

"There is no reason not to admit you enjoyed it."

Raven fell silent, painfully remembering that he had said they could never have a normal relationship, and she had said it didn't matter. But it did matter, more than she had ever imagined. It had been years since she'd had anyone to love—or to love her. She felt content and safe in Taber's arms, and she wanted nothing more than to stay there.

"What are you thinking about, love?" Taber asked, leaning up on one elbow.

"What are we going to do, Taber?"

Taber ran his thumb along her jawline. "I dinna' know yet, love, but put it out of your pretty head. I'll work something out."

"Soon, I hope. I can't stand the thought of being away from you."

"So you're going to be a demanding woman," he teased. "Good, I like a woman with spirit."

As they made their way through the darkness, Raven clutched Taber's hand in a crushing grip.

"Are you all right?" he asked.

"Yes, but I'm glad you insisted on coming with me. I do not like the dark. Isn't that foolish?" she laughed, embarrassed.

"Everyone has something they fear," he said, putting his arm around her shoulder.

"Do you have fears, Taber?"

"Aye, I suppose failing is my worst fear. Helping my homeland has been instilled in me since birth, and sometimes it is a heavy burden."

"You've taken on too much."

"Sometimes too damnably much, but the people depend on me."

"Do they know you will hang if the English

catch you?"

She could feel him shrug. "They can only hang me once."

"Once is more than enough," Raven exclaimed.

Taber laughed at the tone of her voice. "Enough about such morbid subjects."

"I agree. This has been the most wonderful day of my life, and I don't want anything to spoil it," she said.

"Aye, it has been a wonderful day, Raven McClennon. I'll never forget it."

"That sounds like we'll never have another like it."

"I dinna' mean it to sound like that. Here we are," he said, touching the level that opened the door into her room.

Before Raven moved inside, he took her in his arms. "I'm going to be at the cottage for a few more days. Do you think you can get away again?"

"I'll try."

"Try hard," he ordered gently, before kissing her.

Raven backed into the room and let the door close between them. For a moment she laid her head against the paneled wall, wishing she could have stayed with Taber and never returned here.

*　　*　　*

After a sleepless night worrying about what she and Taber were going to do, Raven prepared to join her aunt and uncle for breakfast. She stared at herself in the mirror, thinking no one would doubt that she had taken to her room yesterday because she had felt ill. She looked absolutely terrible.

Dismissing her reflection with a shrug, she reluctantly headed for the dining room.

"There you are, my dear. I was beginning to get worried about you," her uncle said as he pulled back her chair.

"Thank you, Uncle Charles. I'm feeling a little better this morning."

"You look awful. I certainly hope you don't have anything contagious," her aunt said caustically, holding her handkerchief to her nose. "It would be very selfish of you to expose me to some God-awful disease."

"I assure you, it's nothing contagious, Aunt Caroline."

Charles took Raven's hand in his. "Your aunt and I are leaving this morning for Waterford. I had hoped you would feel up to the trip."

Raven struggled to retain her happiness. This would give her a chance to be with Taber for a few days. "I'll go if you think I should . . ."

"I'm not riding in close quarters with that girl when she is so ill," Caroline exclaimed,

177

just as Raven had hoped. "Look at her, she is flushed and glassy-eyed."

"Be quiet, Caroline. If Raven feels up to the trip, she will go."

"Perhaps I shouldn't, Uncle Charles. I do still feel a little feverish." Raven tried to keep the excitement from her voice.

"Then maybe we should stay here until you're feeling better. Denseley should be able to handle this matter."

"No!" Raven exclaimed. "No, please, I'll be fine. I have the entire staff here if I need anything."

"I don't like leaving you when you're ill," her uncle said.

"You promised me this trip," Caroline bristled. "I've already sent a message ahead to the dressmaker . . ."

"Your concern for our niece is overwhelming, Caroline," Charles said sarcastically. "Are you sure you'll be all right, Raven?"

"Of course she'll be fine," Caroline said in a clipped voice. "The villains already took everything of value, so she shouldn't be bothered with intruders."

Raven ignored her aunt's contemptuous remark. "I'm positive, Uncle Charles. I plan to return to my bed after I have some tea and toast. By the time you return, I'll be fine."

Her uncle kissed her on the forehead. "All right. I agreed to let Molly have a few days off to travel with her brother to market to sell their stock, but May will be here and so will Fergus O'Brien.''

Raven had forgotten that Molly mentioned she was worried about Colin traveling by himself so soon after his injury. She was glad her uncle had given her the time off. "Don't worry about me. I cannot imagine needing to bother Fergus or anyone. Do you have any idea how long you'll be gone, Uncle Charles?''

"I'm not sure, dear. Walter has a lead on some of our horses.''

"Oh . . ." Raven's teacup rattled in the saucer. "I'm so glad to hear that. I hope you find the mare, Devil Lady. I have missed riding her.''

"Have you ridden the lovely mare Walter Denseley sent over for you?" Caroline asked, knowing Raven had refused the horse.

"I would rather walk," Raven answered coldly.

"Why that nice man bothers with you I'll never understand," Caroline exclaimed. "Your rudeness to decent people knows no bounds. That poor man tries to be kind to you . . .''

Raven pushed her chair away from the table. "I hope you have a nice trip, Uncle Charles. I'll see you on your return.''

Caroline's sniff of disdain was clearly audible as Raven left the room.

Charles watched his niece make a hasty

retreat, then he turned on his wife. "Let me give you a warning, my dear wife, it's time for you to stop making Raven's life miserable."

"What is that supposed to mean?" she asked haughtily.

"It means if you're wise, you'll leave Raven alone, or you'll learn what it means to be miserable," Charles said before storming from the room.

Raven paced her room, then finally fell across the bed, where she stared up at the ceiling. Her aunt and uncle would be gone for several days, giving her the perfect opportunity to spend some time with Taber, but what would she tell the staff? She couldn't very well just disappear.

She jumped up at the sound of the carriage leaving and hurried to the window. Forgetting her decorum, she gave a loud whoop as the sound faded down the cobblestone drive. She was free—free to do whatever she wanted, even if it was only for a few days.

Suddenly her lighthearted mood disappeared. There was still the question of the servants, she puzzled. Leaning her head against the cool glass, she tried to think of some excuse to keep them out of her room. Oh God, suppose she went through all this to go to Taber, and he wouldn't want to see her.

"What's taking you so long?" a voice asked from behind her.

Raven spun around to find Taber leaning against the secret panel, his thumbs hooked nonchalantly in his belt.

"You hurt me, love. I thought you'd be on your way to meet me as soon as your aunt and uncle were in the carriage."

"How did you know they were leaving?" Raven asked, her heart singing now that she knew he wanted her to come to him. "I just found out myself this morning."

"The little people told me," he said, his eyes twinkling. "They liked you and me making love in their green fields yesterday, so they told me they'd arranged for your aunt and uncle to go away so we could continue our assignation."

"I don't believe a word of it," she laughed.

"Saints be preserved, already you are questioning my word."

"Taber, how did you know?" Raven persisted.

"I went by the Devlins last night after I left you, and learned that Molly was going to accompany Colin to Kerry since your aunt and uncle were going to Waterford. The only thing I dinna' know for sure was if you were going along with them. I was relieved to see them alone and that all my efforts hadn't gone in vain."

181

Raven didn't pay any attention to his last statement. All she heard was that he was glad she hadn't gone. "You were hoping I wasn't going with them?" she asked tentatively.

"I was holding my breath, lass."

Suddenly Raven remembered that her uncle was going to Waterford to check on his stolen horses. "Taber, do you know why my uncle is going to Waterford?"

"Aye, he thinks Denseley has tracked down some of his stolen horses."

"Aren't you worried about that?"

"Why should I be? His Lordship will find nothing. Come, lass, get some things together. We're wasting precious time."

"There is one problem, Taber. I cannot just disappear, leaving the servants in a panic about my whereabouts."

"I've already taken care of that." He smiled. "May is going to say you're still ill and will be taking your meals in your room until your uncle's return. The servants will be glad for a chance not to have to work so hard."

Raven's eyes widened. "May is also one of your people?"

"May is a friend. Now stop asking questions. Are you coming with me or not?"

"Will we return here tonight?" she asked.

"It's up to you," Taber answered.

"What do you want me to do?" she asked, suddenly feeling embarrassed.

Taber took Raven by the shoulders and pulled her to him. "Sweet Raven, don't you know I want you with me forever. I'm certainly not going to let you away from me for at least a couple of days. After that we'll take one day at a time."

"One day at a time," she repeated.

"We will make this a time we'll never forget," Taber promised.

His words reminded Raven how fragile their relationship was. They may both profess their love, but neither knew what tomorrow would bring.

Taber smiled at Raven, his eyes bright with love. "Come now, Raven McClennon, I'll not tolerate a frowning face for the next couple of days."

"I promise, you will not see a single frown," she laughed. "Sit down while I put a few things in my bag. I will only be a minute."

Taber sat on the bed, leaning back against the post as he watched her. "Do you wish to go to Blackmoor House or the cottage?" he asked amiably.

"Oh, the cottage," Raven said emphatically. "I want us to be alone."

Taber smiled. "I was hoping you'd say that." He began to whistle a happy tune as he watched Raven throwing clothes into a small sachel. "You won't need that," he said, grabbing a white nightshift from her hands.

Raven looked devastated. "Then you don't want me to stay the night?"

"I want you to stay, love," he said, pulling her onto his lap, "but you won't be wearing anything in my bed."

"Oh," she giggled, "suppose I get cold?"

"Sweet, it could get thirty degrees below zero and snow ten feet deep, and I'd still promise you, you won't get cold."

"Well, then I suppose I have everything I need."

"Bring something to wear to ride. I want to show you a little of the countryside."

"Where will you get horses?" Raven asked.

"There you go questioning me again, lass. When will you ever learn."

Fergus O'Brien sifted through the papers on Lord Montgomery's desk, hoping to find something that would be of interest to Peter Muldane. He was in a very enviable position having access to Lord Montgomery's papers, yet he had been able to supply the Brotherhood with only trivial bits of information. Information that even Molly Devlin had privy to. What he needed was something important. Something that would make him look good in Peter's eyes, and more importantly in Brenna's eyes. He was tired of her telling him about how important and powerful Taber O'Flynn was.

Damn, there was nothing, he fumed. Walking around the room, he sifted through books and articles on a table in front of the window. Suddenly something moving outside caught his eyes. He pressed his nose to the pane of glass and strained to see. The courtyard below had been neglected and was overgrown with trees and shrubs, but he was sure he had seen a movement of color.

"I'll be damned," he swore, recognizing Taber and Raven as they slipped through a gate. "This may be better than a stackful of secret papers."

Fergus rushed from the office and down the steps to the rear entrance. He found himself on the wrong side of the house from the garden he had been overlooking, and there didn't seem to be a pathway to it. Taber and Raven were out of sight by the time he circled the huge house. He followed the path at a run and finally caught sight of them as they topped the hill. They were holding hands and chatting away as if they didn't have a care in the world.

Hiding in a stand of trees, Fergus watched in puzzlement as Raven and Taber stopped at a small graveyard, where they stood and talked.

"Do you always carry garden tools with you?" Taber laughed as Raven retrieved a trowel from her bag.

"Not always. Connor loaned this to me. When I was here yesterday I decided to try to clean around the headstones."

Taber pulled Raven into his arms. "How did I ever get so lucky? Beauty and a kind heart too. No man could fight such a combination."

"You're not supposed to. You're supposed to see that I am perfect for you," Raven teased.

"You dinna' have to convince me, love. I realized that the day I met you."

What in the world, Fergus wondered, as he watched them pulling weeds away from several headstones. Why would they be doing that?

A half an hour later Taber and Raven were on the move again. Fergus had thought they would probably head back to Riverside House, but they were now crossing the field toward the river. He was amazed as they went into a small cottage in the woods. The place had to have been there for a long time, but he had never known of its existence before.

"Taber, what have you done?" Raven exclaimed as she looked around the cottage.

Where there had been a well-worn quilt on the featherbed before, now there was a beautiful fur throw. A small table set with crystal and china had been placed before the fireplace, and the aroma of potato soup permeated the air.

"Do you have a woman living here with you?" she asked suspiciously. "This place has been cleaned since yesterday."

"The little people were here while I was gone." He smiled.

"Taber, the truth . . ."

"I had one of Tomas's staff who lives near here clean up the place a bit, and she's also agreed to cook for us for a few days."

"Will that mean we'll have someone here all the time?" Raven asked.

"I'm not a fool, my love. Ellen will come and go when we're away from the cottage."

Raven smiled sheepishly, relieved that they were to have their privacy. "You did all this for me, when you weren't even sure I was going to be left behind at Riverside House?"

"I believe in being prepared," he said as he threw a log on the fire, even though the windows were wide open.

"But you asked me if I wanted to come here or go to Blackmoor House. How did you know I would choose the cottage?"

"I didn't for sure, but I had a feeling you would choose the cottage."

"Oh, Taber, I'm so glad I did. Everything is lovely, and what a delicious aroma."

"Potato soup and fresh-baked bread," he said, pulling a chair out for her. "If m'lady will sit, I'll serve."

"You'll spoil me," Raven laughed as she sat down. "You may find it difficult to get rid of me."

"Precisely my plan. We'll stay right here and forget that anyone else exists. I'll hunt and fish for our food and you can cook and clean our little Utopia."

A sad look came over Raven's face. "It sounds wonderful, but we both know it's a fantasy."

Taber removed the porcelain cover from the tureen and dipped out a bowl of steaming soup for each of them. Then he took his place across from her. "I suppose it is a fantasy to think it would last," he said, taking her hand, "but for the next few days we will live that fantasy, my love."

"And think of nothing else," Raven said in a determined voice.

Taber filled the crystal goblets with a deep red wine. He held his glass up. "To us, Raven my love."

Raven touched her glass to his. "And to our fantasy." She smiled with love in her eyes.

I heard a bird at break of day
Sing from the autumn trees
A song so mystical and calm
So full of certainties
                    Percy

Chapter Nine

Fergus O'Brien knocked at the O'Neill door, smug in his new confidence to win Brenna.

"Fergus, what are you doing here?" Brenna asked. "I thought Lord Montgomery kept you busy during the day."

"Lord Montgomery went to meet Lord Denseley in Waterford. They think they have a lead on the stolen horses."

"Does Taber or Peter know that?"

"Of course," he answered in a clipped voice. "That's not why I'm here, Brenna. Can you walk with me?"

Brenna looked back over her shoulder at her mother scrubbing the hearth. "Aye, I suppose. What is this all about, Fergus?"

"You know I'm doing very well at Lord Montgomery's," he said proudly. "The English are very generous with people they like and trust."

Brenna glanced at Fergus as they walked, wondering what he was up to now. "Dinna' forget why you are there," she warned.

"The Brotherhood is always uppermost in my mind," he snapped. "Unlike some people I know."

"And who would you be meaning?" she asked defensively.

"Oh, certainly not you, love," Fergus quickly explained.

"Well I should hope not. They may treat me like dirt, but still I am loyal to them—at least to Taber and Peter."

"That's why I'm here, Brenna," Fergus said, taking her hand. "To tell you that Taber O'Flynn does not deserve your loyalty or your love."

Brenna yanked her hand free and walked a few steps away. "We've been all through this before, Fergus. One of these days Taber will come to his senses, and when he does, I will be there waiting for him."

"It will never happen," Fergus warned. "What is it going to take to make you realize Taber isn't in love with you? How long has it been since he's even been around here?"

"He has to be very careful who sees him,"

Brenna said, undaunted.

"My God, girl, don't you know he's in love with the Scottish lass?"

"What are you talking about?" Brenna turned on him angrily.

"Listen to me, Brenna. I'll forget that you have slept with him. We'll get married and have a family . . ."

"Tell me what you meant." Brenna yanked at his arm.

"At this very moment Taber is entertaining Lady Raven McClennon at a little cottage near the river."

"You're lying. Taber is away on a mission."

"That's what he told you, but I've seen him with my own eyes with Raven McClennon. I followed them when they stopped at the O'Flynn family cemetery and then went on to a cozy little cottage by the sea."

"That bastard," Brenna hissed.

"I'm willing to offer you marriage, Brenna. I've been saving money. Didn't I buy you that nice jaunting cart?"

"I dinna' want a secondhand cart, you fool. I want away from this place. I want to live in a fine house and have beautiful, expensive clothes, and a carriage drawn by fine horses."

"If you'll be patient, love . . ."

"Dinna' be a fool. You'll never have the things I want," she said in exasperation.

"And you think Taber O'Flynn will?" he

laughed. "You're living in a fantasy world, Brenna O'Neill."

"Taber has the power behind him to do whatever he wants," she insisted. "His family were once the royalty of Ireland as were mine. When the Brotherhood gets rid of the British, the people will make Taber and me their rulers." Brenna's eyes gleamed as she thought of it. "We will rule Ireland together."

Fergus stared at Brenna, shaking his head. "You're daft, girl. The time of royal families in Ireland is past. Taber will never have any more than he has right now, and neither will you if you dinna' come to your senses."

Brenna was silent, considering what Fergus had said. She hated to admit it, but it was possible he was right. Taber didn't seem to care about the things that really mattered. All he thought about was his precious Ireland. Well, maybe it was time for her to move in a different direction—to take care of herself. Perhaps she should seek someone different to help her with her goals. Someone like Walter Denseley. He certainly struck her as a very ambitious man. He wanted power, and he had the money to pay for it. Brenna smiled to herself. Perhaps together . . .

"I can't do it," Raven shrieked, dropping the worm she was supposed to be putting on the hook.

"All right, all right," Taber laughed. "I'll bait your hook this time, but if you're going to be my woman, you're going to have to learn. Fishing is one of my favorite pastimes."

Raven stared down at the worm. "I'll try again," she said with determination, "but I don't know why a fish wouldn't bite at a piece of potato. It would certainly be a lot less messy."

Taber roared with laughter. "What's it going to be like when I teach you to clean the fish we catch?"

"Clean? You mean they come from the river dirty?"

"Oh God." He doubled over with laughter. "Raven, you have led a sheltered life," he said, holding his sides.

Ignoring Taber's fit of laughter at her expense, Raven managed to get the worm on the hook. While Taber still rolled with laughter, Raven dropped her line in the water. In a flash a fish hit the hook, nearly pulling her off her feet. "Taber, help me," she shrieked.

"Hold him, hold him," Taber shouted, jumping to her side. "It's a big one."

"Take it," Raven pleaded, trying to hand Taber the pole. "It's going to pull me in."

"Dig your heels in," he instructed.

By now Raven was in knee-deep water. "I do not want to dig my heels in. I want you to take this thing," she insisted. "My arms are tired."

"You're soft, Raven McClennon. Some people fish all their lives and never land one like this. I couldn't take that pleasure away from you."

"Thanks," she shouted, now in waist-deep water. "Put that on my tombstone after I've drowned."

"All right, I'll help," he laughed. "I'll start gathering in the line. You just hold that pole."

Taber waded farther into the river, gathering up the line. Then suddenly he completely disappeared.

This time it was Raven's turn to laugh as he came up sputtering.

"Dinna' let it go," he still shouted.

Raven felt as if her arms were going to fall off any moment. She could barely hold the pole and the fish was still pulling her farther into the water. The weight of her wet clothes added to her exhaustion. "Taber," she shouted as she was dragged under.

Taber grabbed her around the waist and pulled her to shallow water. The fish and pole were both gone.

"It's a good thing . . ." She gasped for air. "A good thing we didn't eat all the potato soup."

Taber started laughing again as both of them struggled to reach dry ground. "I have never had such a good time fishing," he said as he collapsed in the grass.

"Nor gotten as wet." Raven giggled, collapsing beside him. "You should have believed me when I said I couldn't fish."

Taber rolled over and stared down into her face. "Aye, I should have. It would have saved us both a dunking."

Suddenly his expression changed. "Do you know how beautiful you are all wet and looking like a sea nymph?"

"I do not believe a word you say," she said softly.

"I have a little cottage not far from here where you can dry."

"Oh no, I've heard that before," she laughed, trying to get away from him.

Taber wrestled Raven to the ground and pinned her beneath him. "I dinna' plan to let you get away, my sweet." He pushed a strand of her wet hair away from her face. "I think I like you best like this. You're a siren of the sea, my lady." He turned her face up to him and kissed her gently, then moved to her eyes, her throat, and back to her mouth.

"Taber," she whispered against his mouth. "I hate to tell you this, but it's raining."

"Raining?" Taber repeated, lifting his head to feel the drops pelting his face. "My dear, we dinna' have rain in Ireland. Only soft weather. Haven't you seen the silvery mists drifting down the mountains carrying the scent of sea and heather?"

"Rain or mist, I've always found it depressing," Raven sighed.

"Then you haven't spent a rainy evening with the right person. Just imagine snuggling under a fur throw while the rain plays a rhythm on the roof."

"Did you say rain, sir?" Raven teased. "You mean when the mist plays a tune on the roof."

"I stand corrected, m'lady. Or should I say I lay corrected. Whatever, we're wasting time." Taber stood up and offered Raven his hand. "Let's go back to the cottage and I'll show you how you should spend a rainy evening."

Raven woke with a start. Taber's arm was thrown possessively about her waist as he slept beside her. She thought of their evening of lovemaking. He had sated her with kisses, caresses, and intimate touches before slowly and expertly making love to her over and over.

A low rumble of thunder sounded in the distance seconds before a bright flash of light lit the room. Making love while it rained had been a delightful experience, but it still didn't change her feeling of melancholy as she listened to the wind and rain beat against the little cottage. It seemed ominous. As if the heavens were telling her that her happiness with Taber O'Flynn was not to be.

Easing gently from the weight of Taber's

arm, Raven slipped from the bed. He stirred slightly, but remained asleep. She slipped the discarded quilt around her shoulders and moved to the windows. A bright bolt of lightning lit the sky, silhouetting the outline of the bending trees. Rain pelted the glass as the wind howled. Raven placed her finger on the cool pane and followed a rivulet. Why had this uneasy feeling invaded her happiness all evening? Everything had been perfect. Taber was a sensitive, considerate lover. Maybe that was the problem, she thought sadly. He was everything she wanted in a man, but she had to keep reminding herself that theirs was not going to be a normal relationship.

Raven laid her head against the cool pane. Aye, there was the problem. They were trying to live a lifetime in a few days. Oh God, what was she going to do? She loved him so much.

Suddenly a pair of warm arms circled her waist. "Are you all right, love?"

"Yes . . . no." She turned in his arms and clung to him. "I'm afraid, Taber. What is to become of us? I cannot bear the thought of being apart from you."

"I know, love. I feel the same way, but we said we weren't going to think about it for a few days," he said softly against her ear.

"I know, Taber, but I can't help thinking that every minute that passes brings us closer to parting."

"I will work things out," he promised. "Come back to bed," he urged. He led her to the bed then slipped under the fur throw with her. "I've been thinking about our situation too," he said gently, caressing her face. "I realized today that I can't live without you. I have a very important mission to complete one night this week. When it's finished, you and I will go away."

"Can you do that, Taber? Can you walk away from it and never look back?"

Taber was silent for a long moment. "I dinna' know about never looking back, but I know I want to be with you."

"And when the passion fades, what will you feel then? Will you hate me then because I made you turn your back on your people?"

"I could never hate you, Raven," he said, kissing the palm of her hand.

"But the regrets would fester, Taber. You would feel you had let your family down, that you hadn't revenged their deaths . . ."

"Damnit, Raven," Taber shouted, suddenly sitting up. "I dinna' know what I'll feel, but I now have an obligation to you also."

"An obligation?" she asked, confused.

"Oh, love, don't you realize you could already have the seed in you that could produce our child? If I hadn't meant our relationship to be a permanent one, I would have been more cautious."

Raven turned her face away. Of course she had realized the possibility, but she loved him.

"Does the thought of carrying my child upset you so much?" Taber asked softly.

She turned and gently touched his face. "I would love having your child, but I could never raise him in Ireland to grow up hating the way you do."

"I wouldn't want him to, love. Perhaps by then things will be different." Raven stared silently at Taber. "Oh hell," Taber ran his hand through his hair. "I know it won't happen in our lifetime."

"Taber, if you really think you can change things, I'll stay here with you. I'll become a member of your Brotherhood, if they'd let me. I'll spy, steal, or whatever it takes . . ."

"Shh," he said, placing his finger to her lips. "Have I told you lately how much I love you?"

"It's been a few minutes . . ."

Taber sought her mouth in a deep, tender kiss. "I love you, Raven McClennon. God help us, but I love you more than life itself."

The next morning they both acted as if they didn't have a care in the world. And acting it was. Their conversation had continued into the early hours of the morning, yet nothing had been solved.

"I'm glad the sun is shining," Taber said lazily.

"Aye, so am I," Raven replied, taking a bite of her scone. "These are delicious."

"I thought you would enjoy them. Ellen is a wonderful cook."

"I hate putting her to all this trouble."

"Dinna' worry about it, love. I provide her family with fish and game whenever I catch anything."

Raven grinned. "I hope she wasn't planning on anything yesterday."

Taber laughed. "Today I'll teach you to hunt. Maybe you'll do better at that."

"Oh no, Taber," Raven exclaimed. "I could never shoot an animal."

"My softhearted lass, if it meant the difference between starving or killing an animal, I think you'd change your mind."

"Maybe, but since I'm not starving . . ."

"All right," he laughed. "You'd probably end up shooting me anyway."

"I didn't say I couldn't shoot. As a matter of fact, I'm an excellent shot. One of my cousins taught me while I stayed with them. I just couldn't shoot a living creature."

"Then we'll pass on the hunting or fishing today. What would you say to a ride about the countryside?"

"A ride?" Raven asked.

"I told you to bring riding clothes," Taber reminded.

"Aye, I did, but I haven't seen any horses."

"There you go questioning me again. When are you going to believe?"

"When I see horses," Raven laughed.

"I'll do better than that. You change clothes and I'll be back in a few minutes."

Raven cleared the table, then put some cream in the cat's bowl. "What do you think, Emmet? Can your master really produce horses? He did seem very sure of himself. Perhaps I had better change into riding clothes just in case."

Instead of the usual elegant riding habit, Raven donned a pair of buff riding pants tucked into shining cordovan riding boots, and a bright yellow silk shirt. She plaited her long hair into one single braid that hung down her back.

Moving about the cottage, she studied the titles of the books on the shelves. Apparently he did a lot of reading. Many of the books were classics, but most were written about Ireland and its patriots. There were also several books of poetry, she noticed with pleasure.

She smiled to herself as she realized it had been quite some time since Taber had gone in search of horses. "So much for Taber O'Flynn's miracles," she said, patting Emmet's furry head.

The words had no more than left her mouth when she heard horses. She opened the door to greet him. "I'm a believ—" She stopped in midsentence, staring at the white mare. "Taber, that's Devil Lady."

"Aye, love. I would have returned sooner if I had chosen just any horse for you, but I thought you'd enjoy your own."

"I can't believe you are so brazen as to keep the horses you stole right under the noses of the offended."

"Where better to keep them?" he laughed. "They would never expect them to be this close. Besides, I only have a few here."

"The best ones, of course. I see you are riding Nighthawk."

"Of course," he said, amused.

"Oh, Taber, you take such chances. If my uncle or Walter Denseley ever learned—"

"Do not worry yourself on my account, lass. I thoroughly enjoy making fools of the English. Now let me take a look at you," he said, walking a circle around her. "Hmmm . . ."

"I'm sorry if you don't like it," Raven said, assuming he didn't approve, "but I will not ride sidesaddle. This outfit is much more practical."

"And more flattering, I might add," he said, patting her derriere.

"You approve?" Raven asked in surprise.

"Very much so. I canna' imagine you riding this beast sidesaddle."

"To be honest, I never have," she laughed. "Even when I wore a riding habit, I'd ride like a man and just pull my skirt around my legs."

"Your aunt would have fainted at the sight if she'd seen that," Taber laughed. "Here, you hold this wild animal while I change her saddle."

They spent almost an hour in the hills before coming out in a clearing above the sea.

"We'll rest here," Taber said, tossing her an apple. "We're going to have a long walk after we ride down the hill."

"A walk? Do you mean to walk on water?" she asked, seeing nothing but water below them.

"Look again," Taber said as he settled on the soft grass, leaning on one elbow so he could watch her.

Raven shaded her eyes, and this time could make out gray turrets rising from the ruins of a castle. "There's a castle. Is that where we're going?" she asked with girlish excitement.

"Aye, now sit down and rest," he laughed.

"Oh, Taber, this is a bonny spot," she exclaimed as she sat down beside him. "I love anyplace near the water."

Taber wrapped his arms around her. "I'm glad to hear that, lass," he said, nuzzling her neck. "There is something about the sea that

203

has always drawn me, too."

"Maybe someday we'll have a house that overlooks the water, and you can fish right in your own front yard. It will be a white house sitting on a knoll, and there will be stables." She turned to him with a laugh, even though there were tears in her eyes. "Listen to me go on. What a dreamer I am."

"If we dinna' have dreams we have nothing," Taber said, rubbing his thumb along her jawline. "Keep those dreams, Raven McClennon. Someday I'm going to make them come true."

"Promise?"

"I promise," he laughed. "Come on, we better ride down if we're going to see the castle. The sky is beginning to look dark over the mountains."

"More of your soft weather," she teased.

They rode down through the valley, closed in on three sides by mountains and on the fourth side by the sea. It had all the peaceful quietude of a fairy kingdom. As they rode closer, Raven realized the castle was actually built on an island in the cove, accessible only by a narrow land bridge.

"It was built by the Normans," Taber pointed out, "probably around 1170. It was designed to withstand siege by medieval warriors on horseback, armed with sword and dagger. What they hadn't foreseen was the advent of gunpowder and cannons. It has fallen a half dozen times to its enemies since the advent of such weapons. Cromwell was one of those conquerors.''

"And now it sits deserted," Raven said sadly.

"Aye, the English were the last to occupy it, but some say the ghosts of owners past make living there impossible. When I was a boy I used to come here and spend time with the old caretaker. He knew more about the castle than anyone. He told me about one family who had lived here for years. They had fifteen sons, all who left the castle one morning to join the army of King James II against William of Orange at the Battle of Boyne. Every one of them was killed. The old caretaker claimed the wives and sweethearts of those young men still wander the castle waiting for their return.''

"Oh, that's so sad," Raven said, looking up at the dark gray walls.

"Come, sweet Raven, I dinna' want to make you sad today. Let's explore the place on foot. The view from the turrets is breathtaking.''

"You mean to climb up there?" she asked, staring up at the towers in awe.

"Can you fly?" he asked, a twinkle in his eyes.

"You know I cannot."

"Then we better start climbing," he said, grabbing her hand.

"This tower is known as a keep or donjon,"

he explained as they climbed the spiral staircase in the massive stone tower. "They always circle to the right so the attacker is hampered by the center wall, but the defender is not."

"That's incredible that they would have thought of that," Raven exclaimed.

"They needed every advantage they could think of to protect themselves. There was always somebody challenging them for their property, or just wanting to do battle."

"Not much different from today," she said solemnly.

They walked along the wall, looking through the parapets to the sea stretched out before them. Raven stopped and leaned against a stone embrasure. "You would never know there was any trouble in the world standing up here where it is so quiet and peaceful."

Taber leaned against the opposite wall, staring at Raven as she looked off in the distance. The wind was blowing her dark hair around her flushed face, and he thought if he should ever be parted from her, this would be the way he would remember her.

Without saying a word, he turned her around to face him and kissed her deeply. When he raised his head, he smiled down at her. "I love you, Raven McClennon."

Raven wrapped her arms around his neck. "This place must have cast a spell over us. I was just going to tell you the same thing."

"I need no spell to know how I feel."

Raven turned, leaning back against him as she looked back out over the sea. Once again she tried to shake her feeling of melancholy. "This is such a beautiful place. I can see for miles and miles."

"I thought you would like it," Taber said, tightening his arms about her waist. "I used to come here as a boy and dream about my future and the future of Ireland. There were times at sea when I would close my eyes and see this place against the green hills, and I would long to be home."

"Have you always loved the sea?" she asked.

"Aye, my father taught me the love of the sea. He was smuggling guns into Ireland from France when I was born, and I've been doing it off and on since I was old enough to sail."

"Smuggling," she exclaimed, turning in his arms to face him. "You're a pirate?"

"Nothing so exciting, love."

"Do you have a ship?"

"Aye. She sits in a hidden cove waiting for my return."

"Can I see her sometime, Taber?"

"I'll take you there one day soon," he promised.

Raven stared across the sea. "We could go anywhere we wanted and start a new life."

Taber kissed her on top of the head. "And

where would you be wanting to go, Lady McClennon?"

"America. I've heard it's a wonderful place. They say it's the land of opportunity."

"Aye, I remember the day of the fair, you told me you wanted to go to America. I hate to be the one to tell you, but they're having their own troubles with Britain right now."

"Aye, I had heard my uncle mention it. He was hoping to be called back to London so he could become involved in it."

"You mean he'd give up persecuting the Irish in favor of persecuting the Americans?" he asked in mock surprise. "I'm hurt."

"Don't tease, Taber O'Flynn. You'd probably instigate a war between England and America if you thought it would pull the British out of Ireland."

"Aye, you're right, lass. But it will never happen. The English have always been at war with somebody and it's never lessened their hold on Ireland."

An uneasy wind moaned restlessly through the castle parapets causing Raven to shiver. She wasn't really cold, yet there was a feeling of gloom that hung over her. "It looks like we're about to have more of your Irish mists," she commented.

"Aye, it looks that way. We better head back to the cottage before we get caught in it."

"Are you going to admit it looks like a storm

coming?'' Raven laughed as they started down the steps.

"No. I just want to spend a repeat of last evening.''

By the time they reached the horses the weather had already changed drastically. A fog rolled off the sea and a light mist began to fall.

"I'll race you back to the cottage,'' Raven challenged.

"You'll never win,'' Taber laughed, undaunted, but before he could say more, Raven was several lengths away. She rode leaning forward over Devil Lady, but in moments Taber drew abreast of her, restraining Nighthawk from going ahead. They rode this way for a while, but the weather increasingly worsened.

"Slow down before you break that pretty neck,'' he ordered.

She quickly brought her horse under control, wary of the fog that had become so thick. She could see Taber as long as he stayed beside her, but little else. "How far are we from the cottage?''

"Anxious to be under that fur throw with me, uh,'' Taber grinned.

"Oh, you are so conceited,'' Raven exclaimed, laughing.

"It's true, isn't it, lass?'' he persisted.

"I'll not make your head any bigger, Taber O'Flynn.''

Taber laughed. "This is where we were fishing yesterday, so we're not far."

Suddenly a rider emerged from the mist directly in front of them. Taber reined his horse sharply in front of Raven to protect her. The stallion reared his forelegs wildly in the air.

"My God, Taber, I'm sorry. I dinna' mean to startle you," Patrick said, staring down the barrel of Taber's gun.

"Where the hell did you come from?" Taber asked irritably.

"I stopped at the cottage and when you weren't there I decided to try the place where you like to fish."

Raven felt embarrassed as Patrick glanced at her and nodded. She hadn't seen him since the night of the fair when he told her she should stay away from Taber.

"What are you doing here, Patrick?" Taber asked as they rode.

"May asked me to tell you that Lord Montgomery is on his way back to Riverside House. He should be there by morning. Also our contact wanted me to tell you that our target arrived a day early. He wants to know what time you want to rendezvous."

Patrick saw the look of despair that passed between Taber and Raven and wondered how deeply involved his friend was. "Everything is set as you planned," he said, glancing at Raven as if wondering if he should be talking in front of her.

"Raven, why don't you fix Patrick a cup of tea while I rub down the horses," Taber suggested when they reached the cottage. "The fire will feel good after your long ride, Patrick."

Patrick silently followed Raven into the cottage. Ellen had already placed covered dishes on the table for their dinner. Well, there would be no romantic dinner this evening, she thought sadly.

Patrick threw a couple of logs on the fire, then took a seat where he could watch Raven.

After she put the kettle over the fire, she took the other chair and faced him. "Thank you for letting us know my uncle is returning," she said.

"No problem," he answered, then fell silent.

Raven stared into the fire trying to think of a way to clear the air between them. "Patrick, why don't you approve of me?"

"Because you're playing a dangerous game with my friend," he answered bluntly.

Raven met his accusing stare with wide eyes. "I wish to God this were a game. But Taber and I both know it isn't."

"What is it you want from him? Taber doesn't have a lot of money . . ."

"Money!" she exclaimed. "In a month I'll have more money from my own inheritance than you could ever imagine. The reason I want Taber is because I love him."

"If you love him you'll give him up," Patrick persisted.

"Give him up," she repeated. "Why should I give him up?"

"You're putting him in grave danger. Not only from his enemies, but from the Brotherhood. They dinna' take kindly to outsiders meddling in our affairs, and there is already great concern that Taber's mind is on you instead of the business at hand."

"If that is true, I'm sorry, but when you're in love that sometimes happens."

Patrick leaned forward, his face only inches from Raven's. "Listen to me, lass. You're a beautiful woman and I can understand why Taber is smitten with you, but you could bring an end to his life with a casual word to the wrong people."

"So could you, Patrick. So could anyone Taber knows. I would be the last person to betray him, because I love him."

"You're a stubborn lass," he said, a tinge of admiration in his voice.

"Aye," Raven said softly. "If I thought my not seeing Taber would protect him from his enemies then I'd never see him again, even though it would probably kill me. But in all honesty, I cannot see how it would help. Taber has had little enough happiness in his life. He deserves this time and so do I. And who knows, maybe in time the Brotherhood will come to accept me."

"I wish to God it were that easy," Patrick said tiredly.

"Why must everything be so difficult for you Irish?" Raven asked, losing her patience. "I've offered to become one of you, to do your bidding, even spy for you if I have to. All I ask is that I be allowed to love Taber O'Flynn without meeting resistance at every turn."

"Does Taber know you feel this way?" Patrick asked, surprised by her words of loyalty.

"Of course he does," Raven admitted, but neglected to mention that they had also talked of the possibility of leaving Ireland.

Patrick said nothing. He stared into the fire for long, uncomfortable seconds. The expression on his face looked as if a battle were being waged inside him.

Raven began to pace. She didn't know if she had gotten through to him or not, and for some reason it was important that Taber's best friend approve of her. "I don't mean Taber or anyone else any harm, Patrick. Fate seems to have thrown us together, and now that I know his love, I could never walk away from it without at least fighting for him."

Patrick turned and faced her. "I think I understand why Taber loves you."

Raven smiled. "I hope you do, Patrick, because I know how much Taber values your friendship. I want you and I to be friends."

"You are right about Taber needing some happiness in his life, and if you can give him that, I'd be honored to consider you a friend."

Raven threw her arms around Patrick's neck and hugged him.

"I leave you alone with my woman for five minutes and that quick you try to move in," Taber said from the door.

"It wasn't like that, Taber," Patrick quickly began to explain, before seeing the twinkle in his friend's eyes. "And you damn well know it," he laughed.

"Aye, I dinna' trust you, but I trust Raven."

"We just became friends," Raven said.

Taber wrapped his arms around Raven's waist. "I was hoping that would be the case."

"Did you plan this, Taber O'Flynn?" she asked, pushing playfully at him.

"I was sure when Patrick got to know you he'd like you."

"And he'd probably have run me through if I hadn't," Patrick laughed.

"Did you know that Patrick has been courting Molly?" Taber asked Raven.

"No," she exclaimed. "She hasn't given me the slightest hint anything so wonderful was going on in her life."

"Our relationship is still pretty new. I guess

both of us are a little hesitant to broadcast it just yet."

"I think it's wonderful. I know you'll both be very happy."

"Aye, I hope so. I had planned to stay a bachelor, but the lass wanted me . . ."

"Dinna' believe a word he says," Taber laughed. "He begged Molly to marry him."

Raven smiled. "Would you stay for a bite to eat, Patrick? There is more than enough."

"Thank you for asking, but I've got to start back. Just the cup of tea will be fine."

After pouring them tea, Raven excused herself to give Emmet some cream. She was sure the two men would be more comfortable talking business without her hovering over them. She wondered if Taber would be going back with Patrick. If only they had had more time, she thought as she knelt on the stoop to pet the cat as he rubbed against her leg. "You're lucky to have such an uncomplicated life, Emmet."

She'd only been outside a few minutes when the cottage door opened and the two men appeared.

"Take care of yourself, lass," Patrick said. "I'll look forward to seeing you again soon."

"You take care of yourself too, Patrick. I shall pray for your safety on your mission."

Raven glanced at Taber, expecting him to also tell her good-bye, but he said nothing.

"Will you be going with Patrick?" she asked softly.

Taber put his arms around Raven's shoulders. "We still have some time. I'll join him later."

She smiled up at him. "I'm glad. I was afraid you were preparing to leave."

"Not until I have to," he said, kissing her on the tip of her nose.

After Patrick had gone, they walked arm in arm back into the cottage. "Did you see Ellen had been here?" Raven asked.

"Aye, I saw the covered dishes."

"Are you hungry?"

"Only for you," he growled, pulling her into his arms.

His mouth sought hers in a kiss so poignantly tender that tears welled in Raven's eyes. When it ended he stared down into her bright eyes. They were warm and glowing with love. A tightness constricted Taber's throat. He couldn't speak, so instead he slid his arm beneath her knees and carried her to the bed. His hands moved over her, slowly, tantalizingly removing her clothes.

Raven laid back against the pillows and enjoyed the feel of his hands roaming her body. "I was afraid you would leave with Patrick," she whispered.

"I wasn't going to leave until I had a chance to tell you how much I love you."

Raven shifted to lie on her side as Taber moved to lie naked beside her. He went still as she ran her hands over his chest and down his stomach.

"I wanted to spend every moment with you until we had to part," she whispered against his mouth.

"It won't be for long," he promised. "Two or three days at the most."

"Is this mission dangerous?" she asked, nibbling at his earlobe.

"Aye, they're all dangerous, but I've always come through them fine. I have nine lives, didn't you know?"

"And I'd be willing to bet you've used up quite a few of them."

Taber laughed deep in his throat. "You're probably right."

"Will you be leaving Cork?"

"No." Taber hesitated a moment, but then decided if he couldn't trust the woman he loved, whom could he trust? "We're going to take a British ship that anchored in the harbor today."

Raven's hands stopped their movement. "Why would you risk so much to take a British ship? You said you had one of your own."

"Aye, but it doesn't have a hold full of gunpowder."

"Oh God, Taber," she gasped. "Do you have to do this?"

"It's my plan, love. What kind of a man would I be if I sent other men to do my work?"

"A safe one," she sighed. "Oh, Taber, hold me. I don't want to think about this."

Taber ran his hand down the small of her back, pressing her to the lower part of his body. "You have the softest skin." He bent his head to trace a burning path around her breast with his tongue. "It's like satin," he murmured. "And I intend to feel and taste every inch of it."

In an attempt to stretch minutes into timelessness, Taber took his time exploring, feeling, devouring. And Raven reciprocated. With words and actions of undying love, they tried to hold on to the night.

When we are parted, let me lie
In some far corner of the heart,
Silent, and from the world apart,
Like a forgotten melody.
Charles Hamilton Aidé

Chapter Ten

Raven lifted the cover of the gold filigree music box and listened to the haunting melody. Taber had given it to her before they left the cottage. It had belonged to his mother, and the thought that he wanted her to have it gave her hope that they had a future together.

The sound of a carriage rolling across the bricks brought her back to reality. She had spent two days in another world. Now she had to wait—wait and pray that she and Taber would be able to work things out, and all the while pretend that nothing had changed in her life.

"They're here, m'lady," Molly said, rushing into the room. "Are you sure you dinna' want me to tell them you're still feeling ill?"

"I would love nothing better than to hide out here and not have to see them, but I'm afraid my uncle would insist on calling the doctor if he thinks I'm still ill."

"Aye, you're probably right. Maybe your aunt will be exhausted from the trip and take to her bed."

Raven laughed. "My hopes exactly. Oh, Molly, I can't begin to tell you how happy I am that we are friends again. It helped so much having you here to talk to this morning."

"I'm glad too, and I'm thankful you understand why I have been acting so strange lately."

"I understand," Raven assured, hugging her friend. "One day soon I hope to make my peace with this Brotherhood of yours."

"I will help anyway I can," Molly promised.

Raven moved to the windows and glanced down at the courtyard. "You are so lucky to be able to openly love Patrick. To have your family and friends share your happiness."

"Aye, I know, m'lady. But you and Taber will have friends."

"Will we, Molly?"

"Of course you will. You'll have Patrick and I, and there will be others. Now we better get downstairs before they come looking for you."

* * *

Walter Denseley returned to his townhouse, furious that the trip hadn't gone as planned. He threw his riding gloves across the room, ignoring the servant who waited to take them.

"Nothing goes according to plan where these damned Irish radicals are concerned," he cursed. "I want a brandy, Sweeney. Make it a double. Then I want a hot bath drawn. I feel as if I have half the dirt of Ireland on me."

"Sir, there's a young lady waiting in the library."

"A young lady? Who the hell is it now?"

"Miss O'Neill, sir. Miss Brenna O'Neill."

"Brenna O'Neill," Denseley mused, remembering a female at the Montgomery party with auburn hair and gold eyes. "How interesting. I'll take my drink in the study, Sweeney," Denseley said over his shoulder.

Brenna jumped to her feet as Walter Denseley entered. "M'lord," she said, and curtsied.

"How nice to see you again, Miss O'Neill."

"Thank you, sir. I wasn't sure you would remember me."

"How could I forget such a beautiful woman," he said, as his eyes lingered on her breasts.

"How very kind of you," she smiled, lowering her long lashes seductively.

"Ah, Sweeney, there you are," Denseley said as his servant entered the room with a tray of refreshments. "Would you like a cup of tea, Miss O'Neill?"

Brenna noticed the decanter of brandy. "If it's all the same, I'd prefer some brandy."

Denseley laughed. "I like a woman who knows what she wants." He handed her the crystal glass and watched with amusement as she took a long gulp.

"I know exactly what I want, Lord Denseley. And I think I know what you want."

He studied her suspiciously. "Perhaps you should sit back down, Miss O'Neill."

Brenna smiled as she sat down, knowing she had his undivided attention.

"Now tell me, Miss O'Neill, what do you think I want?"

"You want to be leader of the Tory administration in Ireland," she said smugly.

"And what has that to do with you?"

"I have the way for you to achieve the position."

Denseley laughed as he stood up. He poured himself another drink without offering Brenna one, then he turned to face her. "Let's stop playing games, Miss O'Neill. Get to the point."

"Would it help your position if you were to capture Taber O'Flynn?"

"Help it?" he laughed. "My dear, it would allow me to name my own terms."

"What would you be willing to pay for that information?"

Denseley's eyes narrowed. "You're serious, aren't you?"

"Very serious."

"So, Taber O'Flynn is here in Cork," he mused, "and I was right about him working with this Hawk character."

"Taber O'Flynn *is* the Hawk," Brenna laughed.

"By God, I knew it!" Denseley refilled Brenna's glass then took the seat across from her. "What is it you want, Miss O'Neill?"

"Money, position, respectability," she answered.

"As I said," he laughed, "I like a woman who knows what she wants."

"My family are the *O'Neills*," she said, feeling more confident by the moment. "They were once the royalty of Ireland."

"I'm afraid I can't make you Queen of Ireland, my dear," he said sarcastically.

"No, but you can make me a very rich woman so I can show them all that they shouldn't have looked down their noses at me. And that's just for starters," she added.

"By God, I believe I've met my match. A woman as greedy as I am."

"You have plenty of money, Lord Denseley. Are you willing to share it to have the power you want?"

"No one ever has enough money, my dear, but I will consider your proposition."

"I'm sorry, m'lord, but if you want Taber O'Flynn, it has to be tonight."

"Tonight," he laughed, rubbing his hands together. "You're prepared to tell me where he'll be tonight?" he asked, still unable to believe his luck.

"Aye, so you must make up your mind now. I will wait here and you can give me the money as soon as you have him."

"Why are you doing this?" he asked suspiciously. "I thought all you Irish stuck together."

"I have my reasons."

"Ah, hell hath no fury like a woman scorned."

"Yes, he rejected me, but he'll regret the day he ever took up with Raven McClennon."

"Raven McClennon," Denseley repeated. "You can't be serious. The Lady McClennon would never take up with the likes of Taber O'Flynn."

"You are mistaken, m'lord. The lady has spent the last two days with Taber O'Flynn at a little hideaway he keeps not far from here."

Denseley threw his glass across the room. Glass and amber liquid stained the wall and floor. "The slut! The damn little slut. She was so goddamned high and mighty."

"Part of my plan is to get rid of her too." Brenna smiled. "But we can let the Brotherhood do that for us."

"All right, Miss O'Neill, let's hear your plan."

In a deserted warehouse on the docks, they went over the plan one more time to satisfy Taber. This time, more than ever before, he didn't want anything to go wrong.

"How much time will you need before we board?" Patrick asked.

"Only a few minutes. Wait until we've taken the first guards. And for God's sake, only use your guns as a last measure. We dinna' want that ship to blow up with us on it. Once we have the guard under control, we'll sail the ship out of the harbor. By dawn we should be able to reach the safety of the cove. Charley, you and Dan will stay with the ship once we've anchored. The rest of you get back to your families and jobs as soon as possible. We dinna' want anyone missing the lot of us."

"It's a good plan," Peter Muldane praised. "In fact it's a masterpiece. I dinna' know why I've been worrying about you, lad. This might be the blow that will make the British reel."

"It will certainly give them something to worry about," Taber agreed. "They'll be wondering when and where their gunpowder is going to be used against them. When Kevin gets back we'll know how many guards were left on board, then we'll move out of the warehouse in twos. Patrick's group will take to the boats, where you'll wait to board over the side of the British ship. The rest of you will go with me."

The man, Kevin, who had been sent to do surveillance came quickly back among them. "I dinna' believe it, Taber, but there only seems to be a skeleton crew. I saw no more than four men on board."

Taber looked at Peter Muldane. "I dinna' like it. I've never known the British to be careless."

"Perhaps they're trying not to draw attention to the ship," Peter suggested. "No one is supposed to know it's loaded with gunpowder."

"Are you sure your source knew what he was talking about?" Patrick asked.

"Aye, Fergus took the message from Lord Montgomery himself," Taber said, rubbing his chin.

"The success of this mission could give the people a real boost," Peter said. "London will be stunned if we can pull it off. The whole world will know about it."

"I know all that, Peter, but I still dinna' like it," Taber said, fighting the feeling that something was wrong. He was surrounded by men who worshipped him, and whom he trusted with his life, yet something nagged at him.

"I want to check this out myself. It will delay us a few minutes, but I dinna' want to take any chances."

The night was sweet and cool. Taber took a deep breath, wondering if he was being overly cautious because of Raven. The gun running had always been exciting to him. Even when he had been captured before, he had taken great delight in making the British look like fools every chance he got. They hadn't known who he was, and that had given him an advantage over them, but tonight was different. His palms were sweating and his heart was beating faster than usual.

"What's going on?" Patrick asked, coming up alongside him.

"Something isn't right."

"You think we're walking into a trap?"

"Possibly. Fools like you and me have been walking toward a prison cell since the day we were born, but tonight I can almost feel the cold bars."

"Jesus," Patrick hissed. "I dinna' want to die now. I finally found me a woman I want to settle down with."

"I know the feeling, my friend." Taber stared up at the ship. He could see the watch lights swaying, and see the outline of one man

227

leaning against the rail.

"Have you got a bottle with you?"

"Sure. You need a drink?" he asked, taking a bottle from his jacket pocket.

"We're going to become rousing drunk, my friend."

"That sounds good to me."

"The only thing is, we're going to do it cold sober."

"Aw hell, Taber, you take all the enjoyment out of life."

Taber laughed deep in his throat. "When we get to the ship I'm going to try to get invited on board. You stay on the dock, pretending to be too drunk to make it."

"I don't like this," Patrick warned. "Maybe we should get the others."

Instead of answering, Taber started singing an Irish song. Patrick quickly joined in as they stumbled toward the ship. They stopped at the gangplank and danced a little jig, then Patrick collapsed to the ground laughing.

"Your old lady is going to be mad as hell when you get home, Dooley, me friend," he warned.

"Ah, the devil take her. Every man should be able to get away with his friends and get roaring drunk."

Taber glanced at the man still standing at the railing. "You up there. Are you looking to hire for your unloading tomorrow? We're two strong lads who could use the money."

"That's him," a feminine voice whispered from the deck of the ship. There was silence for a moment.

"Tell them to come aboard," another voice whispered.

"You'll have to talk to my captain, mate. Come aboard."

"If I give the warning, get the hell out of here," Taber told Patrick.

They both stumbled toward the gangplank, but Patrick tripped and fell into a pile of crates and pretended to have passed out.

"Come on, man, get up," Taber ordered in a slurred voice. "We'll get us a job and have money to drink all the whiskey in Ireland."

When Patrick didn't move, Taber stumbled toward the gangplank by himself. "The hell with him. I'll get me a job." He stumbled and grabbed the rope, singing as he climbed aboard the ship. The hair on his neck bristled, adding to his fear that he was walking into a trap, but it was too late now. If he turned and ran, he and Patrick both would be shot down.

"Where's the captain?" he demanded, then stumbled toward the rail. "I dinna' have all night."

"Quite a performance, Mr. O'Flynn," a male voice said from the shadows.

Taber gave a shrill whistle as a warning to Patrick.

"Get the other one," Denseley ordered, before turning his attention to Taber. "Where are the rest of your men?"

"I dinna' know what you're talking about. I have no men."

"You can stop the pretense, Mr. O'Flynn. It was a good plan, and probably would have been successful if Lady McClennon hadn't informed us of your scheme."

Taber stared at Walter Denseley, unable to utter a single word. He felt numb all over, and flashes of Raven's face flooded his mind. She couldn't have . . . oh God, she wouldn't . . .

Taber let out a bloodcurdling scream and lunged for Walter Denseley's throat. It took three men to pry his hands loose.

Denseley rubbed his throat, where red welts already appeared. "She must have given a very convincing performance."

"You're lying, you English bastard."

"Am I?" he laughed. "It was all a setup, my gullible friend. She told us how you went out through the garden, then stopped at your family's cemetery plot."

"No!" Taber shouted, struggling against the hands that held him.

"Oh yes, Mr. O'Flynn. The only reason she spent two days with you at your cottage was so she could learn your plan. You don't think a woman like Lady McClennon would waste her time on the likes of you."

"The other one got away," one of the sailors said, "and there's no sign of anyone else."

"Now surely you didn't plan to pull this caper off all by yourself."

"I told you, I'm here alone. I have no men."

"It doesn't matter, Mr. O'Flynn—what Lady McClennon doesn't tell us, you will. What a brilliant stroke of luck. When they hang you, England will rid itself of Taber O'Flynn, the Hawk, and Lord Fitzgerald, all in one swing of the rope."

"You'll have to hang me first," Taber said savagely.

"Oh we'll hang you, but not until you beg for death, you arrogant bastard."

"I heard him, Peter," Patrick said, an anguished look on his face as he paced. "Oh God, I heard him loud and clear. He said the Lady Raven McClennon had been his informer. I still can't believe it."

"I believe it," Peter spat. "I knew all along that woman was going to be trouble. I tried to tell him." He paced, throwing his hands up in despair. "Damn, this ruins everything. Somehow I've got to convince Lord Montgomery that Tomas Fitzgerald knew nothing about his cousin's activities or we'll lose Blackmoor House to the English bastards. Damnit, we needed this coup for the people's morale."

"The hell with the people," Patrick swore. "What are we going to do about Taber?"

Peter Muldane got a strange look in his eyes. "You know, it might just be possible that it will have the same effect on the people if they do hang Taber," he mused. "It's this type of thing that captures the Irish sense of pride in their fellow countrymen."

Patrick grabbed Peter Muldane by the shirtfront. "We've all done your dirty work for years, Muldane. All for Ireland. This time though we're going to help one man—Taber O'Flynn."

"It's impossible," Peter said, straightening his clothing. "He's the most valuable prisoner they've had since Robert Emmet. They're not going to let him escape."

"Maybe they'd like to have you in exchange. I'm sure they'd be happy to know that the man they trust gives the orders to the Brotherhood."

Peter's eyes narrowed dangerously. "Dinna' be a fool, man. You can get yourself killed talking like that."

"Have you got the guts to do it, Muldane, or will you send someone to kill me in the shadows?"

"Get out of here, Casey."

"I will, Muldane. This place suddenly stinks!"

Patrick walked down the dark street, his hands jammed in his pockets. God, he could use a drink, but Taber had taken his bottle. It was probably a good thing, he thought angrily. He needed to have a clear head to help Taber. There had to be someone he could talk to—someone beside Peter Muldane.

"She wouldn't do it," Molly shouted, tears rolling down her face. "She loves Taber."

"If I hadn't heard it with me own ears I wouldn't have believed it either."

"Maybe it's a trick, Patrick," Colin suggested. "Someone who knew what went on the last couple of days could have used the information to trap Taber."

"Why?" Patrick asked. "They caught Taber. What possible reason could they have for lying about who their informant was?" he asked, bewildered.

"Sometimes you dinna' think, Patrick Casey," Molly said, exasperated. "What better way to defeat a man's spirit than to have him think the one person he loves has betrayed him."

Patrick stared out the window, letting what Molly said sink in. Finally he turned and faced her. "You really think she's innocent?"

"Aye. She has no reason to deceive Taber. She hates what the British are doing to our people."

"I have to agree after talking with her last

night I thought the same. She even said she'd work for the Brotherhood if it meant she and Taber could be together."

"There, does that sound like a woman who is about to turn her lover over for hanging?"

"We need to get to her tonight, Molly."

"Get to her?" Molly asked, misunderstanding his meaning.

"Get to her to talk," Patrick explained. "If you want your friend safe, we have to warn her. Half the Brotherhood already thinks she was the informant."

"How could they think that so soon?" Molly asked.

Patrick looked sheepish. "Because I shot my big mouth off when I got back to the warehouse."

Molly touched Patrick's cheek. "That's understandable. You thought Raven was guilty. How do you plan to get to Raven? We can't just walk up to Lord Montgomery and demand to see her."

"Sometimes you dinna' think, my sweet Molly. Have you forgotten the tunnel?"

"I want my money now," Brenna said, nervously pacing the room. "I'm going to leave Ireland in the morning."

Denseley poured them both a drink. "I thought you wanted position and respectability here," he laughed.

"You can laugh. You have nothing to fear, but if anyone saw me tonight . . ." Brenna downed the whiskey in one gulp.

"There's nothing to fear, my dear. If you'd feel better you can stay here for a few days."

"Do you mean it?"

"Of course I mean it. I want to know more about the Brotherhood's activities and who other members are."

"I know nothing else," Brenna said, turning away. "Taber was my lover and that's the only reason I knew about his plan tonight."

"Surely he has mentioned other members."

"No. He's never mentioned anyone," she insisted. Turning Taber in had taken every ounce of courage she had. She wasn't going to take a chance by exposing anyone else.

"Perhaps I can jostle your memory," he said ominously.

"What about Lady McClennon," Brenna asked, hoping to change the subject. "When are you going to tell her uncle about her affair with Taber O'Flynn?"

Denseley had already decided to use this bit of information to bring Raven to her knees. She'd have to agree to marry him and then he'd have her money.

"There's no need to tell her uncle. As you said, the Brotherhood will take care of Raven."

"Suppose they don't?" Brenna asked nervously.

"My dear, you were hiding in the shadows

when I announced for all the world to hear that Lady Raven McClennon had been our informer. Of course they will take care of her. If there is one thing the Irish hate, it's an informer." Denseley turned and gave Brenna an evil smile. "Perhaps you should keep that in mind, my lovely."

"I want my money now," she said, backing away from him.

"Do you now?" he laughed. "You haven't finished earning it yet, my dear."

Gone, gone, forever gone
Are the hopes I cherished
Changed like the sunny dawn
In sudden showers perished.
Author Unknown

Chapter Eleven

Taber bit through his lower lip as the whip cut into his flesh at the jailer's count of five. He hadn't even been taken to a cell before they started with the punishment.

"Lord Denseley said we was to welcome you. I think twenty strokes should be welcome enough," the jailer said, and laughed sadistically.

This wasn't a new experience for Taber. He had been under the lash once before, but the pain was worse than he'd remembered. He tried to focus his mind on something—detach himself from his body, as someone once told him. Raven's face came to mind and he decided to concentrate on what he would do to her if he could get his hands on her at that moment.

"Eight," the jailer called out.

Taber tasted his own blood as his teeth mangled his lips each time the whip tore into his flesh. He kept the face of Raven fixed in his mind. *Bitch, whore, deceiver, liar,* he cursed in his mind as the jailer counted each stroke. Through his pain-fogged mind he could hear the butcher telling him if he begged he would go easier. But he'd never beg. He'd die before he begged an Englishman for mercy.

The jailer, disappointed that he hadn't made his victim beg or scream out in pain, went to work with a new determination. Taber's body slammed into the wooden post with each explosive blow. His blood covered the walls and dripped to the floor.

It was her fault. He had let her into his mind and heart instead of using her for his lust as he should have. He would kill her—strangle her slowly, hold her beautiful neck in his hands. He could see her face smiling seductively at him. *Slut, whore, bitch.*

God, let me lose consciousness, he prayed silently, sagging against the chains that held him. He could feel the blood running down his arms, and he wondered if his wrists had separated from his hands. Unconsciousness began to drift over him. Blessed, sweet, blackness . . .

"Beg, you bloody bastard." The jailer struck again.

"You better cease, Green," another jailer advised. "If you kill the bastard, Lord Denseley will have you hanging up there. Besides you've already passed twenty strokes." The jailer lifted Taber's head then let it fall back against the wooden post. "This bloke doan know what's going on now. He's out cold."

Raven stared straight ahead as if she were in a trance. "Did you hear me, Raven? They've captured Taber," Molly repeated.

Raven looked at Patrick, who was leaning against the windowsill, waiting for him to deny what Molly said. "They will hang him. Oh God, they'll hang him." Jumping from the bed she began pulling clothes from the armoire.

"Raven, what are you doing?" Molly asked.

"We've got to do something. I'll beg my uncle to help him."

Patrick laughed bitterly. "Do you have any pull with Lord Denseley? Because that's who has taken him. And there is something else you should know . . ."

"He wasn't wounded?" she asked, closing her eyes.

"That would probably have been kinder,"

Patrick said, staring out the window as the sky began to lighten with dawn.

"For God's sake, what is it, Patrick? Tell me," she begged.

Patrick turned and faced her. "Taber believes you betrayed him."

Raven stared at him in disbelief. "Me . . . why would . . . that isn't possible . . ."

"I heard Denseley tell him that his plan to capture the ship would have been successful if you hadn't tipped them off."

"No!" Raven screamed. "You had to have heard wrong."

"I dinna' hear wrong, Raven, and neither did Taber. He went berserk when Denseley told him that."

A wave of nausea hit Raven. She stumbled back to the bed and clung to the post. "How could he think I'd betray him? I love him."

"A new love is always fragile, Raven. Neither of you knew each other long enough to be able to trust without a shadow of a doubt."

"Oh God, he's sitting in prison thinking I've betrayed him," Raven cried. She looked up at Patrick, her eyes pleading. "Please, Patrick, think of something. We have to get him out of jail."

"That's easier said than done, lass. I've already talked to the Brotherhood, but most of them are afraid to get mixed up in this right now, particularly since I've come to you."

"Would it help if I begged them?"

"I dinna' think so, Raven. Besides, my concern right now is for you."

"Me? Why should you be concerned about me? Surely you don't think . . ."

Patrick took Raven by the shoulders. "Molly and I dinna' believe you betrayed Taber, but I'm afraid we're the only ones who feel that way. And that's my fault."

Raven brushed the tears from her eyes. "How could it be your fault?"

"I'm afraid I blurted out what I heard Denseley say before I considered the consequences. Molly made me see that Denseley probably told Taber you were his informant to crush his spirit."

"So you're saying that Denseley learned about Taber and me and used it to his advantage."

"Aye. So now you are not only in danger from your own people for associating with Taber, but you're in danger from the Brotherhood because they think you betrayed him."

"We know you weren't the informant," Molly assured, "but someone had to know you two have been together. Patrick even heard Denseley mention the O'Flynn cemetery."

"But who?' Raven said, pacing the room. "May knew, but Taber seemed to trust her implicitly."

"No, I canna' imagine May ever betraying

Taber. She owes her son's life to him," Patrick said. "Did Fergus travel with your uncle to Waterford?"

"No, he was here. Surely you don't think . . ."

"It's worth checking out," Patrick replied.

"Fergus has seemed troubled lately," Molly added.

"Molly, do you think you can get him up here without anyone knowing?" Patrick asked.

"I can try," she said, leaving the room.

"Is there any possibility of seeing Taber?" Raven asked.

"I'll inquire in the morning, but you're going to have to stay in this house until we have our informant. There are too many people who would love to be able to say they eliminated the person who informed on Taber O'Flynn."

Raven sat on the edge of the bed, totally devastated. "He has to know that I didn't deceive him."

"Try not to worry, lass. We all need to keep our heads about us. Somehow we'll come through this thing."

But will Taber, she wondered, staring vacant-eyed at the secret panel, where only ten hours ago Taber had left her. How could their lives have changed so drastically in so short a time?

*　　*　　*

"What is this, Casey?" Fergus asked, irate that he should be summoned to Raven's room. "And how in hell did you get in Lady McClennon's bedroom?"

"Sit down, Fergus," Patrick ordered, towering menacingly over the smaller man. "You're the one who is going to answer some questions."

"If you're caught up here, I won't be held responsible . . ."

"Did you know Taber was arrested tonight?" Patrick asked.

"God no," Fergus said, coming up out of the chair. "How? What happened?"

"That's what we'd like to know. Lord Denseley was waiting for him at the docks. When they captured him, he told Taber that Lady McClennon had informed on him."

Fergus's eyes flew to Raven's face accusingly.

"I didn't do it," she said irritably. "What we want to know is who led Taber into a trap using my name."

The color left Fergus's face as he sat back down. "Holy mother of God . . ."

"You know something, don't you?" Raven asked.

"No. I was just thinking about poor Taber in prison. Was anyone else taken?"

"No, thank God. Taber had a feeling something was wrong and he insisted on checking it out alone. I was hiding in a crate and heard everything."

"We could all be in danger," Fergus said, fear in his eyes. "This informant could name us one by one."

"Why would they do that? Why not turn us all in at one time?" Patrick asked suspiciously.

"Who knows. I suppose money or vengeance." Fergus quickly stood up, afraid he had already said too much. "I've got to get back downstairs before Lord Montgomery misses me. If I hear anything I'll let you know."

"I dinna' think he is the one," Molly said after Fergus had gone.

"No, but I think he knows who is," Patrick said.

"I had the same feeling," Raven agreed. "He seemed so nervous."

Patrick paced the floor. "We're going to need more help. Someone who can be trusted."

"Colin will want to help," Molly said.

"Good. Then we'll keep things between the four of us."

"If we're right about Fergus, shouldn't someone keep an eye on him?" Raven asked.

"Aye, that's what I'm going to have Colin do. It seemed to me that he was afraid of the person when he was talking, so I dinna' know if he'll try to make contact or not."

"Aye," Molly agreed. "It just doesn't make sense."

"Nothing makes sense," Raven said, rubbing her temples. "If my uncle knows I've been seeing Taber, why hasn't he been up here yet. I would think he'd want to wring my neck."

"At the least," Patrick said, "but maybe Denseley hasn't told him yet. I suggest you go down as usual. If there is a problem, Molly will come for me. I'm going to see what the word is around the streets."

Patrick kissed Molly, then kissed Raven on the forehead. "Have faith, lass."

He was dreaming, lost in the memory of the day at the river. He could smell the scent of wildflowers and hear the sweet sound of the birds. Raven's body blended with his in every way, her soft lips parted sweetly, returning his passion innocently. He could feel the satin of her skin. The softness of her silky hair flowed across his body as her mouth touched his burning skin.

Taber suddenly opened his eyes and stared at the dirty pad beneath him. He began to tremble violently as the pain enveloped him. The pain in his back and the pain in his heart.

Put her out of your mind, he willed himself. The surroundings, yes that should do it . . . concentrate on your surroundings. He could hear groans and labored breathing not far from him. He tried to raise up, but the effort was too much. His face pressed into the filthy mat as he was seized with a spasm of pain. His lips were raw and split, and he needed water desperately. Surely there was water . . .

"Here mate," someone said, putting a metal cup to his mouth. "Sip slowly or it will come back up."

The water tasted like iron, but it quenched his thirst, and Taber was grateful to whoever had offered it. "Thank you," he whispered hoarsely before losing consciousness.

For two days Raven waited for someone to confront her about her relationship with Taber, but to her amazement, no one said a thing. Her uncle was elated with the prospect of returning to London now that the leader of the Insurrectionists was finally behind bars.

Raven was beginning to think Patrick must have heard wrong. Even Walter Denseley was unusually pleasant to her, as was her aunt. Why then did she have this feeling of impending doom?

"I dinna' know what to make of it," Patrick said as he met with Raven and Molly in her room. "Denseley has to be planning something."

"Let's forget him for now," Raven said. "Have you any news of Taber?"

"I've learned that he is still here in Cork."

Raven stared at him. "Did you think they'd take him someplace else?"

"Aye, they usually transport important prisoners to Dublin immediately. Cork only has a small jail."

"Then that's to our advantage," Raven said hopefully.

"Aye, you would think so, but they have every inch of it heavily guarded."

"Do you think any of these guards could be bribed to help us?"

"I've already checked that out. There is an old night guard who is ready to retire. I would think the prospect of a little extra gold in his pocket would appeal to him. He was at least willing to talk to me last night. That's how I learned Taber was still there."

"Were you able to find out anything about his condition?" Raven asked. Out of the corner of her eye she saw Molly shake her head. "You know something, Patrick. What is it?"

"Taber is strong, lass. He'll be fine."

"What is it, Patrick? What have they done to him?" she persisted.

"Taber's been under the whip."

"Under the whip." She closed her eyes and swayed. "Oh God, that's what Denseley meant when he said he was sure Taber would eventually talk. They mean to torture him until he does."

Raven turned to Patrick, clutching his wide

247

shoulders. "We have to help him . . . we've got to," she pleaded, tears streaming down her face.

"We will, Raven, but we have to find a way first. Colin is with some members of the Brotherhood who want to help. Maybe one of them will come up with some ideas."

"In the meantime, Taber will be tortured."

Patrick pulled Raven into his arms. "Lass, if I could walk in there and free Taber, you know I would, but we'd both only end up prisoners. You and I both know that isn't going to help."

"I realize that, Patrick. I would never willingly place you in danger."

"I know you wouldn't, lass, but please, be patient. And keep your ears open. You're in the best position to learn something that could help us."

Raven tried to smile. "I will."

Taber's spirit was at its lowest. He had endured the lash, and the torture, but the grief he felt at Raven's deception ate at him, making him sick inside. The only reason he wanted to live was the need for revenge. Someday, somehow he would make her pay.

Taber carefully leaned back against the cold stone wall. When he went to trial, he would plead the cause of the Irish people. Perhaps his words would help someone. A sick feeling came over him as he realized no one had mentioned a trial. Surely the Brotherhood would put pressure on the British for justice. How long had it been now, four or five days? God, he was already losing track of time.

He glanced at the other two prisoners. One was an Englishman who had murdered his commanding officer. The one who had given him water was called Delaney. It seemed he had worked for an Englishman, until he was caught stealing. At least a woman they loved hadn't betrayed them, he thought bitterly. A woman with raven black hair and sky blue eyes, who one moment swore she loved you and the next spied on you.

Taber pulled his legs up to his body and leaned his head against them. How could she have done it? he wondered. She had actually given up her virginity to him so she could learn information that would help the British. Wasn't that above and beyond the call of duty? he snorted harshly. She had been convincing—oh God, had she been convincing. He would have done anything for her, even leave Ireland. What a fool he had been.

It had been five days and still they hadn't come up with a way to help Taber escape. The waiting and not knowing what condition

Taber was in was driving Raven insane. She leaned her head against the cool glass of the window and stared out into space. "Taber love, please know that I did not betray you."

Raven was lost in thought when there was a light knock at her door. "M'lady," May whispered. "Your aunt and Lord Denseley request your presence in the library."

"Where is my uncle?" Raven asked.

"He's out, but I dinna' know where."

Raven glanced in the mirror at herself. Her coloring was gray and her eyes were bright with unshed tears. Not the sight of a calm, stable person, she thought.

"May, when Molly returns, please tell her where I am."

"Aye, I will, m'lady. Good luck to ye."

Raven squeezed the woman's hand. "Thank you, May."

"Ah, my dear, come in," Walter Denseley greeted.

Raven glanced at her aunt sitting on the settee, a malicious smile on her face.

"I thought it was time we discussed our wedding plans," he said, leading her to a chair across from her aunt.

Raven willed herself to stay calm. "I think I've made my feelings on that subject quite clear."

"Yes, you have, my dear, but I have a feeling you will change your mind this time."

Raven had a sick feeling in the pit of her stomach as she glanced at her aunt. The ax was about to fall.

"I cannot imagine anything that would make me change my mind," she said, struggling for an air of confidence.

Denseley's expression became cold and hard. "We can stop the pretense now, Raven. Your aunt and I know all about your alliance with Taber O'Flynn."

"Alliance? Your choice of words is strange, m'lord. I met Taber O'Flynn only once at the party Uncle Charles gave. You remember, when we all thought he was Lord Fitzgerald."

"Liar," her aunt hissed. "We know you've whored for the murderer."

"He is not a murderer!" Raven said, jumping to her feet.

Denseley grabbed Raven roughly by the shoulders. "Listen to me, you little fool. I'm giving you a chance to have respectability. You are ruined. A soiled slut, but I'll keep that quiet."

"Respectability with you?" she spat. "I'd rather die."

Denseley slapped her hard across the face, knocking her back into the chair.

"No, Walter, don't mark her," Caroline grabbed his arm. "You don't want Charles to become suspicious."

His eyes glittered with anger. "Perhaps she'd like to see her lover tortured until he dies very slowly." He smiled at the satisfaction of seeing the terror in Raven's eyes.

"Are you telling me that if I marry you, you'll release Taber?"

Denseley laughed. "Don't be a fool. Taber O'Flynn will have to pay for his treachery against England, but I can see that he isn't hung, and that he's treated in a more humane fashion."

Raven collapsed against the chair. Her face had gone stiff with revulsion. "Uncle Charles will never believe that I have agreed to marry you without pressure."

"Your uncle will disown you if he finds out what a tramp you are. At least this way you will still get your inheritance," Caroline said.

"How could you do this to me?" she asked her aunt. "I've never done anything to you."

"You were born. That was enough," her aunt spat hatefully. "Now get on with this, Walter. Charles will be returning soon."

Denseley took a paper from his pocket. "This is our marriage agreement, my dear."

Raven stared at the paper giving him control over her inheritance. She stood up and bravely faced him. "I need time to think about this."

"You don't have any time," her aunt said sharply.

"Now, Caroline, if she wants to take her time, let her. I must admit I've been enjoying my little sessions with Taber O'Flynn. He's been a hard devil to break, but I'm close. The man barely has flesh left on his body, yet still he persists in remaining silent. Such a challenge," he clucked.

Raven swayed, gripping the chair for support. "You are the murdering traitor," she hissed. "It's you who should be in jail."

"But I'm not, my dear. It's your beloved Taber O'Flynn. So what is it to be?"

"I want to see him first."

"That's impossible."

"How do I know he's even alive?"

"Take my word, Raven, and save yourself the unpleasantness. He's not a pretty sight."

"Either I see him or I don't sign the papers."

"Let her see him," her aunt encouraged. "What difference does it make?"

"He's to be moved to Dublin tomorrow so it will have to be tonight," Denseley said, unaware he had given Raven the information she had been waiting for.

"I'll get my cape."

"Patience, my dear. First you must sign the papers."

"Do I have your word that you will take me to Taber and that your harsh treatment will cease?"

"Of course, my dear. As long as you are cooperative."

Raven quickly signed the papers. "Fine," Denseley said. "I'll send for you later this evening—if you're sure you want to see what's left of your lover."

"I'm sure," Raven said, leaving the room.

"That was much simpler than I'd expected," Denseley laughed.

"Don't become overconfident, Walter. We still have to be very careful."

"Of course, dear Caroline. And on that thought, I must leave. I have some unfinished business at home."

"Haven't you gotten rid of that girl yet?"

"She's been a delightful diversion, but I'm afraid she has outlived her usefulness."

"Has she given you any more information?"

"No, she still denies knowing anything else about the Brotherhood, but it doesn't matter. Taber O'Flynn will eventually tell us what we want to know."

Caroline laughed. "You are an evil man, Walter."

"You've been an excellent example, Caroline. But my plans are going to turn out better than yours did."

"You swore never to speak of that again," she said, her face turning white with fear.

"Who would be interested in knowing that you had the wheel of Anne McClennon's carriage sawed through so she would die at the bottom of a cliff?" he asked, a cruel smile on his face.

"Shut up, Walter. The walls have ears in this place."

"Poor Caroline, your plans didn't include killing the man you loved, did it?" he laughed.

"I should never have told you," she said between gritted teeth.

"No, you shouldn't have, Caroline," he said as he left the room.

"We should have known he'd try something like this," Patrick fumed. "Well, don't you worry, lass, we'll get Taber out of there and then you won't have to sign any stupid papers." Raven moved away from him and stared out the window. "What is it, lass?"

"I've already signed the papers. It was the only way he'd take me to Taber."

"Well, no matter, Taber won't let it happen once we have him out of prison."

"I hope you're right," Raven said, yet she had the ominous feeling that it wasn't going to be like that. "What's important now is that we know when Taber is going to be transported, and that's when we'll make our move."

"You sound like you have some ideas already, lass."

"Aye, I do. The guards will be told that

Taber is to be moved. If I can find out the exact time, we'll get the jump on them and move him a few minutes before the appointed time. I'll have a letter with my uncle's signature on it for you to give to the guard. You'll need to get hold of uniforms for you and Colin, and anyone else you can recruit."

"Many of the members of the Brotherhood have said they want to help any way they can, but I've been reluctant to involve too many people."

"Pick just a few you know you can trust. It would look strange to the guards if just two of you showed up to transport such an important prisoner."

"I'll take care of it," Patrick said.

"Do you think you can get your hands on a prison wagon?" Raven asked.

"You get that letter from your uncle and I'll take care of the prison wagon," Patrick assured.

"We need some way to tell Taber we're ready to make our move," Raven suggested. "I'm hoping Denseley will let me be alone with him, but if he doesn't, is there some word I could use that would make him understand we are planning to help him?"

"Aye, if you use the word *Inisfail*, he'll know I'm involved."

"What does that mean?" Raven asked.

"It was one of the first names Ireland was known by hundreds of years ago. It means *Isle of Destiny*. It is also the name of Taber's ship, but only a few people know that."

"Then *Inisfail* it will be." Raven forced a smile.

When he was ready to leave, Patrick produced a small pistol from his pocket. "Take this with you, lass. If it is possible, slip it to Taber."

Raven stared at the silver gun. "Let's just hope he doesn't use it on me."

"You'll be able to make him see that you had nothing to do with his imprisonment, lass. Stop worrying about it."

"I hope you're right, Patrick."

Raven threw her arms around Patrick's neck and hugged him. "I want to thank both of you for your friendship. I will never forget your kindness."

"You're talking like you'll never see us again," Molly said, tears in her eyes. "Everything is going to work out just fine. Patrick and I have talked about it. Taber is going to have to leave Ireland this time, so Patrick and I want to go with you. We'll all start a new life in America."

"Aye, I have Taber's crew standing by to sail at a moment's notice," Patrick added. "They're all good men willing and anxious to follow

Taber wherever he goes."

"Taber should be very proud that his men would feel that way."

"Aye, lass, they'd give their life for him, as I would."

And as I would, she thought silently.

*This was the most
unkindest cut of all.*
Shakespeare

Chapter Twelve

Nervously Raven waited, pacing between the window and her bed. Things she and Taber had said to each other kept rushing through her mind—words of love and of hope. She drew a deep breath, trying to steady her nerves. Please, let him be all right, she prayed. And let this plan to free him be successful.

She jumped as a knock sounded at her door. She was surprised and disappointed that it was Fergus O'Brien instead of Walter Denseley.

"Lady McClennon, I need to talk with you for a moment," he whispered.

"Please, Fergus, not now. I'm expecting someone."

Fergus ignored her protest and stepped past her, closing the door behind him. "I think I know what is going on, and I want to help."

"I don't know what you're talking about."

"If there is a plan under way to help Taber escape, I want to be involved." He didn't mention that he felt partially to blame for Taber's being in prison.

"Perhaps you should talk to Patrick," Raven suggested.

"I've tried talking to him, but he treats me like his enemy. Please help me, Lady McClennon. I would never knowingly do anything to bring harm to Taber. He's always been a good friend."

Raven stared at Fergus. He sounded so sincere she didn't have the heart to refuse his offer. "Do you think you could get my uncle's signature on a document ordering the transfer of Taber?"

"There is already such a document on his desk to be used in the morning."

"Do you know what time?"

"Aye, just a few minutes after the change of the guards. That would make it around eight."

"Suppose we had our own document and showed up at six o'clock. Do you think the guards would believe us?"

"They would if I sent a message tonight telling them the time had been moved up."

"You would do that?"

"Aye."

Raven was silent for a moment. "We could both be in a great deal of trouble if we are discovered," she warned.

"I'm aware of that."

"Walter Denseley is to take me to see Taber tonight, so you must wait until after our visit. In the meantime, you can deliver the forged document to Patrick, and explain everything to him."

"Dinna' worry, I'll take care of it," Fergus promised. "And Lady McClennon, I promise, you won't be sorry you trusted me."

"I pray not," she answered.

A knock at the door silenced them both. "Just a moment," she called.

Raven opened the secret panel and hurried Fergus into it. "Don't let Taber down, Fergus," she whispered.

Opening the door, Raven faced Walter Denseley. "I'm ready."

"I still strongly recommend that you forget this folly."

"I want to be sure he's alive," she answered, moving past him.

"You could take my word."

"I'd rather trust a snake," she spat.

Denseley laughed. "It's going to be a pleasure taming you, my little spitfire."

Raven trembled as they descended the stone stairs. The corridor was dark except for a torch, which threw everything into eerie shadows.

261

Moaning noises echoed all around her, sounds of pain, and of the poor souls who had lost their minds. She screamed as a hand reached out of one of the cells, grabbing at her cape.

She wanted to turn and run, but she forced her fear down and followed Denseley toward a cell lit with several torches.

When Denseley stopped, Raven peered into the cell before them, but she didn't see Taber. "Where is he?" she whispered.

"I told you he wasn't a pretty sight, my dear."

Raven's eyes went back to the bearded man lying on a bed of straw. "Taber," she whispered.

He was staring at her, his eyes dark sockets in his gaunt face, but she couldn't tell if he knew who she was.

"I want to talk to him alone." She turned pleading eyes on Walter Denseley.

"I'm sorry, my dear, but that's impossible."

At the sound of his chain rattling, Raven stepped closer to the cell. Taber was struggling to his feet, clinging to the wall for support.

She cried out as she saw there was not an inch of his flesh that wasn't bleeding or a raw scar. "Taber, oh God, Taber," she cried, reaching through the bars toward him.

He steadied himself against the wall. "Did you come to gloat?" he asked, his voice barely a choked whisper. "Take a closer look," he ordered, stumbling as far as his chain would allow him. "You should have been here earlier. You could have enjoyed Denseley's handi-work."

"No!" She turned on Walter Denseley. "You promised—"

"As soon as we are married he will be taken care of," Denseley answered, his voice devoid of emotion.

"So that's your reward. Marriage to Lord Walter Denseley for the head of Taber O'Flynn. You made a poor deal, you conniving bitch," he growled.

Raven cringed at the hate in his voice. "Taber, you must know I had nothing to do with your capture."

"Liar," he hissed. "How could I ever have believed you? It makes me sick to remember that I lay with you."

"Taber, I love you," she said, holding her hands out to him. "Please believe me," she begged.

Denseley laughed. "There is no reason to keep up the performance, my love. Mr. O'Flynn knows why you pretended to be in love with him."

"He's lying, Taber. Can't you see that. I love you . . ."

"Lying bitch. Get out of my sight."

"Taber, listen to me," she begged, trying to get close enough to drop the gun within his reach.

"Enough," Denseley said, pulling her back from the bars. "You did a good job tormenting him. Now we have to go."

"Taber, please listen to me."

"Shut up, Raven," Denseley ordered.

"You deceived me," Taber shouted hoarsely, "and one day I'll make you pay."

Raven stopped struggling and stared at him through tear-filled eyes. "No, you deceived me, Taber. You deceived me by not believing."

"Come, Raven," Denseley said, dragging her roughly away.

"No." Raven struggled against him. "Not yet." She broke away and ran back to the bars. "Taber, listen to me." Taber turned his back to her. "For God's sake, listen to me," she pleaded. "Does Inisfail mean anything to you?"

Taber spun around and stared at her.

"Inisfail," she screamed as Denseley dragged her away.

Raven rode in silence, devastated by the turn of events. She had failed to make Taber understand that she hadn't betrayed him, and she had failed to get the gun to him.

She tried to ignore Walter Denseley's gloating remarks, but he continued to taunt her. "Don't even think about going back on our deal, my dear.''

"Dealing with you is like dealing with the devil,'' she spat.

"Perhaps,'' he said, smiling, ''but you have no other choice.''

"I'm not so sure of that.''

"What did you think you were telling O'Flynn when you kept saying Inisfail?'' he asked suspiciously.

"It's an Irish word that means *believe in me,*'' she lied.

"Well it didn't work,'' he sneered. "I would have thought you had more pride than to beg and grovel to that Irishman.''

"I love Taber O'Flynn,'' Raven retorted. "I would have done anything to make him believe me.''

When the carriage pulled up in front of Riverside House, Raven tried to open the door, but Denseley stopped her, twisting her wrist painfully until she cried out.

"Don't do or say anything foolish, my dear Raven. Or your lover will have to pay for it.''

"Are you beginning to see the error of your way, m'lord?'' she asked sarcastically. "My uncle will have your head . . .''

Denseley rapped on the roof and ordered his driver to continue riding until he told him to stop.

"Let me out, you bastard,'' Raven struggled to get past him.

"Not until we finish our business. Now sit back and shut up before I hurt you."

Raven gave up the struggle and sat back, glaring at Walter Denseley. "When my uncle learns you have treated me this way . . ."

"He will do nothing, my dear. I hold all the cards now. I've already been in touch with Lord Beatty. Your uncle will be recalled to London, and I will take his place here."

"Wonderful. That's what he wanted all along," Raven said, trying to act calm. "But he still will not tolerate the way you have treated me."

He smiled an evil smile. "You're such an innocent in so many ways, Raven. Have you forgotten I hold the paper that you signed, agreeing to marry me of your own free will. And if that isn't enough, I have some information about your family that would ruin you all, and probably kill your uncle."

"My uncle has never been involved in a scandal," Raven said curtly.

"No, he probably hasn't, but your aunt has."

"Nothing she has done would surprise me," Raven said, turning to look out the window.

"Oh, I think this would, but no matter. We have other things to discuss. Tomorrow you will meet with your uncle and tell him you wish to accept my offer of marriage."

"He'll never believe me," Raven laughed.

Denseley grabbed her by the chin and forced

her head around to stare at a knife he held up to her face. "You need a lesson here and now," he hissed through gritted teeth. "When I'm through with you, you will never cross me again."

My God, he was going to kill her, she thought in horror. She was completely taken by surprise when he shoved her back against the seat and lifted her skirt.

"No!" she struggled, flailing him with her fists.

"Bitch," he hissed, striking her hard across the face, stunning her long enough for him to cut away her stays and undergarments.

"I'll show you things that that Irish low-life wouldn't even know about . . . ways of pleasuring," he said, as his breathing became labored. He was delighting in causing her pain everywhere he touched and prodded.

Raven shook her head, trying to remain conscious. She had to stop him . . . this couldn't be happening, she sobbed. As she tried to clutch her clothes to her, she felt the weight of the gun in the pocket of her cloak.

"This will be the last time you defy me," he growled. "Do you understand me?" he asked, slapping her again. "Tonight your lover will die. If you don't want to join him, you'll become my submissive wife."

"No!" She struggled to sit up. "You promised—"

"The devil doesn't make promises. He takes what he wants and to hell with everyone else."

Raven was able to feel the cold steel of the gun, but her arm was pinned under the weight of Denseley. "Please help me," she shouted, hoping the driver would come to her rescue.

Denseley laughed. "Ains is in my employ, Raven. He isn't foolish enough to cross me." As he spoke, he raised up to undo his pants, enabling Raven to get her finger on the trigger of the gun.

"No!" she screamed, as he positioned himself to enter her. A muffled explosion vibrated the carriage. Walter Denseley stared at her, his colorless eyes wide with shock. Then his full weight collapsed on top of her.

Raven felt sick and disoriented. She could feel his blood, warm and sticky, on her own skin. With all her strength she pushed him off, then sat up. To her amazement, the carriage was still slowly moving. Her first instinct was to bolt and run, but she forced herself to sit a moment until she had her senses about her.

Glancing out the window she realized they were not far from Riverside House. She tapped on the roof and spoke to the driver. "Lord Denseley is not feeling well. He'd like you to take me home, then drive him around until he tells you to stop."

There was no answer, and Raven held her breath until the carriage slowed and turned into the drive of Riverside House. She trembled as she climbed over Denseley's body. When she stepped down from the carriage, she gathered her torn clothes around her as best she could, and stumbled toward the steps.

As she opened the massive door, she heard the carriage begin to move away. It would only be a matter of time before the driver realized Walter Denseley was dead, and then they would come for her.

Raven stood at the foot of the stairs listening to the silence. There was nothing to do but talk to her uncle, she decided. She had to make him understand.

Clutching the railing for support, she slowly climbed the stairs. The night had been a disaster. Taber didn't believe her . . .

Oh God, Taber. She froze midway up the steps. She couldn't do anything to jeopardize his escape. She looked over her shoulder at the clock. It was a little after two. If everything went as planned, in four hours he would be free. Raven collapsed on the stairs. He would be free, she sobbed, and she would be a prisoner.

"Raven, is that you, dear?" Charles Montgomery asked from the top of the stairs. "What is it, child? What's wrong?"

"I've killed him, Uncle Charles," Raven sobbed. "He was going to . . . I couldn't let him . . ." she sobbed incoherently.

Charles knelt beside his niece and took her in his arms. "Who are you talking about, Raven?"

"He was going to kill Taber," she sobbed. "He said if I didn't do what he wanted he'd kill me too . . . I had to kill him, Uncle Charles . . . you see that, don't you?"

"Raven, for God's sake, what are you talking about?"

"How can I make you understand?" she sobbed. "I had been seeing Taber O'Flynn and Walter found out. He and Aunt Caroline forced me to sign a marriage agreement. He's been beating Taber . . . oh God, it was terrible. He promised if I agreed to marry him, he would stop torturing Taber, but he lied." Her voice was getting higher as she was near hysteria.

Charles heard movement at the top of the stairs. "Come, my dear, let me take you to your room and we'll talk there."

"They're going to be coming for me, Uncle Charles," she said as he helped her up. "They're going to take me away and put me in a dark place."

"I'm not going to let anyone take you away, Raven. You should know that."

They didn't see Caroline standing in the shadows as they moved down the hall toward Raven's room. After they passed, she silently crossed the hall and headed for the servants quarters.

Between sobs Raven told her uncle the whole story, except for the fact that Taber's friends were going to try to break him out of prison.

Charles listened to Raven's story in numb silence, patting her hand or giving her a hug as she talked.

"I am so sorry, Uncle Charles," she sobbed when she was finished. "I've caused you nothing but trouble since I came to live with you."

"Nonsense, my dear. This is partly my fault. I knew Walter had hopes of marrying you, but I had no idea he or Caroline would resort to such extreme methods."

"But the law isn't going to care about the pressure I was under or the fact that Walter Denseley was trying to rape me. All they will care about is that I killed him."

"Unfortunately you are right, my dear," Charles said, rubbing his chin in thought. "But if I can get to Walter's driver before he goes to the authorities, I'm sure I can make him see the wisdom of saying someone off the street shot Walter."

"Do you think he would agree to that?" Raven asked hopefully.

"He's certainly not going to want to admit that he ignored the pleadings of a young lady in trouble. Besides I'll make it worth his while."

"It's too late for that," Caroline said from the doorway. "I've already sent May for the authorities."

"You did what?" Charles asked, grabbing his wife.

"I knew she'd go too far one day," she smiled smugly.

"No, *you* went too far, Caroline. I think the authorities are going to be more interested in what I have to tell them about what happened in Scotland, than what happened here tonight."

A look of fear crossed Caroline's features. Her eyes darted from Raven's face to Charles's. "You couldn't . . ."

"I couldn't what, Caroline? I couldn't know what happened, or I couldn't turn you over to the authorities?"

"This isn't the time or the place to discuss this, Charles."

"I disagree with you, my dear. I think it is finally time Raven knew what really happened to her parents."

"You're bluffing. You don't know anything," Caroline said, wringing her hands.

"Uncle Charles, what are you talking about?" Raven asked.

"Tell her, Caroline," Charles ordered.

"I don't know what you're talking about," she lied.

"Excuse me, m'lady," May said from the doorway. "Did you mean for me to go for the authorities right away?"

Charles laughed triumphantly. "No, it's all right, May. Lady Montgomery made a mistake. Isn't that right, Caroline?"

"You little fool." She turned on the servant. "You knew very well I meant for you to go right away."

"I'm sorry, m'lady. Sometimes I get confused," May said with a curtsy.

"Get out of my sight," Caroline snapped. "I should have known you'd be useless."

"Just a moment, May. I wish to speak with you." He turned his attention back to his wife. "Go back to your room and stay there, Caroline. You and I have much to discuss."

"I want to know what happened to my parents," Raven said, stepping forward.

"I will tell you everything, my dear, but right now we have other more pressing matters."

When Caroline left, Lord Montgomery turned to May. "Thank you for your loyalty to Raven. Now I want you to pack all of her belongings, and it must be done quickly. Raven will be leaving here tonight."

"Yes, sir." The maid curtsied and hurried

from the room.

Raven stared at her uncle for an explanation. "There is a ship leaving with the morning tide, Raven. The captain is a friend of mine, and he'll see that you are delivered safely to friends in America."

At the look of devastation on her face, Charles took her in his arms. "I wish there were some other way, Raven, but we can't trust the authorities in this area. Denseley had too many people in his pocket."

Raven forced a smile through her tears. "I've always wanted to go to America."

"You are a very rich young lady, Raven. You will be able to live very well in America. The friends I am sending you to are Doctor Jordan Mitchell and his daughter, Elayne. Jordan grew up in London and knew your mother when she was young." He smiled down at Raven. "As a matter of fact, he was quite smitten with your mother before she met and married Evan. You will like him, I'm sure. Jordan's letters rave about the area where he settled. It is a beautiful little village on the Chesapeake Bay in Maryland. Now go get cleaned up and properly dressed for a sea voyage. I have messages and letters of introduction to write."

After hugging her uncle, Raven headed for the door. Before opening it, she turned back to face him. "What happened to my parents,

Uncle Charles?''

"I will explain everything, Raven, but we only have a few hours before Captain Sullivan sails, so we must hurry."

There had been time to do little more than say a tearful good-bye. Her uncle had pressed a letter in her hand, telling her it would explain everything. Then, as the sky turned a pale shade of pink, the ship weighed anchor and they prepared to sail. She stared back at the green hills and cliffs of Cork, realizing she was totally alone. The sails filled with a strong gust of wind, and the ship moved swiftly away from land. As the docks and piers began to disappear from sight, she thought of Taber. She would probably never know what happened to him, but maybe that was best. He had certainly made it clear how he felt about her. Somehow she had to make a new life for herself, and the only way she could do that was to put Taber O'Flynn out of her mind, and out of her heart. It sounded so easy, she thought bitterly.

Raven glanced down at the letter clutched in her hand. It was time to find out what her aunt and uncle had been talking about, she decided as she made her way to her cabin.

Removing her fur-lined cape, Raven sat on the edge of the bunk and opened the letter. She read a few lines, explaining that her inheritance was in a trust in her name in the Bank of England, and when she was ready to transfer it to America, he would see that it was done immediately. He explained that Captain Sullivan was also holding a good sum of money for her in his safe, to be handed to her on their arrival in Maryland, along with her letters of introduction.

The next paragraph took her breath away as if she'd been hit in the stomach. She read the words over, but it was the same:

Caroline was in love with your father. When we visited your family in Scotland, she apparently told your father of her feelings, and he rejected her. We left quickly, if you remember. Caroline told me that she had had words with May, and she would not stay in the same house a minute longer. There wasn't any reason for me to doubt this since they had never gotten along. What I didn't know was that Caroline had paid someone to tamper with the axle on your mother's carriage, thinking that if May were out of the way, Evan would turn to her. I suppose she planned to get rid of me next, but that is neither here nor there. Caroline hadn't planned on your father being with your mother when her carriage broke away from the horses and plummeted down the cliff.

Please believe me, my dear Raven, I didn't know any of this until we were in Ireland and I overheard Caroline telling Walter Denseley what happened. My only reason for not confronting her right away was because I wanted to spare you. I knew you were anxious to be on your own as soon as you were eighteen, and since the time was so close, I decided to hold off. Forgive me if I was wrong. Now I want you to put all of this out of your mind. You have your whole life ahead of you, my lovely niece. I want you to think only of the future—and to be happy.

Your devoted uncle,
Charles

Tears ran down Raven's face. She was feeling a mixture of confusing emotions—hate, loss, abandonment, and sadness for her uncle, who now had to deal with Caroline—but happiness wasn't one of them, and she doubted she would ever know it again. Happiness had been lying in Taber's arms, fishing with him on the River Lee, or looking out to sea from the parapets of a deserted castle.

Oh God, why was she doing this to herself? she sobbed. She had to put him out of her mind—just as he had put her out of his life.

I stand a wreck on Error's shore,
A spectre not within the door,
A houseless shadow evermore,
An exile lingering here.
Menken

Chapter Thirteen

The trip was relatively uneventful. Raven stayed in her cabin at first, too depressed to do more than sleep or pace. Worried that the girl would become physically ill, Captain Sullivan insisted upon her taking a stroll each morning and afternoon. The clear blue sky and invigorating effects of the salt air quickly brought Raven out of her doldrums. The latter part of the trip she spent most of her time on deck learning everything she could about the ship and navigation. Captain Sullivan had turned out to be a wonderful teacher and friend, thoroughly enjoying his inquisitive young passenger.

Raven stood at the railing of the ship as they

sailed up the Chesapeake Bay. It was dawn, and the cool air hung with the scent of pine and salt air. The bay surface rippled like silk as they slipped through the water with no more than a whisper of a sound. A faint wind coming out of the east rustled the canvas, and a sea gull made a sound as if it were laughing at them as it swooped over the ship. It was all so different, Raven thought as she watched the sandy shoreline in the distance. She had never seen anything like the tall sea grass, the pine trees, and the hardwoods with their crimson and gold leaves. "There's another British ship," Captain Sullivan pointed out on the starboard side. "They seem to be everywhere."

"Are we in danger?" Raven asked.

"I don't think they'd try anything this close to Fort Severn," he said, studying the ship through his telescope. "Privateers have been using Spa Creek of late. That's probably what they're interested in. If they're not careful, one of those privateers will be hauling them into Annapolis as a prize," he laughed. "The reward for British ships is growing everyday. A seaman can become rich overnight if he captures the right ship."

"I heard your seamen talking about the British ships impressing American sailors right off their own ships. Is that true?"

"Afraid so, Lady McClennon. Thousands of our fine young men have been torn from their country and from everything dear to them. They've been dragged aboard British ships and exposed to the severities of British discipline, exiled to the most distant and deadly climes, and forced to risk their lives in the battles of their oppressors."

"That's terrible. Can't anyone stop such actions?"

"That's what this war is all about. President Madison has condemned Britain for their actions and has informed them America will no longer tolerate the impressment of its citizens or the seizure of goods in international waters. Now he has to back those words up with actions."

Raven stared across the bay towards land. "Why is peace so hard to find, Captain Sullivan?"

"It's not hard to find, m'lady. It just has to be earned and sometimes that's easier said than done."

Raven felt the ship change course. The morning sun was out now, burning the remains of the fog off, and ahead, blurred and indistinct, she could see houses and steeples. "Is that it, Captain Sullivan? Is that Annapolis?"

"That it is, m'lady. The tall building with the cupola is the State House."

Inside her a slow excitement stirred, letting her forget for a moment the unhappy events that had brought her there. As they sailed nearer, she could see the sheltered harbor with ships anchored in the calm water, their tall masts reaching toward the sky from out of the blue water. Closing her eyes, she breathed deeply of the salt air, and thought she could smell the aroma of bread baking from somewhere onshore. She scanned the dock area, taking in the brick houses and church steeples. It was all so beautiful, she thought excitedly.

As they approached the town quay, Raven forgot the steeples and houses of Annapolis, staring instead at the tall ocean-going schooners that Captain Sullivan pointed out. "They slipped through the blockade in the fog," he said proudly, as if he had accomplished the feat. "The small boats surrounding them are all anxious to purchase wine, coffee, and sugar. That's what has brought everyone out so early this morning."

"Do the British ever come up in the harbor or bother the townspeople?" Raven asked.

"They haven't ventured up this far, but they've been a plague to the small crafts fishing in the bay, often confiscating a day's catch. I suppose just their presence in the area has kept everyone in a state of turmoil."

"You don't think I will have any problems, do you, Captain Sullivan?" Raven asked, worried about her British connections.

"Your uncle explained to me that you were to be introduced as Lady McClennon of Inverness, Scotland. Most people here know the Scots people have been persecuted by the British, so I don't think you'll have any trouble."

"I hope not. I so want to belong someplace, and I have a feeling this place is just what I've been looking for. If only . . ."

"If only what, m'lady?"

Tears came to Raven's eyes. "I was just missing the friends I made in Ireland."

"You'll make lots of friends here. Annapolis is a very social town. Something is going on all the time. Once you get settled in at Doctor Mitchell's house, I'm sure you'll be caught up in the midst of it all."

Raven smiled at the man who had become such a dear friend. "Thank you for everything, Captain Sullivan, but especially for being a good friend."

"It has been my pleasure, m'lady," he said, bowing over her hand. "You know I wish you all the best in America. Now you'll have to excuse me, Lady McClennon. I have work to do now," he said, leaving her alone at the railing.

Shivering, Raven pulled her cape closer. Fall was definitely in the air, she thought. Raven studied the activities on the docks, wondering if being caught up in the midst of social activities was really what she wanted. Even after having weeks alone, trying to put some direction in her life, she couldn't decide what she wanted to do. Taber's handsome face would always come to mind, reminding her that she had thought he would be a part of her future.

She forced her attention to the street crowded with carriages and horses. It was strange to her that two ships could bring so much activity to the docks. Captain Sullivan anchored a short distance from the privateers, and she could catch snatches of conversations on buying and bidding on the supplies aboard. The ships will surely sink if one more person boards, she thought, watching the activity.

"If you are ready, m'lady, we already have your belongings in the dory," Captain Sullivan said at her side.

When they were ashore, and Captain Sullivan had hired a carriage, Raven began to feel uncomfortable about showing up unannounced on the doorstep of Doctor Mitchell. "Is there a hotel or boarding house I could go to first, and then send a message to Doctor Mitchell?"

"Don't worry, m'lady, the Doc is a wonderful man. He'll be very happy to have you when he learns you're Lord Montgomery's niece."

"I feel like an intruder," she murmured, staring out the window at the brick row houses. They had only ridden a few minutes when the carriage stopped in front of a large red brick house on the corner of East and Prince George Streets.

"Would you like me to speak to him first," Captain Sullivan said, and smiled in understanding.

"Yes, please. And if he has any reservations about my staying here, I want to know."

Raven waited nervously. What if he didn't want to bother with her . . . she would be a woman alone in a strange country. She took a deep breath. This was what she had always wanted—to be independent. She had money, and she was intelligent. For God's sake, Raven McClennon, there is no reason in the world for you not to be able to take care of yourself. What kind of a spineless creature are you? she scolded herself.

She jumped as the carriage door opened, and a handsome middle-aged gentleman stared at her. She could have sworn there were tears in his brown eyes. "Forgive me for staring, my dear, but you look so much like your mother."

"I have often been told that," she said, and smiled.

"Forgive my manners, I am Jordan Mitchell. Welcome to my home, Lady McClennon," he said, offering her his hand.

"I do not wish to impose . . ." She hesitated.

"Nonsense. I would be offended if the daughter of Anne Montgomery accepted hospitality from anyone other than myself while in Annapolis."

A black servant stood at the large double doors while two other servants collected her belongings. "If I can just stay for a couple of days until I decide what I'm going to do," she explained, wondering if the doctor thought she was moving in lock, stock, and barrel.

"It will take much longer than that for us to get to know each other," he said, taking her hand. "I want to know everything about you. When I heard Anne had died, I wondered what had become of you."

"You were concerned about me?" she asked in disbelief.

"Of course, my dear. I was going to invite you to come here, but my contact in London told me you had already settled in with the Montgomerys."

"That was very kind of you to have been concerned about me." As they climbed the stairs, her hand in his, Raven suddenly felt at ease. She found herself anxiously looking forward to discussions with him about her mother.

"I'm going to give you the third-floor bedroom on the front. It's a bright sunny room, and you can see the ships in the harbor from there. It also has a pleasant sitting room."

"You are very kind, but please do not go to any bother for me. I will only be here a few days.''

Jordan Mitchell stopped midway up the stairs. ''Now listen to me, young lady. For twenty years I wondered what became of Anne Montgomery, and if she was happy. If you think you're going to get away from here before I learn everything, you are mistaken. Please humor an old man and stop this talk of leaving. You just got here and I intend to show you off to all my friends and acquaintances.''

Raven smiled. ''When you put it that way, how can I refuse?''

''Exactly,'' he laughed warmly, pulling her up the curved stairs. ''Bonnie, where are you? We have a guest,'' he shouted. ''Bonnie is my housekeeper,'' he explained. ''She's from Edinburgh. Where are you when I need you, woman?'' he shouted again.

''Stop that bellowing,'' a female voice with a Scottish burr said from above them. ''I know we have a guest, that's why I'm up here seeing that the rooms are ready.''

''Bonnie has a way of putting me in my place,'' he whispered to Raven. ''She thinks I would fall apart if she didn't take care of me, and she's probably right, but I can't let her know that. God knows, she's difficult enough to live with.''

''Stop that whispering and bring that sweet bairn up here. She must be near exhausted.''

When they reached the top of the stairs, a

heavyset woman with a robust look greeted her warmly. "Lady McClennon, is it now? That's a good name, m'lady. Wear it well," she said.

"You have known McClennons?" Raven asked.

"Everyone knew of the McClennons of Inverness," she said, leading Raven into the room. "When you are rested we will talk. Now I hope this will be satisfactory, m'lady."

The room was white with gold drapes and a beautiful flowered gold damask bedspread. There was an oriental carpet in front of the fireplace that picked up the same colors. A beautiful Chippendale writing desk set before one of the long windows, and in front of the fireplace was a big comfortable-looking chair. It wasn't as large as some rooms Raven had occupied, but it was surely the most beautiful.

"It takes my breath away," she said.

"Does that mean you like it?" Jordan Mitchell laughed.

"Oh, Doctor Mitchell, it is beautiful."

"I'm glad you approve. Now while Bonnie shows you where everything is, I'm going to the dining room to read Charles's letters. Come down as soon as you're ready and I'll have Katie fix you some breakfast."

"Please, sir, you're going to too much trouble. I do not want to be an imposition."

"Nonsense. We are going to have a great

time, as soon as you stop arguing with me," he laughed, showing beautiful, even white teeth.

Jordan Mitchell had just finished reading the letter from Charles Montgomery when Raven appeared.

"My dear, I can't tell you how sorry I am," he said, leading her to a chair. "It's all so incredible. Poor Charles, to think he's married to that woman. She has to be quite insane. Who would ever have believed she could hate Anne enough to kill her, and to make your life miserable for all these years . . ."

"I suppose she hated me because seeing me reminded her of what she had done," Raven sighed.

"I doubt that, Raven. An insane person doesn't have a conscience. They can rationalize everything they do." Jordan shook his head. "If only someone had realized how sick she was . . . well, it's all behind you now, Raven. Your uncle wrote that you are a very wealthy young lady, so you shouldn't have a problem in the world."

Raven laughed bitterly. "You would think not."

"I know a young man who is a genius when it comes to investing money. If you'd like to talk to him, I'll arrange it."

"Yes, I suppose I should," Raven said, sipping her tea. "Did my uncle say any more in the letter?"

"He explained about this Walter Denseley incident, if that is what you're concerned about. You did what you had to, my dear. No man has a right to force himself on an innocent. Put it out of your mind."

"I wish I could, but sometimes I see his face in my sleep, and it all comes back so vividly . . ."

Jordan placed his hand over Raven's. "The past is the past, my dear. This is another world, and you're about to begin a whole new life."

"Aye, the past is the past," she whispered.

"Ah, here is your breakfast," Jordan said as his cook entered with a plate heaped with food.

"I'm not very hungry," Raven apologized, smiling at the black woman as she set the plate before her.

"Katie insists that we all have good appetites around here," Jordan teased. "She may let you get away with not cleaning your plate this morning, but you better be hungry by dinner."

Taking a bite of a biscuit dripping with honey, Raven suddenly realized she was famished. "This is delicious," she exclaimed.

While Raven ate, Jordan made small talk. He laughed as she accepted seconds from his smiling cook. "You will get along just fine with Katie."

"How long have you known my uncle, Doctor Mitchell?" Raven asked between bites.

"Since we were boys," he answered. "You must call me Jordan, my dear. Only my patients call me Doctor Mitchell."

"All right." Raven smiled.

"Charles and I were inseparable until I fell in love with his sister. He gave me a fit when I tried to court her. He was the typical protective brother."

"You actually courted my mother?" Raven asked in surprise.

"Yes, for all it meant. I had the family's approval, but I never had Anne's heart. She was honest, and very sweetly told me she didn't love me, but I still had hopes. Then one evening there was a ball, and in attendance was a young, handsome Scottish Lord named Evan McClennon. When I saw the way they looked at each other, I knew I'd lost her."

"I'm sorry," Raven said, touching his hand.

"Don't be, my dear. I know now it would have been hell having Anne as my wife, but not having her love. It probably sounds trite, but knowing that she had found the man she loved made me happy."

"And were you happy in your marriage?" Raven asked. "Did you love your wife?"

Jordan was silent for a moment. "Not the same way I loved your mother, but we were comfortable together. Sometimes I think it's more important to be good friends with the person you marry, than to be so much in love you're blind to their faults. When you know their faults and still love them, then you have something very special that will last through the years. Listen to me," he laughed. "My God, maybe I should have been a philosopher instead of a doctor."

"Is that your wife's portrait in the parlor?" Raven asked.

"Yes, Catherine wasn't a beauty, but she was a fine woman, and she came to me with a very large dowry."

"Uncle Charles mentioned that you have a daughter."

"Yes, Elayne. Her aunt took her to Washington to buy some clothes, but they are due back this afternoon. She'll be delighted to find someone near her age to talk to."

"I will also enjoy her company."

"Elayne is only a year younger than you, but she isn't nearly as mature. I'm afraid I have been overprotective since her mother died. Elayne was only fourteen, and the responsibility of raising a young girl that age has sometimes been overwhelming. She loved her mother very much."

"She is very fortunate to have you," Raven commented.

"I've had some help from Catherine's sister, but there are times I think I'd have been better off without it. Rebecca is a spinster and set in her ways. I'm afraid Elayne is becoming just like her."

"I'm sure Elayne is a lovely young lady," Raven said.

"I have a feeling you'll be good for her, Raven. Now the first thing I want to do is have a party to introduce you before everyone gets involved in the holiday parties. By the new year, you'll be the toast of Annapolis."

"Please don't go to a lot of trouble for me, Jordan."

"Trouble? I can't wait for my friends to see you. This town hasn't seen anything as pretty as you in a long time. Besides, it's time Mitchell House came alive again. Isn't that right, Katie?" he asked his smiling cook.

"It sure is," Katie agreed as she cleared the plates. "This young lady is going to be good for more than Miss Elayne," she said, winking at the doctor.

They spent the day touring Annapolis in Doctor Mitchell's fine carriage. He pointed out Madame LaFrancois's dress shop, the millinery shop, the goldsmith's, and the leather goods shop where fine saddles and elegant boots were made.

Raven found herself thoroughly enjoying Jordan's company. He was a delightful companion, knowledgeable about everyone and everything in the lovely town. It wasn't until they were nearly back to Mitchell House before Raven realized how tired she was.

"Well, it looks like Rebecca has returned with Elayne," Jordan said as they pulled up in front of the red-brick house. "Don't be intimidated by Rebecca," he said as they reached the door. "She isn't nearly as fierce as she pretends."

When Jordan Mitchell had said his sister-in-law was plain, it was an understatement, and his daughter looked like a small miniature of her aunt, dressed in the same drab gray, and with her hair pulled back in a severe bun.

The young girl was delighted to have a house guest from Europe, but Rebecca Sowers made no attempt to hide the fact that she disapproved of Raven's being there.

"I want Elayne to return to Washington with me for a while," she said while having tea. "It's time she was introduced to society in the capitol city."

"Perhaps after the first of the year, Rebecca, but right now I am going to need Elayne's help planning a party to welcome our house guest."

"You can't mean to have it here," his sister-in-law said, horrified. "You're still in mourning."

"My dear Rebecca, Catherine has been dead for three years. The time for mourning is past."

"How can you?" Rebecca said, dabbing at imaginary tears.

Raven suddenly stood up, feeling like an intruder in a family argument. "If you have no objections, I believe I'm going to retire early this evening."

"Of course, my dear," Jordan said. "I've been very inconsiderate. I should have realized you were exhausted from your trip."

"Yes, I think it has just caught up with me."

Raven stood at the bedroom window, staring at the starlit sky and pondering the strange fate that had brought her to America. As she did several times a day, she wondered if Taber had escaped prison. At first she had told herself it was better not knowing his fate, but she finally admitted to herself she couldn't put him out of her mind until she knew. But how, she wondered. She couldn't very well ask her uncle. "Molly," she exclaimed out loud.

Sitting at the desk, Raven took out a piece of stationery and began to write. She meant to keep the letter brief, but she found herself explaining how Taber had reacted to her visit, and then about the experience with Walter Denseley. When she finished Molly's letter, she wrote one to her uncle thanking him for his help, and for sending her to Jordan Mitchell.

When the letters were finished, Raven

returned to the window and stared into the darkness. Biting her lip, she fought to hold back the image of Taber's face and the look of raw hatred she had seen in his eyes.

She had to stop thinking of him, she told herself. But a little voice answered: *You may as well stop breathing.*

He who has once been happy
is for aye
Out of destruction's reach.
Blunt

Chapter Fourteen

Rebecca Sowers returned to Washington
once she realized she wasn't going to change
her brother-in-law's mind about having a
party. Raven seemed to be the only one at
Mitchell House concerned about the woman's
reaction. The whole household staff was
already shining and polishing while Jordan
and Elayne discussed what guests to invite.
Deciding maybe this was what she needed to
take her mind off Taber, Raven became
involved too.

Raven accompanied Elayne to the house of a
friend who would write out the invitations.
Her first opinion of the girl changed as Raven
got to know her. She was sweet, and anxious to
make Raven feel welcome. She also had a

contagious enthusiasm for everything, which kept Raven from thinking of her own problems.

By the time they returned to Mitchell House, they were both in good spirits. They were laughing about something as they entered the house, but when Elayne saw her father's guest, she suddenly became very quiet.

"Raven, this is Adam Lawrence," Jordan introduced the tall, good-looking young man. "Adam is the gentleman I wanted you to talk to about investing your money."

"Thank you for coming, Mr. Lawrence."

"My pleasure, Lady McClennon," he said, kissing her hand. "Elayne, how are you today?" he asked politely.

Elayne's face became red and she mumbled something, and then to Raven's amazement she dashed up the stairs. Jordan didn't act the least bit surprised by his daughter's actions.

Jordan had tea served in the parlor, and while Adam Lawrence asked questions, he paced the floor in front of her. He wasn't at all as she'd expected. Light blond hair tumbled over his forehead in an unruly manner, making him look younger than she was sure he was. When he inquired about her interests, his blue eyes showed surprise when she mentioned breeding horses.

He finally sat down long enough to read the letters her uncle had written pertaining to her inheritance. When he looked up, he smiled warmly. "You're in a very enviable position, Lady McClennon."

"Am I, Mr. Lawrence?" she answered, wondering if he'd think so if he knew a little more about her life.

"Give me a few days to mull over this, then I'll make some suggestions."

"We're planning to have a party to welcome Lady McClennon a week from Friday," Jordan said as he walked the young man to the door. "I hope you'll be able to come."

Adam Lawrence smiled at Raven. "I wouldn't miss it. I'll stop back day after tomorrow around ten, if that's agreeable, Lady McClennon."

"That will be fine. I'll plan to be here."

A few minutes after Adam Lawrence had departed, Elayne reappeared munching on an apple.

"Where did you disappear to?" Raven laughed.

"I remembered something I had to do," she answered nonchalantly. "Well, what did you think of father's money wizard?" Elayne asked.

"He seemed very nice," Raven replied.

"More importantly, he knows his business," Jordan added.

Elayne moved a porcelain statue back and forth on the table. "He's handsome too, don't you think?"

"Yes, very handsome," Raven agreed.

"And he's not married," Jordan said, laughing. "But if either of you are interested, you better move quickly. Adam just purchased Rosehill, the mansion on Church Street, so there are a lot of mothers pushing their unmarried daughters at him. The poor man has been besieged with invitations for teas, dinners, and parties."

"And now we've added to his problems." Raven clucked her tongue in mock sympathy. "I guess he could always refuse our invitation."

"Oh, I hope not," Elayne exclaimed, then turned red at her outburst. "I mean, since he's the most eligible bachelor, besides Father of course, he should attend our party."

"Oh, so now I've become an eligible bachelor," Jordan laughed.

"Well you have, Father. When we took the invitations to Mrs. Winslow for printing, she said she was glad to hear you had finally called an end to your mourning. She also said you would now be considered an eligible widower."

"Well, I have no intentions of remarrying," Jordan said emphatically. "I have a lovely daughter," he said, taking Elayne's hand, "and now a lovely . . . shall I say ward?" he asked, smiling at Raven.

"Let's just say friend," Raven suggested.

"You're still a nice-looking man, Father. I'm sure a lot of women will be interested in you. Especially since you are wealthy too."

Jordan laughed. "That's a daughter for you. What do you think, Raven? Am I too old to attract a beautiful young woman?"

"Of course not. You're a very handsome man," she admitted honestly. "Anyone who could attract your attention would be very lucky."

"I'm glad to hear you say that." He smiled.

Something about the way Jordan was looking at her made Raven suddenly uneasy.

"I'm not sure I'll ever marry," Raven exclaimed too quickly.

"Of course you will. You're a beautiful young woman with a lot to offer a man," Jordan said, puzzled by her reaction.

"Is there someone you are in love with?" Elayne asked, knowing there must be some reason for Raven's declaration.

"Yes, there was a man in Ireland," she answered, knowing it was best not to keep any secrets from them. "We had talked of marriage . . ." Tears came to her eyes. "Things just didn't work out."

"But you are still in love with him?" Jordan asked.

Raven brushed away the tears and forced a laugh. "It's ridiculous, isn't it? But they do say time heals all wounds, so I have hope . . ."

"We'll do everything we can to help you forget," Elayne said, hugging Raven.

"Would you rather we didn't have this party?" Jordan asked, concern in his brown eyes.

"Oh no. I'm planning on throwing myself into all the activities you've talked about. I am not going to let this ruin my life."

Jordan put his arm around Raven's shoulder. "You remind me so much of your mother."

Raven was greatly concerned that she was replacing her mother in Jordan's mind, and she didn't want to do that. He was too kind a man to ruin his life by hanging on to a memory.

"All right, everybody perk up," Elayne ordered, saving the day. "Katie has demanded that we give her the final menu for the party."

"Then we better do it," Raven laughed.

October was quickly slipping by and the evening of the party was upon them. Raven kept remembering the last party she had prepared for. It was the night she discovered Taber's true identity.

She opened the music box he had given her and listened to the melody. Then she closed her eyes and glided around the room, remembering what it had felt like to be held in his arms.

Suddenly she stopped. "Oh God, let him be safe," she whispered.

"Here we are, lass," Bonnie said, carefully carrying Raven's freshly pressed silk dress over her arm.

"Thank you so much, Bonnie. It looks beautiful."

"'Tis a pleasure handling such lovely material. Unfortunately, Miss Elayne has the same taste for plain clothing that her mother had, so I don't see elegance like this very often."

"Has anyone ever taken Elayne shopping other than her aunt?" Raven asked as she stepped into the lavender silk gown.

"No, I suppose not, but I'm not sure it would help if they did. I offered to style her hair a little while ago, but she chose to wear it in the same unflattering style."

"She's young," Raven said, turning her back for Bonnie to fasten her.

"And you're very kind, m'lady. Elayne is such a sweet thing, but she's never going to attract a man if she doesn't try to do something to improve her looks. I just hope some of your style and sophistication rubs off on the lass."

"Style and sophistication?" Raven laughed. "If I have it, I don't know where it came from."

"Probably from your mother. She was with you long enough to have made an impression. And from what Jordan says, she was quite a beautiful lady.''

"The memories become vaguer all the time, but I do remember how special she was.''

"I'm sure she was, lass, and I know she'd be very proud of you.''

"I've enjoyed talking about my mother and father with you and Jordan. It has brought back so many pleasant memories.''

"I'm glad, lass,'' Bonnie said, hugging Raven. "Memories should only be pleasant.''

The magnificent mansion of Jordan Mitchell shone from top to bottom. His staff had wanted to make sure everyone knew Mitchell House was once again a house for the living. And there was no doubt about it. It was packed to overflowing with elegantly dressed guests who had come to meet the young lady from Scotland.

No matter how hard Raven tried, she couldn't enjoy herself. Instead, she kept watching the clock and wishing the evening would be over. She found herself constantly surrounded by well-meaning people until she thought she would go crazy. At the first opportunity she tried to blend in with a few people at the punch bowl for a few moments' peace.

"Raven, there you are.'' Jordan smiled tremulously. "I haven't seen you dancing for the last ten minutes."

"I was trying to catch my breath," she said, smiling back, knowing how important it was to him that she enjoy herself.

"I'll give you a moment, but I'm here to claim the next dance."

"Does the line form here?" Adam Lawrence asked as he joined them. "I've been trying all evening to speak with Lady McClennon, but the crowds have been too thick around her."

"Annapolis is the friendliest place I've ever been in," Raven said. "The people are so kind."

"There are a few exceptions, but I'm sure Jordan didn't invite them," Adam laughed.

"From the looks of this crowd, I'd say Jordan invited everyone in town," she said as she was jostled by a couple trying to get to the punch bowl.

"May I have this dance, Lady McClennon?" Adam asked.

"No you don't," Jordan said, taking her hand. "I've already spoken for this one, but if it's agreeable with Raven, you may have the next one."

"It is agreeable," Raven replied.

"I'll try to be patient." Adam smiled warmly.

Raven glanced across the room to where Elayne stood talking with several couples, and an idea came to her. "I noticed Elayne is without a partner this dance," she said, hoping

Adam would ask her to dance.

"Is that a hint, Lady McClennon?" he asked, a twinkle in his blue eyes.

"Just a small one," Raven said over her shoulder as Jordan led her to the dance floor.

"Everyone likes you, as I knew they would," Jordan commented as they danced.

"They've all been very kind to me, but I think they're just as happy to see you entertaining again."

"We used to have some lovely parties here before Catherine became ill. Even President Jefferson came to one of our parties when he was visiting friends in Annapolis," he said proudly.

"Three years was a long time to stay in mourning," Raven commented.

"I suppose it was. It was a comfortable niche to be in. I didn't have to deal with well-meaning friends playing matchmaker, and it also gave me time to spend with Elayne when she needed me."

Raven glanced over at Elayne dancing with Adam Lawrence, and she wondered if she had made a mistake suggesting he dance with her. Elayne looked very uncomfortable.

Jordan also noticed his daughter's uneasiness. "She's such an intelligent young lady, but when it comes to men, she's totally at a loss."

"I saw her dancing with another young man

a few minutes ago, and she seemed fine."

"I don't know what it is, Raven."

"Perhaps it's because she hasn't been exposed to the social scene enough," Raven offered.

"If that's true, perhaps by the time the new year comes around she'll be more comfortable. Dozens of invitations to holiday parties have already arrived. And they all include you, I might add."

"It doesn't look like I'm going to have much time to feel sorry for myself," Raven said, smiling.

"That's the plan," he said as the music stopped. "Well, I suppose I have to turn you over to Adam now, but I'd like to keep you to myself all evening."

Raven was surprised by his words. "Now that wouldn't be fair to all the women waiting to dance with you." She forced gaiety in her voice.

"I believe this is my dance," Adam said at her side.

"Is there any possibility I could talk you into getting a breath of fresh air instead of dancing?" she asked.

"Of course," he agreed. "As long as I have your company, I'll be content."

"That's very kind of you," Raven said, moving toward the door. "I'm beginning to feel like the room is closing in on me."

They stepped out onto the brick path leading through the gardens. Oil lamps had been lit and there was a warm glow, even though the night was cool.

"Will you be warm enough, Lady McClennon?" Adam asked.

"I'll be fine. I just need a few minutes. Why don't we stop being so formal. It would be much nicer if we used first names, since we are going to be working together."

"I suppose it would be less formal," he agreed.

Raven leaned against the garden wall and stared up at the sky. "It's a beautiful night."

"I bet I can guess what you'd like to be doing right now," Adam said.

"I doubt it." She smiled.

"You'd like to be riding a horse across the fields, with your hair loose, and the wind blowing in your face."

"How could you possibly have known that?" Raven exclaimed in delight.

"It suits you." He smiled. "Also you told me that you loved horses, so it's natural to assume you'd enjoy riding anytime of the day or night."

"Whenever things began to close in on me, I'd go riding, and it always seemed to help."

"Are things closing in on you here?" he asked.

"I came to America with a lot of problems,"

she admitted. "But Jordan and Elayne have been wonderful trying to help me forget."

"Perhaps I can help too," he ventured.

"I don't understand . . ."

"Would you consider going riding with me tomorrow? I have several business investments I'd like you to see, so we can combine business and pleasure."

"Would you mind if I asked Elayne to join us?" Raven asked.

"No, but I doubt she'll go," Adam laughed. "For some reason she seems afraid of me."

"Perhaps she is infatuated with you."

"I hope not. She's a very sweet girl, and I wouldn't want to hurt her feelings."

"Do you have someone you're serious about?" Raven asked as she began to walk back to the house.

"I didn't have," Adam answered as they entered the crowded house.

Jordan Mitchell was putting his cape on while Bonnie stood by with his medical bag. "I'm so sorry to have to disappear for a while, my dear, but Martha Timmons decided to have her baby tonight. Very inconsiderate of her, wouldn't you say?" he laughed.

"I want to go with you," Raven said. "Perhaps I can be of help."

"Nonsense. You stay here and enjoy yourself. Bonnie is going with me."

"Please, Jordan, I want to go," she pleaded.

"Bonnie, you wouldn't mind, would you?"

"Of course not, if it's all right with Doctor Mitchell."

"All right, come along," he agreed.

"I'll go along too," Adam volunteered. "Maybe I can give James some moral support."

Martha Timmons was a woman in her early twenties, and already had three daughters. She and her husband, James, had a candlemaking shop on Main Street. Their house was not fancy, but it was a very comfortable place that seemed to be filled with love.

Jordan sent James Timmons out of the room to entertain Adam Lawrence, then he sat on the side of the woman's bed. The frown that creased her pretty face eased as Jordan squeezed her hand.

"It's going to be all right now. You should be used to this by now."

"I don't think you ever get used to the pain. Oh God, here it comes again," she cried.

Without being told what to do, Raven washed her hands in the basin of water set on the table, then sat on the opposite side of the bed from Jordan. He had propped the woman's legs up and placed a sheet over her. Sweat was pouring off her face as she twisted and turned on the bed.

"Easy now, Martha," Jordan advised. "You don't want to hurt that baby."

"I don't want any more children. I can't

stand this pain," she sobbed. "If James ever comes near me again, I'll kill him."

"You say that every time, Martha," Jordan laughed. "Just remember, it will all be over soon, and maybe this time you'll have a son."

Raven gently wiped the woman's face with a damp cloth, all the while giving her words of comfort and encouragement.

"You're Doctor Mitchell's house guest," she said between pains.

"Yes." Raven smiled. "I'm Raven McClennon."

"I heard about you . . . from Scotland, isn't it? Oh God," she cried out as another pain seized her.

"Hold on," Raven encouraged, taking Martha's hand. "Your daughters are beautiful," she said, hoping to take the woman's mind off the pain, "and I'm sure this one will be beautiful too."

"Do you have any children?" Martha asked, gasping for breath.

Raven hesitated a moment before answering no. She touched her own stomach, aware for the first time that it was a possibility that she could be carrying Taber's child. She hadn't had her bleeding cycle since Ireland.

"Raven, wipe her head again," Jordan instructed, bringing her back to the problem at hand.

"Where is James?" Martha screamed.

"Adam Lawrence is keeping him company," Jordan said.

"He's a nice young man," Martha gasped, "but I hate men . . ."

Raven thought the girl would surely break her fingers as she gripped her hand.

"All right, Martha, it's time to bear down. Take a deep breath and push each time the pain comes."

Raven felt tears running down her own face as the girl screamed in pain. She felt inadequate just wiping her face and holding her hand, but there didn't seem to be anything they could do to help.

"Here it comes. Push, Martha. Take a deep breath and push," he encouraged. "Raven, pour some of that hot water in the basin so you can wash the baby down as soon as he makes his entrance to the world."

"Is it a boy?" Martha gasped.

"I can't tell yet," he laughed. "It's almost over now, Martha."

The girl twisted in pain, screaming out as she clutched the bed covering. "Push now . . . that's the girl . . . here it comes . . ."

Raven stared in wonderment at the tiny baby as he made his entrance into the world squirming and flailing his arms and legs. "It's a boy, Martha. It's that son you've been waiting for," he laughed, as excited about it as if it were his own. Turning the baby upside down, he smacked his bottom, eliciting a loud cry before handing him to Raven.

"All right, Lady McClennon, clean the little fellow up and wrap him in a blanket so his mother can have him. I'll make Martha comfortable so James can come in. I can't wait to see the expression on that man's face when he learns he finally has a son."

Raven handled the baby as if she thought he would break. Very gently she washed him with the warm cloth and he stopped crying instantly. "He's beautiful, Martha," Raven said as she finished washing him. Martha was too exhausted to do more than smile.

The little face stared up at her and Raven found herself prolonging her chore. It would be wonderful to have a baby, she thought as she touched his fingers. If she had Taber's child to love, she would always feel she had a part of him. Wrapping the child in a blanket, she placed it beside Martha.

"I think you'd like a child of your own," the woman said. "You were looking at him with such love in your eyes."

"Yes, I suppose I would," Raven agreed as she sat on the side of the bed. "Maybe one of these days. Look at all the hair," she pointed out. "I thought babies were born bald-headed."

"All my babies have had a lot of hair when they were born." Martha smiled.

Raven stood up as the proud father rushed

into the room. Standing in the shadows she watched as he knelt beside the bed and took his wife in his arms. Whispered words were exchanged between them as he lovingly examined his son. The scene made Raven realize how alone she was. Even if she had Taber's child, she'd never have the opportunity to experience anything like the scene before her. Suddenly she rushed from the room and out the front door.

Adam found her leaning against the carriage wheel sobbing. "Raven, what's wrong?" he asked, turning her into his arms. She shook her head, unable to explain her feelings.

"I'm going to take you home. Jordan will come later," he said, helping her into the carriage.

"No, please, I don't want to go back to the party," she protested.

"You've been here for over three hours, so everyone should be gone by now. If they're not, I'll sneak you in the back way."

"Thank you," she sniffled.

Adam put his arms around her and drew her against him. "Relax, I'm just comforting you," he told her when she tried to draw away. "There isn't a woman in the world who doesn't want to be held when she's crying."

Raven accepted the handkerchief he offered and dabbed at her eyes. "How do you know so much?" she asked.

"Believe me, I've had experience," he laughed. "I have seven sisters."

Raven had to laugh. "I suppose I'm in good hands then."

"Do you want to tell me what's wrong?"

"It was such a beautiful moment, and I realized I would probably never experience it with the man I love," she said, turning her face into his shoulder.

Adam was silent for a moment. "You say *love*, as in present tense . . ."

"Yes, past, present, future, I don't think it will ever change. I love a man I left in Ireland."

"Why did you leave him?"

"He was about to be hung . . ."

"My God," Adam exclaimed. "What had he done?"

"He wanted Ireland free of British rule."

"And they'd hang a man for that?"

"Aye, he'd been a thorn in their sides for a long time. When I left, there was a plan to help him escape, but I don't know if it was successful."

"Wouldn't he contact you if he'd been set free?"

Raven shook her head no. "He thinks I'm the one who betrayed him," she whispered.

A friend is one
who comes in when
the whole world
has gone out.
Author Unknown

Chapter Fifteen

It seemed that all of Annapolis buzzed with rumors and speculation about Lady Raven McClennon. Dowagers whispered about the good doctor being in love with the young beauty, while others were willing to place their money on the handsome Adam Lawrence winning her heart. She was seen at all the best functions on the arm of one or the other.

For Raven, romance didn't enter the picture. She was very fond of Jordan Mitchell, but she knew his infatuation with her was because she reminded him of her mother. Adam was a little different situation. After the night he had comforted her, she considered him a friend and confidant. She knew he wanted more, but he didn't push her, and because of that, Raven always felt relaxed in his company.

Her desire to have Taber's baby had been dashed a week after she had witnessed the birth of Martha Timmons's son. She had been devastated when the bleeding started, and she spent almost a week in bed feeling sorry for herself. The culmination of the past several months seemed to suddenly catch up with her. Not being pregnant made her face the fact that her dream of holding a part of Taber by having his child had been foolish. There could be no substitute for the man she loved.

At Jordan's insistence, Raven finally pulled herself together and rejoined the whirl of activities that seemed to take place daily. She swore to herself that somehow she would put Taber out of her mind, but there still wasn't a night that he didn't appear in her dreams. What really concerned her though was when she thought she saw him on the streets of Annapolis. She had been coming out of the goldsmith's shop with Adam when she glanced across the street and met the dark eyes of a bearded man. Just at that moment a carriage passed and when it was gone, so was the man. She tried to dismiss it to tiredness caused by too many parties, but she couldn't put it out of her mind.

To add to her irritation, she hadn't received an answer from her uncle or Molly Devlin. When she mentioned this to Jordan he suggested that she write again, since the mails were often confiscated and destroyed by enemy ships. She did write a second time, but for some unknown reason she was sure she would not get an answer this time either.

One cold morning in late November Raven and Adam were on their way to a shipyard that he felt would be a good investment, when he mentioned the success of privateers working for the Americans.

"There is one in particular who for the past month has established himself as one of the most skillful captains to privateer in American waters."

Raven, only half listening as she stared out the carriage window at the ships anchored in the bay, nodded, "That's nice."

"There's a need for sleeker, faster ships," Adam continued. "That's why I think this would be a good investment for you. There's a young fellow named Alan Hartge working there who has a brilliant design for a new ship, but the present owner is an old man and doesn't see the need to experiment."

"If you think it's a good idea, Adam, then buy it. I trust your judgment implicitly."

"You could show a little enthusiasm about this venture," he said. "I know it didn't excite you to buy the warehouses and property on

Compromise Street, or the tobacco farm outside the city, or the town's newspaper, but damnit Raven, this should be exciting to you. You told me once you loved ships and the sea."

"I'm sorry, Adam. I don't mean to be such a stick in the mud. You're right. If this war is going to continue, as everyone says it will, then good fast ships are needed. Is this Hartge fellow interested in staying on if I buy the place?"

"Yes, as a matter of fact, he's very excited about the prospect of someone backing his designs. I've seen them and I think they are very good."

"Can these privateers afford to buy new ships?"

"The one I was talking about a few minutes ago has made a small fortune by capturing British merchant ships, and as I said, he's only been at it a month."

"How does privateering work?" she asked.

"A captain takes out a letter of marque from the American government. Then if he meets a British cruiser, it legally gives him the right of capture."

"What if he doesn't have this letter of marque?"

"Then he's pirating, and could be hung for it."

"So the government is making pirating legal," Raven mused.

"Only during wartime, and only on enemy ships," Adam explained. "The cargo on the ship is the captain's to sell, and then the government pays him for the captured ship. Nice little profit, wouldn't you say?"

"Maybe we should go into privateering," Raven laughed.

"I think you can make more money building ships for them. Besides, when this war is over, your ships will still be in demand. A privateer will have to look for another line of work."

The decision to purchase the shipbuilding company was quickly made, and on the carriage ride home, Raven proclaimed that she was going to become involved in this business.

"That would be a good idea," Adam agreed. "I think you need to become involved in something."

"What is that supposed to mean?" she asked defensively.

"You go to all the parties and socials, yet I have this feeling that you're drawing further and further into yourself. The gaiety and laughter are forced, Raven. You're only pretending to enjoy yourself."

Raven turned away and stared out the window. "I'm trying, Adam, but his memory won't leave me alone."

Adam took her hand. "Some memories never die, Raven, so you have to learn to live with them."

"I know, Adam. I tell myself that constantly, but it doesn't work."

"I think if you let yourself, you could be happy with me, Raven." Raven's eyes flew to his face. "You realize I'm falling in love with you," he admitted.

"Oh no, don't say that, Adam," she pleaded. "Don't complicate things. You're my friend, my dearest friend . . ."

"It's a fact, Raven. There's nothing I can do about it, but you should know by now that I won't put any pressure on you."

"I don't want to hurt you, Adam. You deserve a very special woman. A woman who idolizes you like—"

"Like you idolize this lover of yours?" he questioned, a tone of irritation in his voice.

"Yes," she answered, but that hadn't been what she was going to say. She was thinking of the way Elayne felt for Adam Lawrence.

They were both silent as the carriage traveled the road along the bay. At a bend in the road, Raven noticed a farm surrounded by a white board fence. She peered out the window to see the house. It was a white house sitting on the bluff overlooking the bay, and behind it she could see barns and stables. The fence went as far as she could see in either direction.

"Adam, who does this place belong to?"

Adam glanced out the window. "It's the Faraday place. It used to be one of the most elegant homes in the area, but Thomas Faraday lost his wife a few years ago and he's let it run down. He's been living with a brother in Baltimore for the past six months. I've heard rumors that he's interested in selling the place."

"Please stop the carriage. I want to look around."

When they stepped out of the carriage, instead of going in the direction of the house, Raven headed for a pier extended out into the bay. She stood for a long moment remembering the day she and Taber had discussed having a home on the water where he could fish from his yard.

Suddenly she turned to Adam. "I want this place."

"But you haven't even seen the house."

"I can tell it's a wonderful house, and I'd have room for horses. It's just what I've wanted, Adam. I can't stay with Jordan and Elayne forever."

"I agree with you there. I don't like the way Jordan looks at you."

"Jordan is a friend, nothing more," she said as she walked toward the fence. "How much land do you think is here?"

"A lot. Are you sure you want a place this big? It's going to take a lot of work just to get it back in shape. And you better consider what it's going to take to run a place like this."

"I'll hire people," she answered, standing on the wrung of the fence so she could see farther. "Will you look into it for me, Adam? I'm willing to pay whatever Mr. Faraday wants."

Adam shook his head. "I should know by now there's no sense arguing with you. I'll have someone contact Faraday."

Raven threw her arms around Adam's neck and hugged him. "Thank you, Adam. I don't know what I'd do without your friendship and guidance. You're the brother I never had," she exclaimed, kissing him on the cheek.

"Brother," Adam snorted. "Come along, *my dear sister*, I promised you I'd have you back in time to go to the dressmaker for your final fitting, and I certainly wouldn't want to be the cause of you not being the most beautifully dressed woman at Cameron's party tomorrow night."

"Thank you, Adam." She smiled warmly, wishing she could feel more than friendship for this wonderful man. But she knew it wouldn't be fair to give him hope when she still had such strong feelings for Taber O'Flynn.

Molly smiled as she changed the bandage on Patrick's leg, pleased that it was finally healing nicely.

"It looks good, man," Colin exclaimed. "It

will be no time before you're up doing a jig."

"Just so I'm not doing a jig at the end of a rope," Patrick laughed.

"You're not going to be doing a jig anyplace for a while," Molly scolded. "You're going to take care of yourself."

"I think you have more to worry about from your nurse than from the British," Colin laughed. "Did I ever tell you about the mustard plaster she put on me when I had the sniffles? Lord, she nearly killed me."

"Don't you have something to do, Colin?" Molly asked, swinging playfully at her brother.

"Naw, Patrick needs me here to protect him."

"Protect him from who?" Molly laughed.

"From you, lass," he answered, quickly stepping backward out of the way of her swing.

A knock at the door silenced the three of them. Patrick took a gun out from beneath his covers. "Open it slowly," he whispered.

"Oh, Fergus, you gave us a start," Molly exclaimed. "Come in."

"I thought you'd be wanting to know the British have stopped their search for Taber and his associates."

"Are you sure?" Patrick asked.

"Aye, they've decided everyone involved must have escaped Ireland with Taber."

"Thank God," Molly said, blessing herself.

"There is something else," Fergus said, looking down at his hat in hand. "Brenna's body was discovered buried in a shallow grave behind Walter Denseley's house a few days ago."

"Walter Denseley," Molly repeated. "Are you saying that he killed her?"

"Aye, I think he killed her after he got the information he wanted."

"Do you mean it was Brenna who betrayed Taber?" Patrick asked in disbelief.

"Aye, the last time I saw her she told me she didn't need me or Taber, that she had other ways to get rich. I had no idea she meant to sell information to the British."

"You couldn't have known what she would do, Fergus," Molly said, laying a hand on his shoulder.

"I suppose not, but it makes me sick to think I caused Raven so much trouble."

"We'll get everything straightened out as soon as Patrick can travel," Molly assured. "At least we can be thankful Taber didn't know where she was going."

Fergus shook his head. "He did know," he said, barely loud enough to be heard.

"He couldn't have. His ship sailed as soon as they reached it," Molly insisted.

"Aye, but May, the housekeeper at Riverside House, thought she was doing Taber and

Raven a favor by letting him know where Raven was going. A message from her was waiting when we reached the ship. Taber was in no condition to know what was going on, but Smyth took the message to hold until he did."

"Oh God," Molly groaned.

"Calm down, love," Patrick urged. "We'll get a letter off to Raven immediately."

"It will be too late, Patrick. Taber is probably there by now."

"He won't hurt her, Molly. I've known Taber all my life, and I know he couldn't hurt her."

"I hope you're right, Patrick."

Snowflakes began to fall as Raven and Elayne headed for the dressmaker, but they refused the carriage for a chance to walk in the snow. "Let's stop at the docks and see if we can get some chocolate," Raven suggested excitedly. "Bonnie said a ship bringing goods from South America anchored last night. When we get home we'll have Katie fix us some hot chocolate."

"Oh, that sounds good," Elayne moaned. "It's been so long since I've had chocolate. Thank heavens we have the privateers to bring us goods."

"Aye, prices are high, but at least we haven't suffered too many hardships from the British blockade."

"Did you hear about the ship that is your namesake?"

"My namesake?" Raven questioned.

"The ship is called *Raven*," Elayne replied.

"I'm sure it's named for the bird," Raven laughed.

"They say her captain is becoming very rich with his British prizes. He's captured more British ships in a month than the other privateers put together."

"Adam tells me it's a sure, but temporary way for making money," Raven said.

"I'm told this captain is quite handsome," Elayne added. "Marie Jamerson saw him at the docks yesterday when he brought another prize in. She said she almost swooned and fell into the water when he smiled at her."

"Marie Jamerson is a dolt," Raven laughed.

"I suppose she is," Elayne laughed. "I hear the dashing captain is bringing the Duchess Martine Valette to the Cameron's party."

"He's going to be at the party?" Raven asked in surprise.

"As a matter of fact, several of the privateer captains are to be the guests of honor."

"It should be an interesting party," Raven commented. "I'm anxious to see what this captain looks like that all the women in

Annapolis are interested in."

After paying an exorbitant price for a small package of chocolate, Raven and Elayne strolled along the dock in the snow. "You're so much fun, Raven. I would never have done anything like this with Aunt Rebecca."

"No, I can't imagine Rebecca fighting a crowd to get a bag of chocolate," Raven teased.

"I'm looking forward to Christmas," Elayne said. "Just having you around is going to make it special."

Raven put her arm around the girl's shoulder. "That's the nicest thing anyone has ever said to me. You're going to make my Christmas special too. Speaking of Christmas, have you thought of something you'd like?"

"If Father asks, I'd like a fine gold chain," Elayne exclaimed. "I saw one at the goldsmith's shop yesterday."

"It's on the way to Madame LaFrancois's shop. Let's stop there and you can show it to me," Raven urged.

The item Elayne was excited about was a thin gold herringbone chain. Raven agreed it was beautiful, and intended to buy it for her friend when she was alone.

"Oh, would you look at this," Raven exclaimed. "That's the most beautiful piece of jewelry I've ever seen," she said, leaning over the glass display box. On a white satin pillow lay a gold chain with a pendant sculptured into two gold and jeweled lovebirds kissing. Their eyes were diamonds and their bodies were made of two brilliant rubies.

"I've never seen anything like it," Elayne said in awe.

"That's my finest piece," Mr. Hollaran said proudly. "I designed it myself. The only problem is, it's too expensive for most people to consider in these trying times."

"Aye, I'm sure it is," Raven said, still studying the piece of jewelry.

"I cannot believe you would allow the enemy in your shop," a woman's outraged voice spoke from behind them.

"You are mistaken, Mrs. Perkins," Mr. Hollaran protested. "Lady McClennon is from Scotland."

Raven hadn't been aware anyone else had come into the shop, and she was surprised by the woman's outburst. "Who is she?" Raven asked a shocked Elayne.

"That's Elmer Perkins's wife. He's the owner of the *Daily Gazette*."

"Is that so." Raven smiled.

Raven stepped between the irate customer and the flustered shopkeeper. "There is nothing worse than a rude, obnoxious woman, unless it's a rude, obnoxious woman who doesn't know what she's talking about. Though it's none of your business, madam, I'm from Scotland, not England."

Heading for the door, Raven held it open for Elayne to pass through. "There's something else you may be interested in knowing, my dear Mrs. Perkins. I bought the *Daily Gazette* yesterday, so I'm now your husband's employer."

Raven closed the door and laughed. "That will give the old biddy something to think about."

"Is it true, Raven? Did you really buy the newspaper?"

"Aye, Adam brought the papers by for me to sign this morning."

"You must be the richest woman in Maryland," Elayne sighed.

"I doubt that," Raven laughed. "But Adam has invested my money very wisely."

"He's a wonderful man, Raven, and he loves you," Elayne said with envy in her voice.

"He is a wonderful man, Elayne, and that's why he deserves someone who can return his love."

"Are you sure you can't do that, Raven?"

"I'm positive," she said as they crossed the street.

"I would give anything to have a man like Adam Lawrence in love with me," Elayne confessed.

"Why Elayne Mitchell, I had no idea you felt that way about Adam Lawrence," she teased.

"Are you saying you knew all along that I

liked him?" Elayne asked innocently.

"Of course I did. I could see it in your eyes everytime you looked at him. That is, when you weren't running away from him."

"I know I act like a fool around him, but I knew I didn't stand a chance with him," she admitted. "You forget, I've been traveling in the same circles with Adam for the past year and he has never paid any attention to me."

"I thought he was very attentive to you," Raven commented.

"Only because of you, Raven. Before you came to stay with us, he barely spoke to me."

Raven stared at her young friend, taking in the pretty brown eyes and chestnut hair. It was the clothes, she decided. The drab colors did nothing for her complexion. Bright colors and a less severe hairdo would do wonders for her.

"Would you like me to help you attract Adam?"

Elayne's eyes widened. "How could you do that?"

"With a change in wardrobe and a different hairstyle."

Elayne touched the bun at the back of her neck. "I wear it like this because it's the way I remember my mother wearing hers."

"Yes, but that was several years ago, and your mother was a married woman."

Her eyes went to Raven's emerald green velvet cape, then down to her own gray wool.

"Bonnie has suggested for a long time that I wear brighter colors."

"It would do wonders," Raven promised.

Elayne was silent as they walked, then a sly smile lit up her face. "Do you really think I could attract Adam?"

"You won't know until you try."

"All right. What do we do first?" Elayne laughed excitedly.

"One of the dresses Madame LaFrancois is making for me is an apricot silk that would be beautiful on you. We'll see if she can alter it to fit you by tomorrow night."

"Tomorrow night?" Elayne exclaimed. "Does it have to be so soon?"

Raven laughed. "You've wasted enough time, my friend. Tomorrow night you're going to be the belle of the ball. Who knows, by the end of the party you may decide you like fifty other gentlemen better than Adam Lawrence."

They spent three hours picking out material for six new dresses for Elayne, and having the apricot silk pinned for alterations. When they were finally done, Raven instructed Madame LaFrancois to bill her instead of Doctor Mitchell.

When they left the shop, they were relieved to find the Mitchell driver and carriage waiting for them. The snow was almost an inch deep and coming down harder by the moment.

"This has been a grand day," Elayne exclaimed as they rode. "I think I like the apricot silk the best, but the gold satin is beautiful too. Maybe I'll save that one for the Christmas ball."

"When we get home we'll ask Bonnie to give some suggestions on styling your hair. She is very good at it."

"I feel ashamed," Elayne commented. "She's offered so many times, but I've always refused."

"There's nothing to be ashamed about. You're a woman and you have a right to change your mind."

Raven glanced out the carriage window as they turned off Main Street. "Just look at the snow. Isn't it beauti—" Suddenly she fell back against the seat, her hand over her heart. Her face had gone as white as the snow.

"Raven, what is it? Are you all right?"

"I don't know. I keep seeing ghosts from my past. That's the second time I could have sworn I saw Taber."

Elayne squeezed Raven's hand. "Maybe it's because you want to see him so badly."

"Yes, I suppose you're right. How could I possibly recognize anyone in this snowstorm anyway."

Elayne had been anxious to tell her father

about her new wardrobe, but when they arrived home, he was closed in his library with several merchants from town.

"More talk about the war," Elayne sighed, as she removed her cape. "I heard Mr. Gallagher say they want to construct a new fort on the north shore of the river."

"I thought Adam said they had reinforced Fort Severn," Raven said.

"They have, but a British cruiser was sighted in the channel a few days ago and now everyone has panicked. I've even heard some people say they don't trust Mr. Madison or his administration to protect us, and they don't like being allied with the tyrant Napoleon Bonaparte."

"In my opinion, it's the British who are tyrants," Raven hissed. "If England's superiority on the seas can be challenged, the war can be won."

Elayne laughed. "You sound just like Adam. Shall we ask Katie to make us some hot chocolate now?"

As they headed for the kitchen, they continued to discuss the war. "Did you know there are some cities in the north that wanted to surrender to the British before they were even under attack?" Elayne asked.

"If they ever lived in Scotland or Ireland, they'd know what it was like to be under a tyrant's rule. Most of the people in Ireland cannot own property, they cannot educate their children, or even speak their own language. British lords now live in homes and estates that used to belong to the Irish gentry. It's no wonder there are so many Insurrectionists."

"You really liked the Irish people, didn't you?"

"Aye, I found them to be a warm, loving people, even though they had little reason to be."

"And one in particular was warm and loving," Elayne added as they sat at Katie's kitchen table.

Raven was silent for a moment. "Aye, Taber had more reason than most to hate the British. They'd killed his father and sister, and confiscated everything that had belonged to the family for generations. Then his mother died a few months after watching her husband be hung."

"My God, how could you not hate the people responsible for such actions," Elayne exclaimed. "And then they had the nerve to throw him in prison for retaliating. It's just unbelievable . . ."

"Aye," Raven said softly. "I just pray he's safe."

"You still haven't heard from your friends?" Elayne asked.

"No. Perhaps they're afraid to make contact

with me."

"I bet Adam could find out what happened to your friend," Elayne suggested. "He still has a lot of contacts in Europe."

"I couldn't ask him to do that. I just have to put it out of my mind. Maybe when I have my own place to work on, I'll be too busy to think about Taber."

"Your own place!" Elayne exclaimed. "You don't mean that, Raven. You must stay here."

"I cannot stay here forever, Elayne. The gossips are already having a field day about your father and me."

"Anyone who matters knows there's nothing to that," Elayne persisted.

"It doesn't matter," Raven smiled. "I've taken advantage of your hospitality long enough. I found a place this morning that Adam is going to look into for me. It's a beautiful house that overlooks the bay. There is room for horses and even some cattle if I wish."

"Oh Raven, what will I do without you here. You've been such a breath of fresh air."

"I'm only going to be a few minutes away. We'll still be best friends, and if you want, you can help me pick out furniture and decorate."

"When will this happen?" Elayne asked sadly.

"Not until after the holidays. The house

needs a lot of work before I can move in."

"Does Father know yet?"

"No. I plan to talk to him this evening. I have to admit, I dread bringing it up. I know he's going to be against it, but I have to do this, Elayne. I have to take charge of my own life."

O wind, O mighty melancholy wind,
Blow through me, blow!
Thou blowest forgotten things into my mind,
From long ago.
Todhunter

Chapter Sixteen

Raven was very quiet and subdued at dinner that evening. She tried to be attentive as Elayne excitedly talked about her new dresses, but her mind was on the figure she had seen who looked so much like Taber. How could she put him out of her mind when she kept seeing his face? she wondered.

"Are you all right, Raven?" Elayne asked.

"What?" she asked with a start. "I'm sorry, I'm afraid my mind was a thousand miles away."

"It's that man you saw on the street, isn't it?" Elayne asked.

Raven nodded her head yes. "Somedays I think I'm losing my mind."

"Oh Raven, I wish there were something I could do," Elayne said, placing her arm around Raven's shoulders.

"I suppose I'm just tired. This has been a long day."

"Father and Adam are in the library with one of the shopkeepers in town, so I suppose he's going to be tied up for a while. Why don't you go ahead to bed and I'll give your excuses. We'll play cards another evening."

"I think I will," Raven agreed, "but you must promise me that when Adam comes out of the library you will graciously ask him to stay for refreshments. He needs to see that you can be a charming hostess."

"All right, Raven. I will try my best." Elayne smiled. "Do I look all right?" she asked, turning around.

"You look just beautiful. Adam isn't going to be able to take his eyes off you."

Raven sat on the edge of the bed and lifted the top of the gold music box. The haunting melody brought tears to her eyes. Taber had said he wanted the woman he loved to have it. Their happiness had been short-lived, she thought sadly. The memory of their angry parting stayed with her like a bitter taste in her mouth. He should be here with her. They could have made a good life in Annapolis.

Taber would enjoy the shipbuilding business she had bought today. And the house on the bay—it was just as they had talked about that day when they had sat on the hill above the deserted castle. Raven took a long breath. That was the same day they had made sweet love long into the night. She closed her eyes and remembered the look in Taber's eyes as his fingertips had grazed her breasts and stomach.

Raven suddenly slammed the top down on the music box. God, why was she doing this to herself? Why couldn't she just put Taber O'Flynn out of her mind? Why did she have to keep remembering their nights and days of lovemaking, of the way his hands had been gentle against her skin, and the way his mouth had pleased her in ways that had nearly driven her crazy with desire? She had never imagined that she would ache for him with this feeling of emptiness and unfulfilled desire.

Taber walked back to the hotel in the snow, but he didn't notice the cold. Why did he keep following her? he asked himself. Damnit, he should just strangle her and get it over with. The little tramp was seeing half the men in Annapolis.

He stormed through the lobby and up to his room, pouring himself a drink before he'd even taken his coat off. What the hell was wrong

with American men? he wondered bitterly.
How could they tolerate their women seeing
other men? Here she was living with the doctor
and yet spending most of her time with this
Lawrence fellow. Fools! If they knew what she
was like . . .

Taber sank into the chair. Perhaps they did
know what she was like. How soft her skin
was, and how warm and how inviting her
mouth was to kisses.

"Jesus," he swore, tossing his drink down
his throat. "How could you even think about
the whore? She wanted to have you hung.
She'd probably been there to watch too, if you
hadn't escaped."

And where was her boy friend, Denseley? he
wondered. Had she already tired of him?
Maybe he didn't have enough money to keep
her satisfied, he thought bitterly. By God, she
seemed to have enough money now. Everyplace he went, her name was cropping up.

Taber refilled his glass, then downed it in
one gulp. How could she have seemed so
sincere? He thought he knew women. Now if
Brenna had betrayed him, it wouldn't have
surprised him in the least. But Raven . . . no,
he'd never have thought it of her if he hadn't
seen it with his own eyes.

God, why did he have this pain in his gut
when he thought of her? She was still so

beautiful . . . so desirable. Taber downed another drink, then fell across the bed. "I have got to put her out of my mind," he said, shaking his head. "She's a lying, deceiving bitch." But he would make her pay.

Taber closed his eyes. He felt beaten and exhausted to the very depths of his soul. He needed sleep, but she wouldn't leave him alone. "Go away, Raven McClennon," he shouted in a drunken stupor.

Ignoring Molly's pleading, Patrick stuffed his hat on his head and hobbled toward the cabin door.

"Please, at least let me go with you. You've only been on your feet a few days."

"I'm tired of being an invalid. You've been hovering over me every second since that damned night I got shot."

Tears came to Molly's eyes. "I'm only trying to help you."

Patrick pulled his hat off and tossed it on the bunk. "Come here, love," he said, holding out his arms to her. "What a fool I am. I know I'd be dead if it hadn't been for you. I'm just feeling frustrated because I've been laid up so long. I dinna' mean to take it out on you."

"I understand, Patrick, but I think you should stop and think about how lucky you are. Doctor Leeds wasn't sure you'd ever be able to walk on that leg, and yet you are."

"With the aid of a cane," he said in disgust.

"Aye, but that's better than being bed-ridden."

"It was such rotten luck, Molly. Do you realize if I hadn't been shot the night we broke Taber out of prison, that we would be with him right now—and he would know that Raven hadn't betrayed him."

Molly was silent as Patrick fumed. She was very much aware of the strange events that had separated them that fateful night. Nothing had gone as expected. Taber had been unconscious from a beating he had suffered just before they had gotten there. Then as they were putting Taber in the prison wagon, one of the guards realized he didn't recognize any of them. Patrick had quickly given the orders for the wagon to move on, leaving himself in jeopardy with only the aid of her and Colin. They had barely reached their horses when the suspicious guard opened fire on them. Patrick had been shot in the thigh, and almost bled to death before they could get him to the Devlin house. In the meantime, as soon as Taber had been taken aboard his ship, orders were given to sail, knowing that the British would soon be on their trail.

"If only we had known sooner that Taber

knew where Raven had gone," Patrick said.

"It wouldn't have mattered, Patrick. You couldn't have traveled any sooner."

"Aye, but we could have gotten a letter off sooner warning her."

"Perhaps the letter we sent ahead of us will reach her before Taber does."

"I doubt it. Captain Dubois said very little mail gets through to America. Damn British fouling everything up as usual," he growled.

Molly pushed back a blond curl that had fallen over Patrick's forehead. "We are both worrying for no reason. Taber wouldn't hurt Raven. He loves her."

"Aye, love, I know he does, but if Taber thinks she was on the side of the British, I hate to think what he might do."

"He won't hurt her, Patrick. I just know he won't."

"I hope you are right, love. God, I hope you're right."

Raven stared into the mirror as Bonnie arranged her hair for the Cameron's party. She would have loved to plead a headache and stay home, but she had promised Elayne she'd give her moral support.

"How do you want to wear your hair tonight?" Bonnie asked.

"I think I'd like to wear it down and just caught with combs on both sides," Raven answered. *Now why was she torturing herself,* she wondered. *Wearing her hair the way Taber liked it was only going to make her black mood worse.*

Bonnie glanced at the dress lying across the bed. "That dark blue satin is nice, but you have so many other dresses that are more flattering. Are you sure you don't want to wear your new aqua watered silk?" she tactfully suggested.

"No, this is Elayne's night," Raven sighed. Besides, she felt as if she was in mourning, so the dress was appropriate for her mood.

"I hope you're not making a mistake," Bonnie mumbled.

"A mistake about what?"

"Giving Miss Elayne ideas about Adam Lawrence. The man is obviously in love with you."

"Where I'm going I won't have any need of a man," Raven sighed miserably.

"And where would that be?" Bonnie asked.

"I think I'm going to join a convent."

"Oh come," Bonnie laughed. "It can't be all that bad."

"I suppose it could be worse, but I don't know how."

Bonnie held the dress out for Raven to step into. "Perk up, lass. Life is too short to make yourself miserable."

Raven raised her chin and stared at herself in the mirror. "Aye, you're right, Bonnie. No man is worth ruining your life over."

"Do you like it?" Elayne asked as she came bursting into the room. "I don't know how to thank you, Raven," she said as she did a spin in front of her. "It's so beautiful."

"You're beautiful." Raven smiled. "The dress only highlights your coloring."

Bonnie had parted Elayne's chestnut hair in the middle, then arranged curls to frame her lovely face. The difference in the girl was more than Raven had expected.

Elayne bent to kiss Raven on the cheek. "Are you doing all right?" she asked.

"Yes, I'm fine. Bonnie has talked me out of suicide and the nunnery, so I may as well face the world."

"Good." Elayne smiled warmly. "I need you with me this evening. I'm so nervous. I feel as if this is my first party."

"It is your first party—as the new Elayne Mitchell." Raven hugged her friend. "Just relax and enjoy yourself."

"I'm going to, Raven," she smiled. "But I've decided I'm not really interested in Adam," she lied. "I've been thinking a lot about John

Talbot, and I think I'm going to use my feminine wiles on him tonight."

"You're only saying that because you think I need Adam, but you're mistaken, Elayne. Adam and I are just friends, and that's what we'll always be. Tonight he's going to discover a wonderful woman who does love him."

"He was so sweet to me last night, Raven. He kept looking at me as if seeing me for the first time. Then when he was ready to leave, he asked me to save him a dance tonight."

"I think you should save him more than one dance," Raven suggested.

Tears filled Elayne's brown eyes and she hugged Raven. "I wish more than anything that you could find happiness. You are the kindest person I've ever known."

"Stop this minute," Raven laughed as tears brimmed in her eyes. "You're going to have us both blubbering in a minute." She turned away from Elayne and picked up a crystal flagon from the table.

"The finishing touch," she said, holding up a small crystal bottle. "It's a French scent that is supposed to make men fall over themselves to get to you."

"Well, pour it on," Elayne laughed. "I want all the help I can get."

Raven hesitated a moment, studying the liquid in the flagon. "You know, if we were smart, we'd invent something that would keep men away from us. It would certainly simplify life."

"But would life be worth living?" Elayne asked softly.

Raven was silent for a moment. "I suppose if the truth were known, it is better to have loved and lost, then never to have loved at all."

*Who never doubted never half
believed.*
Bailey

Chapter Seventeen

Adam Lawrence wasn't the only man to stare in appreciation when Elayne entered the room. Proudly Raven and Jordan watched from an alcove as the men swarmed around her.

"It's like seeing a caterpillar evolve into a beautiful butterfly," Jordan said proudly.

"Doesn't she look pleased with herself?" Raven smiled. "I think your daughter has seen the last of her wallflower days."

"If this is any indication of how men are going to react to her, I have a feeling I'm going to be deluged with young men asking for her hand."

"Elayne is interested in only one man," Raven said, taking Jordan's arm as they walked into the room.

"You must know something I don't," he

said, waiting for her to explain.

"Haven't you noticed how she acts around Adam?"

"Adam? Adam Lawrence? But I thought you and he—"

Raven had to laugh. "Adam and I are only friends."

"Does that leave any chance for me?" he whispered, a smile on his handsome face.

"You and I are best friends," she laughed. "Now why don't you go find yourself a beautiful woman to dazzle with your distinguished good looks."

"I'm with the most beautiful woman in the room. Why should I want anyone else?"

"Go on with you," Raven laughed.

"You're not trying to get rid of me so you can dance with one of these dashing privateer captains, are you?"

Raven smiled warmly. "Now how could a lowly seaman possibly compete with you?"

"I think you'll be surprised when you meet these privateers. One in particular is very well educated, and quite a handsome chap. I understand most of the women in Annapolis have been clamoring to meet him."

"How fortunate for him," Raven laughed. "And I suppose he's taken advantage of the situation."

"I don't know about that, but I'm told the Duchess Valette is quite smitten with him."

"Martine Valette," Raven repeated. "Isn't she the woman Adam had been seeing?"

"Adam and half the men in Annapolis," Jordan laughed. "Martine is very beautiful, but not very discreet."

Suddenly a burst of applause sounded throughout the room. "The guests of honor must have arrived," Jordan assumed. "Come, let me introduce you."

"You go on, Jordan. I'll meet the conquering heroes later. Right now I want to see how Elayne is holding up."

Turning away from the young man she was talking to, Elayne smiled as Raven made her way toward her. "Lady McClennon, have you met Carlisle Rogers?"

After introductions were made, Raven asked the young man if he would excuse them for a moment. "I hope you didn't mind my doing that," Raven said, pulling Elayne aside, "but I had to know if you were having a good time."

"I didn't mind at all. Carlisle is a boor. Oh Raven, I'm already enjoying myself so much. Adam and I danced a few minutes ago and he told me he expected me to save him several more dances."

"I've noticed he cannot take his eyes off of you," Raven said.

"I just can't believe it, Raven. He really seems to like me."

"Why does that surprise you? I knew all

along he would."

"Thank you, Raven," Elayne said, hugging her friend.

"How about including me in all this hugging," Adam teased as he joined them.

"Now what would people think if the two of us started hugging you?" Raven asked.

"I don't know, but I'll chance it."

"Go on with you," Raven laughed. "Why don't you two dance. I have to find Jordan. He wanted to introduce me to the guests."

Raven made her way through the crowd to where Jordan stood. As she approached, he turned and smiled at her.

"There you are, my dear. I was just telling the duchess and Captain O'Flynn that I wanted them to meet you."

A smile on her face, Raven turned to speak to the duchess and her escort, but the smile on her face froze. For what seemed an eternity, the room went incredibly still as she stared into Taber's icy blue eyes. His hair was longer, and now there was a scar that ran from his temple to his cheek, but he was still as incredibly handsome as she had remembered.

She could not move or breathe during that endless moment of stunned silence. She felt numb and was afraid she might faint. Taber was alive and standing here before her. Her heart clamored in her throat like the staccato beat of a drum. But why didn't he take her in his arms and tell her how happy he was to see her . . .

"How nice to see you again, Lady McClennon," Taber said in a clipped tone.

"Captain O'Flynn was just telling me that you and he are old friends from your days in Ireland," Jordan broke into the awkward moment. "You should have told me that you knew the fearless privateer that everyone has been talking about for the past month. Captain O'Flynn has been a one-man navy against the British."

He was watching her with an expressionless face that told her nothing except that he was on his guard, and as calmly in control of himself as always.

Captain O'Flynn . . . privateer. She opened her mouth to speak, but nothing would come out.

"Raven, are you all right?" Jordan asked, noticing how pale she was.

"I believe Lady McClennon thought I was dead," Taber said in a cold voice. "I was ready to go to the gallows the last time we spoke. Do you recall that meeting, Lady McClennon?"

Raven remembered his last words to her. *One day I'll make you pay.* That was the reason he was here. He still blamed her for his imprisonment. It didn't matter, she told herself. He was alive and well.

Taber watched the changing emotions on

Raven's face, but he couldn't tell what she was thinking. It was obvious to him that she wasn't overjoyed to see him. She's probably afraid I'm going to interfere with her love life, he thought bitterly.

"I am very relieved to see you weren't hung," Raven said, finally managing to find her voice.

"Are you, Lady McClennon?" he asked coldly.

"Raven, you haven't met Martine Valette, the Duchess of DeLeau," Jordan interrupted. "Martine, may I present Lady Raven McClennon."

Raven met the inquisitive stare of the beautiful woman. "I'm pleased to meet you," she said, forcing a smile. "I've heard so much about you."

"Have you?" the woman asked in a strong French accent. "Strange, I haven't heard a thing about you," she said, glancing at Taber.

"Lady McClennon has only been here a few months," Jordan explained, still wondering about the tension between Raven and Taber O'Flynn.

"You're from Ireland?" the duchess asked.

"No, Scotland," Raven answered politely.

"Lady McClennon has strong ties to England," Taber said sarcastically. "Her uncle is a powerful leader of the British Tory administration. As a matter of fact, he was the one who planned to hang me."

"Really?" the duchess said, one eyebrow raised as she stared at Raven. "I'm surprised that doesn't make your life very difficult in America."

"I don't go around bragging about my uncle's connections with the British," Raven said, glaring at Taber, "and I would appreciate it if you didn't mention it again. You know very well I have no connection with the British," she spat.

"Do I?" he asked, his dark eyes cold as ice. Then he turned a warm smile to the duchess. "Come, *ma chère*, it is time we dance."

Raven was stunned by his rudeness. She felt angry and humiliated. How could he treat her so coldly?

"Excuse me, Jordan. I need to powder my nose," Raven said, fleeing the crowded room.

Raven stood before the mirror, staring at her image. Oh God, she should have been dancing for joy. Taber was alive. But if anything, she felt worse. He had looked at her as if she were a stranger—a stranger whom he hated. How could he? How could he be so cold and heartless after what they'd been to each other?

"Raven, what is wrong? Father said after you met Captain O'Flynn that you seemed distraught."

"Your father is very perceptive," Raven said,

still staring at herself in the mirror. "Taber is the man I had loved in Ireland."

"Raven," she cried, gripping her friend's arm, "I'm so happy for you! How did he find you? Did he come to marry you?"

"Perhaps to kill me," Raven answered as she turned around to face her friend. "He still thinks I betrayed him, Elayne. He treated me like I was a stranger. No," she whispered. "It was worse than if I'd been a stranger. He's been here a month and hadn't even bothered to contact me."

"Did you tell him how much you've missed him?" Elayne asked.

"I couldn't let him know that. Not when he doesn't care for me. I still have a little pride left."

"Does pride really matter when you love him so much, Raven? You've been pining away for him ever since you arrived here."

"How could I have been such a fool? I should have known what he was like when he didn't believe me in Ireland. He's cold, and arrogant. How could I ever have loved him?"

"If that is true, then dry your eyes, Raven," Elayne ordered. "We are going back to the party and you are going to show Captain O'Flynn that you have a life of your own in Annapolis, and if he doesn't want to be a part of it, then he can go back to Ireland."

Raven stared at Elayne in stunned silence.

Then she smiled. "You are right. He would like to see me suffer," she said, wiping away her tears. "I will not let him see me like this. He's going to see a successful woman who can have any man in Annapolis that she wants."

"Except Adam Lawrence," Elayne grinned.

Raven hugged her friend. "Aye, except for Adam Lawrence."

She drank too much champagne and flirted too openly, but she was determined to show Taber that she didn't need him. She tried to keep her eyes anyplace but on Taber, and kept up a constant stream of chatter.

"Jordan, dance with me," Raven asked, as soon as he had joined her circle of friends.

"Of course, my dear," he agreed, noticing how flushed she looked. "You're not feverish are you, Raven?"

"Of course not," she laughed. "I've just decided to enjoy myself. Have you noticed Elayne and Adam are dancing? They make such a handsome couple."

"I'm not sure Elayne is sophisticated enough for Adam's taste," Jordan commented.

"Elayne will do just fine. Having confidence in herself will give her the polish and sophistication she needs."

"I suppose you're right." He smiled down at Raven. "All I can say is my prayers were answered. I had hoped she would take a lesson from you."

Raven gave a bitter laugh. "I wouldn't advise anyone to take a lesson from me. I certainly have messed up my own life."

Jordan looked surprised. "Now why would you say a thing like that? I thought you were happy here. You've certainly made a lot of friends in Annapolis."

"I know, Jordan, and I'm very lucky to have friends like you and Elayne. I don't know what's wrong with me tonight."

"Does it have something to do with Captain O'Flynn?"

"No, of course not. Couldn't you tell we are not the best of friends?"

"I wondered about that."

Raven glanced over Jordan's shoulder and met the dark eyes of Taber as he danced by with the duchess. She quickly looked away, disgusted at the way he seemed to enjoy the look of adoration on the woman's face.

Fool, Raven thought silently. He'll chew you up and spit you out, just as he did me.

When the music stopped, Raven clung to Jordan's arm as they headed for Elayne and Adam.

"Doesn't Elayne look lovely tonight?" Raven asked Adam.

"She looks absolutely beautiful," he answered, smiling at Elayne. "It seems she has grown up overnight."

"With Raven's help," Elayne said, squeezing her friend's hand.

"Before you are surrounded by young men again, how about dancing with your father?" Jordan asked.

Raven watched the expression on Adam's face as he watched Elayne move away with Jordan. "You told me once you hoped Elayne wasn't in love with you because you didn't want to hurt her. Are you having second thoughts, Adam?"

Adam stared down into Raven's face. "Did you do this to ease your conscience?"

"My conscience?" she laughed. "What does my conscience have to do with this?"

"Perhaps you were feeling guilty because you turned me down, so you thought you'd play matchmaker and find me someone."

Raven smiled. "I do think you deserve a wonderful woman who loves you like Elayne does."

Adam leaned over and kissed Raven on the lips in a chaste fashion. "This time I will submit to your matchmaking because you have opened my eyes," he said, smiling warmly at her, "but from here on, let Elayne and me work things out on our own."

"I promise." She smiled through tear-filled eyes. "I'm so happy for you and Elayne."

Taber gritted his teeth as he watched the

tender scene between Raven and Adam Lawrence. My God, how did she manage it? he wondered. Both men seemed to dote on her, yet neither showed any objection to the other. In Ireland he would have killed anyone who had looked at *his* woman like that. But she wasn't his woman, and this wasn't Ireland, he reminded himself.

"Taber darling, I would love some champagne," Martine broke into his thoughts.

"I'm sorry, what did you say?"

"You are ignoring me, darling," she pouted.

As Raven and Adam talked, a young man she'd danced with earlier asked her to dance again. He was very sweet, but her feet still hurt from the last time.

"I'm so thirsty," she exclaimed. "I wonder if you would mind if we just talked, and perhaps had some champagne?"

"That would be wonderful, m'lady. If you'll wait right here I'll get us some."

Raven smiled gratefully. "That would be wonderful."

Making a flustered departure, he disappeared into the crowd, leaving Raven thinking what a shame it was such a nice young man hadn't learned to dance.

She caught sight of Adam and Elayne dancing again. Elayne was radiant as she smiled up at Adam. Painfully Raven remembered a time she had looked at Taber that way. She sighed, forcing her thoughts back to the young man who had gone to get her champagne.

"Lady McClennon, if you have a moment, may I speak with you?" a young man asked. "I know this isn't the proper place to talk business, but I couldn't pass up the opportunity when I saw you alone for a moment. I'm Jeffrey York," he said, holding out his hand to her.

"Hello, Jeffrey York." Raven smiled. "What kind of business do you want to discuss?"

"I understand you bought the *Daily Gazette*," he said. "I want to be a reporter, Lady McClennon, and I think I can be a good one. I'm not shy, and I can almost always get people to talk to me."

"Yes, I noticed," Raven laughed. "Do you have any experience?"

"No, ma'am, but I can make up for lack of experience with enthusiasm and plain hard work."

"Yes, I think you probably could. I'll talk to Mr. Perkins. He still does the hiring, but I think I may be able to influence him to talk with you."

"Thank you, Lady McClennon." He smiled. "You won't be sorry," he said before kissing her on the cheek, then dashing away.

Raven heard the sound of approaching footsteps behind her. "I thought you had forgotten me," she said as she turned.

"I'm trying hard to do just that," a mocking voice answered.

Raven gasped as she stared up in dismay at the tall, velvet-clad form of Taber O'Flynn. He wore a dark brown velvet jacket over a vest of gold and brown, and looked as if he'd been born to dress the part of a gentleman.

"Was that another of your conquests?" he asked, his lips twisted into a faint smile of contempt. "You certainly are a busy young lady."

She could say the same for him, she thought, but didn't say it. She would not give him the satisfaction of knowing she still cared.

"What are you doing in Annapolis, Taber?" she asked, trying to keep the tremor from her voice.

"What, no warm words of welcome, my love?" he asked sarcastically. "I suppose I shouldn't have expected any."

"I cannot believe you would not have visited me when you first arrived in Annapolis," she said furiously.

"You are a glutton for punishment, m'lady. Or is it that you want to have your dealings with me over and done with."

"What is that supposed to mean?" she asked irritably.

"Did you think I was going to let you betray me and leave me for dead without suffering some consequences?"

His voice was like steel, cutting through her confused thoughts. "I didn't betray you!"

"Taber darling, there you are," Martine said, wrapping her arm in his. "I thought you were getting me some champagne."

"Excuse me," Raven said in a rustle of her skirts.

He meant to have revenge, she thought, her mind whirling like a kaleidoscope. Did he mean to kill her, she wondered, feeling sick in the pit of her stomach.

Before Raven could escape from the room, the young man with her champagne found her.

"Here we are, Lady McClennon. I thought I had lost you."

Raven forced a weak smile. "I had about given up on you."

"I'm sorry. I saw you talking with Captain O'Flynn and I didn't think I should interrupt."

"That was considerate of you, Charles, but what Captain O'Flynn and I were discussing was of no importance." Raven quickly drank her champagne, her eyes glancing back to where she had left Taber and the duchess. Thank God, he was no longer in sight, she sighed.

"I've thought of taking up privateering myself," he announced. "The only thing is, it takes a lot of money to get started."

Raven stared at the young man suspiciously. Surely he wasn't thinking that she would give him the money.

"Raven, have you got a minute?" Adam interrupted. "I want you to meet someone."

"You'll excuse us, Charles," Raven said, gladly taking Adam's arm. "Thank you for saving me," she whispered as they crossed the ballroom. "I think he was about to ask me to give him a ship so he could start privateering."

"You're not serious?" Adam laughed.

"I'm very serious."

"Well, then you'll be happy to meet your first paying customer."

"I hope he's the first of many," Raven commented. When she looked up, Taber was standing directly in front of them. "Wait, Adam. I need to—" It was too late. Taber was watching her. She would make a fool of herself if she fled now.

"Captain O'Flynn, I'd like you to meet the woman who had the foresight to go along with Alan Hartge's innovative plans. May I present Lady Raven McClennon."

Taber bowed over her hand, obviously pleased at her bewilderment. "Thank you for your foresight, Lady McClennon."

Raven jerked her hand away. "Adam, Captain O'Flynn and I have met," Raven said, trying to keep her voice steady. "As a matter of fact, we knew each other in Ireland.''

"Well, isn't that a coincidence," he said, a puzzled expression on his face. "You didn't mention that you knew Captain O'Flynn when I was telling you about the prizes he had captured.''

"I don't believe you mentioned him by name. If you had, I would have told you that I knew him," she snapped. Then she looked directly at Taber, raising her chin defiantly. "That is, if you'd mentioned one of the names that I knew him by. Captain O'Flynn has so many different aliases.''

Taber raised one dark eyebrow, an amused expression on his face. "I believe you knew them all, Lady McClennon.''

"You must be pleased for Lady McClennon's success in America," Adam interrupted.

"I've always been amazed by the things Raven does," Taber said sarcastically.

Raven smiled at him for the benefit of anyone watching. "Taber has always doubted my honesty and worth," she said between clenched teeth.

"Well, don't ever doubt anything Raven says she will do," Adam said, feeling as if he were witnessing a war of words. He didn't know if he should leave the two of them or stay there to protect Raven. "This ship being built for you is one of a kind, thanks to Raven having faith in Hartge's design.''

"I just hope it will float," Taber remarked.

"You're jesting, Captain O'Flynn," Adam said. "It will be one of the finest ships to ever sail."

"I don't blame Captain O'Flynn for being concerned, Adam." Raven smiled wickedly at Taber. "It's a wise man who is cautious around his enemies."

At that moment one of the other privateer captains, a Frenchman named deLisle, joined them. As soon as introductions were made, he asked Raven to dance, and she quickly accepted, glad for the opportunity to get away from Taber. Once they were on the floor, she wished she hadn't been so quick to accept his invitation. He held her much too close, and his hand continually moved up and down her back, touching the bare skin at her shoulders.

"Captain deLisle, I would appreciate it if you'd keep your hands where they belong," she said, her blue eyes blazing.

"Ah, *chérie*, I can see in your eyes that you are a passionate woman."

"Passionate enough to slap your face," she warned.

"Ah, a spitfire. I like that in my women," he said as he moved his hand back on her shoulder.

"You overstep the bounds of propriety, sir," Raven exclaimed as she pulled out of his grasp. "I suggest you find someone else to maul."

Raven glanced around to find Jordan or Adam, but neither were in view, and Taber was blocking her exit from the room as he talked with a young blonde. Determined to further avoid him, she turned toward the doors leading to the garden. It didn't matter how cold it was, she thought, she had to get some air. This night was turning into a disaster.

She took several deep breaths, trying to still her nerves. This was never going to work, she thought in exasperation. How can I possibly live in the same town with him?

"Ah, so this is what you wanted," deLisle said as he walked up behind her. "You wanted out of view of the public to protect your reputation, eh?"

"I stepped out here to get away from you," she spat. "Now leave me alone!"

"Come, *chérie*, there is no reason to pretend. I can see a fire in your eyes that invites a man . . ." He pulled her to him, assaulting her mouth.

Raven struggled against him, finally bringing her foot down hard on the top of his instep. "Don't ever touch me again," she warned.

"You little bitch," he hissed. Then a sadistic smile came over his face. "So you like to play rough . . ." He grabbed her by the arm and pulled her hard against his chest. "I like a woman with fire."

"No," Raven gasped as his hand touched her

369

breast. She struggled like a madwoman as the scene with Walter Denseley came to mind.

Suddenly, out of nowhere, a voice froze both of them like the slash of a rapier. "The lady made it very clear she isn't interested in your games, deLisle."

"Stay out of this, O'Flynn. The lady and I came out here for some privacy."

"Take your hands off her," Taber warned.

The Frenchman stared at Taber, confused. "What the hell is wrong with you, *mon ami?*" he asked with a laugh. "I saw this woman first. Go find yourself someone else."

Raven stumbled away from the two men, unable to take her eyes off Taber's face. She watched horrified as he pushed his velvet jacket back, exposing a small pistol.

"Come now, *mon ami*, you don't mean you'd duel over someone you don't even know?"

"The lady and I are *old friends.*" Taber smiled. "Isn't that right, Lady McClennon?"

"Yes," Raven whispered, finding her throat constricted with fear.

"Why didn't you say so," the Frenchman exclaimed, holding up his hands in surrender. "Of course I'll go back inside and leave you two old friends alone," he said, backing away from Taber.

Raven began to tremble violently. She turned her back to Taber and clutched the brick wall. She wanted to object when he placed his jacket around her shoulders, but she couldn't make her teeth stop chattering.

"Come on, let's get you back inside," he said flatly.

"No, I can't go inside like this," she gasped.

Taber stared down at her. She was right; there would surely be questions if anyone saw her at that moment. "Is there an entrance we can use where we won't be seen?" Taber asked.

"Donald Cameron's library . . . this way," she said with chattering teeth.

Raven knelt close to the fire while Taber poured them a brandy. "I hope Mr. Cameron doesn't mind," he said, handing her the amber liquid.

Raven didn't answer as she accepted the glass. The warm glow of the fire and the excellent brandy made her forget for a moment that she and Taber were now antagonists. It seemed so natural being there with him. Perhaps now they could get everything out in the open and work out their problems, she thought hopefully. But then his next words brought everything back to focus.

"You should be more selective in your men, Raven. Jacque deLisle is a dangerous man, and I wouldn't be surprised if he doesn't try something again."

Raven stared at him, unable to believe what he'd said. "More selective in my men," she repeated. She stood up and removed his jacket from her shoulders, then threw it at him. "Yes, I certainly should have been," she spat. "Now I know to stay away from privateers and Irishmen! So why don't you get out of my sight?" she said between gritted teeth.

Taber's jaw hardened and he cursed beneath his breath. "You're the most exasperating woman I've ever met. You should be thanking me for saving you from that bastard, instead of shouting at me."

"No one asked you to save me," she said irrationally. "I could have taken care of myself."

"Aye, I'm living proof of the way Raven McClennon watches out for herself. By the way, what happened between you and your British lover? I thought you and Denseley planned to be married as soon as I was hung. Or did my escape change things for you?" he sneered.

Raven, thinking he knew what happened, stared at him for a moment, her eyes glistening with tears. "How could you?" she sobbed, dashing past him into the hallway.

Taber followed her to the door and saw her run into the arms of Jordan Mitchell.

"Are you all right, my dear?" he asked, looking over her shoulder at Taber's black look.

"I want to go home. Please, Jordan, take me home."

"What did he do, Raven?" Jordan asked angrily.

"Nothing. It was nothing, Jordan. Just take me home," she pleaded.

"All right, get your wrap. I'll wait here for you."

As soon as Raven was out of hearing, Jordan turned on Taber. "What happened in there, Captain O'Flynn?"

"To be honest with you, Doctor Mitchell, I'm not quite sure. It seems I hit a sensitive nerve in Lady McClennon."

Jordan stared at Taber, wondering what it was about this Irishman that irritated him. After a long moment he spoke. "Raven has been through a lot in the past four or five months. She doesn't need any more problems. I don't know what is going on between the two of you, but I suggest you stay away from her."

"Fine," Taber agreed. "I shall leave her in your loving care. Excuse me," he said, walking past Jordan. "I believe the Duchess is waiting for me."

"What the hell is between those two?" he wondered aloud.

*Faith is believing in things when
common sense tells you not to.*
Beringer

Chapter Eighteen

The next morning, after a sleepless night,
Raven decided to attend church services with
Elayne. She hoped it would keep her mind off
the events of the previous evening. They were
to meet Jordan and Adam at the Maryland Inn
afterward for the midday meal.

Raven only half listened to the sermon,
unable to stop thinking about Taber. Why
hadn't Molly and Patrick told him of her
innocence, she wondered, and how had he
found her? Only her uncle knew where she was
going.

A loud "amen" brought her back to the
present as Elayne stood up to join in the
singing of the closing hymn.

"You seemed a million miles away," Elayne
said as they filed out of the church.

"I know, and I'm sorry. I just can't stop thinking about what happened last night."

"Perhaps you should try to talk to him and explain what really happened in Ireland."

"I had planned doing just that, but I don't think he wants to listen to anything I have to say."

"You won't know until you try," Elayne persisted.

"Perhaps you're right . . ."

They were almost to the carriage when a deep voice froze her. "Are you trying to save your soul, Lady McClennon?"

Raven stared in shock at Taber O'Flynn as he sat astride the big black stallion he had ridden in Ireland. Then her eyes were drawn to the spirited animal beside him. Raven's eyes moved from the smug face of the duchess to the white horse she rode.

"That's my horse," she exclaimed. "That's my Devil Lady!"

"She is appropriately named," the duchess said, struggling to keep the horse under control. "I have never ridden such a wild beast."

"How dare you!" Raven turned to Taber. "You're a horse thief on top of everything else."

"Come, come, Lady McClennon." He smiled. "You left your precious horse behind in Ireland, and you know how I feel about excellent horse flesh."

"I can't believe . . . how do you have the nerve . . . you horse-thieving bastard," Raven hissed, her fist clenched at her side.

"Raven," Elayne whispered, clutching at her arm. "Not here."

Raven glanced around, embarrassed as people leaving the church stopped to stare.

"I suggest you go back inside and do a little more praying," Taber said arrogantly.

"I suggest you go to hell," she shot back.

"I've already been there, my love, thanks to you," he said turning Nighthawk away. "Come, *chérie*, shall we finish our ride?"

Raven held her fist to her forehead and closed her eyes. "Don't say a word, Elayne. I know very well I acted like a fool, but I can't believe the gall of the man. That was my horse she was riding."

"What are you angry about, Raven? The fact that the duchess was riding your horse, or that she was with Taber again?"

"Both," Raven answered, "and how did you manage to become so wise so quickly?"

"I've had a good teacher," she answered, hugging Raven. "Come on, Adam and Father will be waiting for us at the Inn. We can decide on a plan of action on the way."

"A plan of action?" Raven asked as she climbed inside the carriage.

"Of course. If you want Taber O'Flynn back,

then we have to decide on the best course of action. It worked for Adam and me.''

Raven had to laugh. "Circumstances are a little different between Taber and me. Adam didn't hate you.''

"Do you think Taber would be showing up everyplace you go if he didn't still love you? He may not realize it, but I think it's obvious.''

Raven stared at Elayne. "No, I'm afraid you're wrong. He hates me, Elayne. The only reason he's showing up everyplace I go is to taunt me—to drive me crazy.''

Elayne laid her head back against the seat, a smug smile on her face. "Have it your way, Raven, but mark my word, he's torturing himself as much as he is torturing you, even if he'll never admit it.''

The Maryland Inn was famous for its Sunday midday meal. Crabs and seafood from the Chesapeake Bay were served, along with duck, pheasant, and smoked hams. Everyone who was anyone made an appearance there sometime on Sunday afternoon.

When Raven and Elayne arrived, they found Adam and Jordan in a circle of friends discussing the horse race that was to take place in a few days.

"It's an annual event," Elayne explained. "It

378

was started as part of the holiday celebration several years ago, and is considered the highlight of the season. The entry fee money and admission fees all go to charity."

"What kind of race is it?" Raven asked as they took a table next to the front window.

"It's a half-mile flat race," Adam answered. "Judge Adams's horse has won the last two years, but I'm told Captain O'Flynn plans to run that big black stallion of his this year."

Elayne glanced at her father, realizing he hadn't told Adam that Taber O'Flynn had been the man Raven was in love with.

"Raven, what are you going to order?" Elayne asked, hoping to change the subject. "I understand the flounder is excellent."

At that moment Raven saw Taber enter the hotel. "Suddenly I've lost my appetite," she said, throwing her napkin down on the table. "I have some unfinished business to take care of. If I'm not back by the time you're through, I'll meet you back at the house."

"Raven, wait," Elayne called after her. "Don't do anything foolish . . ."

"What's going on?" Adam asked.

"Father, why didn't you explain the situation to Adam?" Elayne asked in exasperation.

"I'm sorry, dear. I didn't have the opportunity. When I met Adam in the lobby, everyone was talking about the race, and then you and Raven showed up."

"Will someone tell me what you're talking about?"

"Captain Taber O'Flynn is the man Raven had been in love with in Ireland," Elayne explained.

"I'll be damned. So that's why they acted so strange to one another."

"Apparently Captain O'Flynn still believes Raven is guilty of betraying him," Elayne continued. "She believes he is here to seek revenge."

"I can't believe that," Adam protested. "He seems like a very decent fellow to me. Besides, he has become a local hero to the people of Maryland, not to mention a very rich man because of it. I can't believe he'd do anything to ruin his reputation."

"I hope you're right," Elayne sighed.

"I hope so too," Jordan agreed. "I have to admit, I have an uneasy feeling everytime he and Raven are in the same room."

Adam stared at the door leading to the lobby. "Do you think I should go after her?"

"No," Elayne said, placing her hand on his arm. "Raven still loves the man, so perhaps if they talk things out . . ."

Raven watched Taber as he asked for his key. Then as he climbed the stairs, she followed him. She let him get to his door before she walked up behind him.

"I want to talk with you, Taber."

He turned around, quickly masking the surprised look on his face. Damnit, why did her closeness still have the power to make his pulse race faster? he wondered.

"Of course, Lady McClennon. Step into my parlor," he said, moving aside. "Were you lurking in the shadows waiting for my return?"

"I was in the hotel dining room when I saw you come in," she answered curtly.

"Would you care for a glass of wine?" he asked with icy cold politeness as he poured himself a glass.

"And let you poison me?" she laughed bitterly.

"It's a wise woman who is cautious around her enemies." He raised his glass in mock salute. "What do you want to talk about?"

"I want Devil Lady returned to me. I'll buy her from you if I have to."

"Really?" He gave a short unpleasant laugh. "I'm afraid you're too late, m'lady. I gave Devil Lady to the duchess today. Women are always impressed with expensive gifts."

"You did what?" she asked, her voice rising hysterically. "She was not yours to give."

"Can you prove she was yours?" he asked, one dark eyebrow raised. "Perhaps you'd like to contact the authorities in Cork and tell them you're now living in America and have recently come across a horse you think was yours." At the look of hatred on Raven's face, he smiled. "No, I dinna' think so. You wouldn't want anyone to know about your treacherous past."

Raven's blue eyes blazed with fire. "Is this the way you intend to get your revenge, Taber O'Flynn? Do you plan to make my life miserable by staying in Annapolis to taunt me with what happened in Ireland?"

"For starters, m'lady," he said, a threat in his deep voice. "And to deprive you of everything that you want—including Faraday Farm."

She stared at him in disbelief. "Faraday Farm? What do you know about that?"

"I purchased it this morning, Lady McClennon." For some reason he didn't understand, he didn't get the pleasure he had expected from depriving her of the farm she wanted. Instead the look on her face made him feel like a heel.

"How could I ever have loved you?" she asked in bewilderment.

"Dinna' stand there and tell me you loved me," he growled. "You forget, I bear the scars of your deception!"

"And I bear the scars of yours," she said in a choked voice. She took a step toward the door, then turned back to him, tears streaming down her face. "If this is the way it is to be, then kill me now and get it over with," she whispered, offering him her throat. "I will not play this vicious game of yours any longer."

How dare she play the martyr, he thought angrily. By God, he wanted to strangle her, but that would be too quick. "Dinna' tempt me, you deceiving witch. I'd like to break every bone in your body, but that would deprive me of seeing your life in Annapolis falling down around your ears. I suffered long and slow, and so shall you."

"You're the biggest of fools, Taber O'Flynn," she whispered, "and someday you will regret your actions."

His hands went around her throat, but instead of tightening, he pulled her against him. An ugly smile crossed his face as he moved his lower body hard against hers. She was shocked as she felt him rigid with desire.

"Bitch," he whispered before capturing her mouth in a consuming kiss.

She fought against him, struggling to break his hold. When he began to unbutton her jacket, she sank her teeth into his bottom lip.

"Damn it, woman!" he swore, staring at her in disbelief as he put a handkerchief to his bleeding lip.

"Revenge can be played by two, Taber O'Flynn," she said as she backed toward the door. "Your ship should be ready in two weeks." She smiled sweetly. "If you dare launch her."

"You wouldn't sabotage your own ship. It would put you out of business," he said, a smug smile on his face.

"Wouldn't I?" she said as she left the room.

Taber picked up the glass of wine and threw it at the closed door. How the hell did he let the situation get so out of hand? She was supposed to have been scared to death. Instead she taunted him, telling him to kill her and get it over with. Damnit, why hadn't he done it, instead of letting her get the best of him. When he had put his hands around her throat, he had suddenly remembered how her skin felt like smooth silk when she was naked against him.

"She was right," he said in disgust. "I am the biggest fool!"

Jordan, Elayne, and Adam were still in the dining room when Raven reappeared. "Am I too late to eat?" she asked. "I'm suddenly famished."

Ignoring the strange look from her friends, Raven piled her plate high with food from the bowls on the table. "Adam, I have a favor to ask," she said between bites. "Your friend, the duchess, has a horse that belongs to me. Would you tell her I'm willing to pay whatever she wants to get it back. The horse is a large white mare called Devil Lady."

"I'll see what I can do," he answered, glancing at Elayne.

"And Adam, you can forget Faraday Farm. It's already been sold," she said buttering a roll.

"How did you find that out?" he asked.

"Just moments ago Captain O'Flynn informed me that he had purchased it this morning. I'll just have to get it from him," she said, taking a bite of her roll.

A concerned look passed between the three. "How do you propose to do that, Raven?" Elayne asked.

"I'm going to win it from him by beating him in a horse race," she said matter-of-factly.

"You don't mean—" Jordan choked on his drink.

"Do they have some rule against women in the race?" she asked in wide-eyed innocence.

"No, but still, you can't mean to . . . I mean, you don't think you can . . ."

"I can beat him, Jordan. Nighthawk is a fine horse, but he's a jumper. I think Devil Lady can beat him in a flat race."

"My God, I don't believe this," he laughed.

"Have faith, Jordan. If there is one thing I know, it's horses."

"Think of the interest the race will draw when word gets out Lady Raven McClennon will race," Elayne commented.

"That's right," Raven quickly agreed.

Adam pushed his chair away from the table. "I suppose I better try to get *Lady McClennon* her horse," he laughed. "I have a feeling this is going to be quite a race."

The duchess had no compunction about selling the spirited horse back to Raven. Her title gave her entrance to the best places, but she needed money to keep up appearances.

The next morning Raven appeared at the hotel as Taber was having breakfast. Dressed in a sapphire blue velvet cape trimmed in white fur, she made a stunning sight as she stormed to his side.

"Good morning, Captain O'Flynn," she said loud enough for anyone who hadn't noticed her entrance to know she was there.

Taber looked up in surprise, but said nothing. "I have a proposition for you, Captain."

"And what might that be?" he asked, silently cursing her for being so beautiful.

The room was totally silent as everyone strained to hear. "I'll bet you the ship we're building for you against Faraday Farm that I can beat you in Tuesday's race."

Taber's laughter echoed throughout the room. "You're not serious."

"I'm very serious, Captain O'Flynn. It's simple. If you win, the ship is yours free and clear. If I win, you give me Faraday Farm."

"And what do you plan to race, m'lady?"

"Don't worry about what I'm going to race, Captain. Is it a bet or not?"

"Come on, Captain, how can you refuse the little lady?" someone shouted from another table.

Taber leaned back in his chair and studied Raven. "I hate to take advantage of you . . ."

"It won't be the first time," she said, before turning around and heading for the door.

What the hell was she up to? he wondered as he watched her leave. And how the hell did she suddenly have the upperhand?

The morning of the race dawned cool and clear. Spectators crowded the crossroads where the race was to start. After hearing of the match between the notorious Captain O'Flynn and the Lady McClennon, several of the contestants dropped out, leaving only two other horses racing against them.

Raven hadn't seen Taber since the morning she had challenged him. Now she caught sight of him talking to the reporter she had hired for her newspaper. He was dressed in black riding pants tucked into black boots, and wore a bright red silk shirt. How can the devil be so handsome? she wondered bitterly.

Forcing her attention back to Devil Lady, Raven whispered in her ear. "We're going to beat them, my pretty one. Then you'll have a beautiful place to romp and play the rest of your life."

For all her earlier determination and confidence, she found herself now wondering if she really could beat Taber. She had seen what he and Nighthawk could do in a steeplechase race. Had she been a fool to think they wouldn't do as well in a flat race? she wondered.

"Riders, mount your horses," the starter announced.

Taber glanced at Raven as she mounted the large white horse. He'd been surprised to see that somehow she had managed to acquire the horse. He was beginning to realize the Lady Raven McClennon was cleverer than he had thought, but he'd be damned if he'd give her the chance to win Faraday Farm.

"Come on boy, give me a good race," he said, leaning over the neck of the black stallion. "We're going to have to put the little lady in her place."

When the gun went off starting the race, Devil Lady reared up on her hind legs, almost dumping Raven on the ground. By the time she had her calmed down, Taber had a handsome lead. Raven leaned low over the horse's neck, slowly gaining, but never able to draw alongside. The other two horses were left in their dust. She could see the finish flag ahead of them and urged Devil Lady with her whip, but it was too late. In those few brief minutes, she had lost Faraday Farm and the ship.

Nighthawk pranced proudly back toward her, his rider sitting tall and proud in the saddle. "Very good race, m'lady," he said, giving her a mock salute. "Too bad your horse was spooked at the start. I'll look forward to taking delivery of my ship."

Raven kicked Devil Lady to a gallop and headed back toward her friends. "I'm sorry," she said as she dismounted. "I really thought I could beat him."

"There's no doubt in my mind that you would have if your horse hadn't been frightened by the starting gun," Adam exclaimed. "What rotten luck."

"I never thought about that possibility." Raven shook her head. "I brought her out here every day to get her used to the land. If I'd known . . ."

"You gave it your best, Raven," Elayne said, hugging her friend. "We are all very proud of you, and more importantly we've raised a lot of money for charity."

"I'm glad to hear something good came out

of it," she said, fighting back the tears. "I'm going to ride Devil Lady back to town and rub her down there. I'll see you at the house," Raven said, anxious to be alone.

Elayne watched Taber accepting the praise of everyone around them. When he was finally alone, she walked over to where he was rubbing down the black stallion. "I hope you're proud of yourself, Captain O'Flynn."

"I beg your pardon."

"Haven't you accomplished what you came to Annapolis for? It was to punish and defeat Raven, wasn't it? Are you satisfied yet, or do you still plan to continue this game of humiliating her? Have you thought of the consequences if you push her too far, Captain? Can you live with that?"

"I'm afraid I dinna' know what you're talking about, Miss Mitchell," Taber said, returning to his chore of rubbing down the horse.

"Perhaps you should look deep down inside yourself and see if you're punishing her, or punishing yourself. I have a feeling you'll find the great Taber O'Flynn has a flaw in his character."

Taber watched Elayne Mitchell walk across the field toward Jordan Mitchell's carriage. "What the hell did she mean about pushing

Raven too far? he wondered silently. She doesn't know her very well if she thinks she'd stop fighting me.

Taber stopped in midstroke. Was that the reason he was taunting her? Was it his way of seeing her? "Hell, O'Flynn, if you're not careful, she's going to drive you crazy."

> *Revenge, at first though sweet,*
> *Bitter ere long back on itself recoils.*
> Milton

Chapter Nineteen

Taber entered the lobby of the hotel in a foul mood. Elayne Mitchell's words kept ringing in his ears. She warned him that he may have pushed Raven too far, but wasn't that what he was trying to do. He wanted to punish her for what he'd suffered because of her. But did he really want to break her? he asked himself over and over. Perhaps it was time to call it quits. He had everything she wanted. Besides, revenge wasn't as sweet as he'd thought it would be.

As he crossed the lobby, he heard a familiar Irish accent. He couldn't believe his eyes as he spotted Patrick and Molly standing at the desk.

"Patrick," he shouted. The two men embraced. "Damn, it's good to see you. And Molly, me love, ye look more beautiful than ever," he exclaimed, pulling her into the embrace.

"I'm glad to see you haven't changed, Taber. When we started asking about you, all we heard was how you were a big hero."

"Aye, we imagined all kinds of things," Patrick added.

"Come on, you must be tired," he said, picking up Molly's bag. "Charles, I'd like my friends to have the room next to mine," Taber instructed the desk clerk. "And would you send up some food."

"Right away, Captain."

As they headed for the stairs, Taber noticed Patrick walking with the aid of a cane. "What happened to you, man?"

"You dinna' know?" Patrick asked, surprised.

"No, I haven't been in touch with anyone at home, so I suppose there's a lot I have to catch up on."

"That's why we're here, Taber," Patrick said as Taber opened the door of his room.

"Taber, have you seen Raven?" Molly asked, unable to put off the inevitable any longer.

A scowl came over Taber's face. "Dinna' concern yourself with her, Molly. She has paid for her betrayal."

Molly's eyes widened in fright. "Taber, you didn't. Please tell me you didn't harm her."

"Raven manages somehow to always land

on her feet," he said bitterly. "She's living with one man and seeing another."

"Have you talked to her?" Molly asked.

"I guess you could say we've talked," he laughed bitterly. "This morning I won a ship from her, and kept her precious farm at the same time."

"Taber, Raven was not responsible for what happened to you," Molly said.

"Listen, my friends, I know you mean well, but just leave Raven to me."

"Taber, it was Brenna who betrayed you," Patrick growled. "You should have known Raven wouldn't lie to you."

"Brenna? What the hell are you talking about?"

"Brenna sold us out for money, Taber. Fergus told her about you and Raven meeting, hoping she'd turn from you to him. He had no idea she'd use it against you."

"Did she tell you this?" he asked, still not convinced.

"No, she couldn't," Patrick answered. "Walter Denseley killed her after he got the information he wanted."

"I dinna' believe this," Taber growled. "If what you're saying is true . . ."

"Taber, it was Raven who was responsible for getting you out of prison," Molly added.

Taber stared at her in disbelief, running his hand through his dark hair in frustration. "I dinna' understand any of this . . ."

"Patrick was going to explain everything to you as soon as you were out of prison, but you were unconscious, and then Patrick was shot and couldn't go with you to the ship."

"That's the reason for the cane," Taber said, shaking his head. "God, man I dinna' know."

"We had no idea that you knew where Raven was," Molly continued, "so we weren't too concerned about you knowing the truth until Patrick was recuperated. Then a few weeks later Fergus told us that May, thinking you and Raven were still lovers, had left a message at the ship telling you where her uncle was sending her."

Taber collapsed in a chair, finally realizing what they said was the truth. "She was responsible for getting me out of prison," he repeated.

"Aye, she found out what Denseley's plans were to transfer you, and then she and Fergus set up an earlier time for us to get there. She even forged papers. Everything would have gone smoothly except on the carriage ride after they had paid you a visit, Denseley tried to rape Raven. She ended up having to kill him. After that everything seemed to go awry; you being unconscious, me getting shot."

"That's why she broke down when I asked where her lover was. She thought I knew about Denseley."

"I think it's time you talked to Raven,"

Molly suggested.

Taber shook his head. "Believe me, it's too late. She told me my need for revenge would turn my life into a living hell," he laughed bitterly. "How right she was."

"If she understands why," Molly persisted.

"It doesn't matter what I say now, Molly. I've been a real bastard to her. Besides, Raven didn't waste any time surrounding herself with admirers. From the looks of it, she's quite happy with the two men who escort her every place she goes. It would be kinder for me to leave her alone."

"Where is the Taber O'Flynn we knew in Ireland?" Molly said sharply. "Are you just going to let her fade out of your life without knowing the truth?"

"All right, damnit, I'll tell her the truth, but it isn't going to do any good," Taber argued. "You both may as well come with me. Maybe she'll agree to see me if you two are there."

Raven was in the parlor talking with Elayne and Adam when Taber O'Flynn and friends were announced.

Raven stood up to tell Taber to get out of her sight when Molly appeared in the doorway.

"Molly," she exclaimed, hugging her friend. "I was so worried about you when I didn't get an answer to my letters."

"I did answer, but I'm told very little mail

gets through these days. That's why Patrick and I decided we better come and straighten out a few things."

Raven glanced over Molly's shoulder and saw Patrick standing next to Taber.

"Hello, lass. How are you?"

"Patrick, what happened to you?" she asked, noticing the cane.

"It's nothing, lass. You're looking well," he said, taking in the riding pants and suede jacket.

"Oh," she laughed, realizing how she was still dressed. "I haven't had a chance to change since racing this morning."

Taber stood back and said nothing. The warm camaraderie between Raven and his friends made him feel a twinge of jealousy. There wasn't a snowball's chance in hell that she was going to understand why he acted as he had—much less forgive him, he thought sadly.

"Taber, didn't you wish to speak to Raven alone?" Molly urged.

"Aye, if I could have a moment of your time."

"Anything you have to say to me can be said in front of my friends," Raven said curtly.

"Molly and Patrick brought me news that sheds a whole new light on what happened in Ireland."

"Really?" Raven answered in a sarcastic tone. She could see the muscle in Taber's jaw tighten. "And just what would that be?"

Taber felt uncomfortable as everyone in the room stared at him. "Damn it, Raven, I was wrong and I apologize. I learned today that Brenna was the one who betrayed me."

"Is that all?" Raven asked in a cool tone.

"I know I was a fool, Raven, and I have no defense for what I did. All I can do is ask your forgiveness."

"Forgiveness?" she shrieked. "You were out to ruin me. You gave my horse to that . . . that woman, you stole Faraday Farm from right under my nose, you've insulted and humiliated me every chance you had, and now you have the nerve to ask forgiveness. From the day you were born you've known nothing but hate and violence. I told you I didn't betray you, but you wouldn't believe me. Well, Captain O'Flynn, you have dug your own grave. You and I have nothing further to discuss."

Raven turned to Molly. "I'm sorry to be rude, but I need a breath of fresh air. I'll talk to you again soon."

Raven left a silent room, slamming the front door behind her.

"Forgive the intrusion," Taber said bowing to Elayne. "And Adam, I apologize for not having been honest with you from the first. I should have told you what the problem was between Raven and me. All I can say is Raven is a fine lady, and whether she chooses to marry you or Jordan Mitchell, you're both lucky to be friends with her.''

"Me or Jordan?" Adam laughed. "I think you're a bit confused, Taber. Elayne is the woman I'm going to ask to marry me. As for Jordan, he's been Raven's guardian at her uncle's request.''

"You mean Raven isn't romantically involved with either of you?''

"That's right. When Raven arrived in Annapolis, she made it very clear that she was still in love with the man she'd left in Ireland.''

Taber shook his head. "It seems I have been wrong about a lot of things. God, what a fool I've been.''

"Give her some time, Captain," Elayne suggested.

"I'm afraid time isn't going to solve anything, Miss Mitchell. I dinna' blame Raven for not being able to forgive me." Taber turned back to Adam. "Adam, could I impose upon you to handle some business for me?''

"Yes, of course. What can I do for you?''

"I want to turn the deed to Faraday Farm over to Raven, along with my horse. My plan had been to set up a breeding farm using Nighthawk. Perhaps she'll want to do that. I'll still want the ship I contracted for, but I'll pay the price we originally discussed.''

"Hold on, Taber, I think this is something you should discuss with Raven.''

"You and I both know that wouldn't do any good. I've made a grave mistake, Adam. A mistake that has cost me the woman I love. But I do still have a little pride left. I'll try to make up to Raven for what I've done. Then I'll leave Maryland so she can get on with her life."

"If you don't mind me saying so, Taber, I think you're making another grave mistake."

"I dinna' see where I have a choice, Adam. Raven said I had dug my own grave, and I'm afraid she was right."

"Maybe, but then again, you never know what might change a woman's mind. I have a plan, my friend. Are you willing to give it a try?" Adam asked.

"I'm willing to try anything," Taber answered.

Adam, Elayne, and Molly talked until they were blue in the face, but Raven wouldn't budge. She admitted she would probably always love Taber, but she couldn't spend the rest of her life with a man who had so little faith in those who loved him.

Plan two was put into action: Raven was alone in the house when a young man delivered a package from the goldsmith's shop.

"Do you know who sent this?" she asked.

"No, ma'am," the boy answered. "Mr. Hollaran said he wasn't at liberty to say."

"How very strange," Raven mused as she closed the door. Opening the small box, she stared in disbelief at the gold and ruby necklace she had admired at Mr. Hollaran's shop. Who would send her such an expensive piece of jewelry? she wondered.

Tucked under the velvet padding was a small note:

> Faith is believing in things when common sense tells you not to.

There was no doubt in her mind that the gift had come from Taber. He was trying to ease his conscience, she decided.

Everyday for the next week Raven received a gift, and each day there would be a message about having faith, or forgiving your enemy. A beautiful saddle trimmed in silver came one day, and the next soft leather boots. Another day a beautiful black velvet cape lined with ermine arrived, and the next day a hat and muff to match the cape.

"You have to admit, he has excellent taste," Elayne said, running her hand over the soft velvet.

"Does he really think I'm going to fall all over him because he gives me a few gifts?" Raven said disgustedly.

"More than a few," Elayne murmured, looking at the gold pendant.

Raven rubbed the fur of the cape against her face, then quickly threw it aside. "This doesn't change a thing. I will not let him hurt me again," she said, tears running down her face.

"It seems to me that you are hurting now," Elayne observed.

"Yes, but at least it's of my own doing."

Christmas morning while having breakfast with Jordan and Elayne, Raven received a message that a carriage would be sent for her at eleven o'clock to take her to her Christmas gift.

"This has gotten out of hand," she exclaimed. "I'm not going anyplace today."

"Aren't you a little curious?" Elayne asked.

"No. Nothing Taber could do would surprise me." But she was lying when she said that. She was more than a little surprised that he would go to such lengths to get her to forgive him. If she could just drop the protective shell she had put around herself . . . but she was afraid—afraid of being hurt again.

Raven changed her mind four times before the carriage arrived promptly at eleven. The driver would give her no information about their destination, only that it would not be a long trip. Reluctantly, she accepted his hand and climbed inside. The driver then placed a fur throw over her lap. *The man thinks of everything,* she thought silently as the carriage closed the door.

The carriage headed past the shipwright's shop and down Greene Street. It was only a few minutes before she realized they were traveling along the bay road toward Faraday Farm. The white board fence was the first thing she recognized. The house had a new coat of paint, and at the entrance two stone gateposts had been added.

The carriage stopped outside the gates and the driver opened the door.

"Why are we stopping here?" Raven asked.

"Those were my instructions, m'lady."

Raven accepted his hand and stepped down from the carriage. On the stone gatepost was a shiny new brass plaque that read, *Raven's Gift.*

"Merry Christmas, Raven."

Raven spun around to face Taber. "Is this your idea of a joke?"

"Hardly, Raven. It's the only way I know how to apologize."

"All the gifts in the world won't change what you've done, Taber. All you know is hate and vengeance."

"You have to understand, Raven, it's the only way of life I have ever known. If I had a woman to teach me to trust. A woman who would love me with all her heart . . ."

Oh God, she wanted to trust him. She wanted to run into his arms and tell him to never let her go, but she couldn't. "I did love you that way, Taber. I would have given my life for you, but the first time there was a question of my loyalty, you doubted that love instead of having faith. The fact that you could think I would have betrayed you and sent you to your death is unthinkable, and unforgivable. I'm sorry, Taber, but the damage has been done, and I'm afraid it cannot be erased."

"I'm sorry too, Raven. Well, you can't say I dinna' try. I'll say good-bye now and leave you to enjoy your new home."

Raven's heart skipped a beat. Could she let him walk away? "I don't want your gifts, Taber."

"Humor me, Raven. It will at least ease my conscience if you accept them."

Suddenly the air was split with the sound of cannon fire. "What the—" Taber shaded his eyes against the sun on the water. "My God, the British are just outside the harbor."

"But how—"

"I never did like long farewells, Raven, so I guess this is good-bye." Taber pulled her to him, kissing her soundly. Then he jumped on his horse and took off down the road in a cloud of dust.

"Taber, wait . . ."

Taber found the dock area in total chaos. People were running around shouting and trying to put the small fires out that had been caused by the gunpowder. Several ships in the harbor were still returning the British gunfire even though they were burning.

"Taber, I was hoping to find you," Adam shouted, trying to be heard over the din of the noise. "Where is your ship?"

"She's tied up to the dock," Taber answered. "Come on, we've got to get her out of the harbor where we can maneuver."

The gangplank had already been taken up and Taber's ship was alive with activity. Taber jumped the space between the dock and his ship with ease.

Adam hesitated for a moment. "What the hell," he said as he jumped. He balanced precariously for a moment, then finally fell forward onto the deck.

As he got up and brushed himself off, he felt the ship move beneath his feet. They had already cast off, and Taber was barking out orders. He joined him at the helm, ready to take orders like the rest of his crew.

"It looks like three British ships in the harbor and a fourth waiting about a mile off shore," Taber said as he eased *The Raven* behind one of the burning ships. "One of them looks disabled, but the other two are still doing a lot of damage."

"What are you going to do?" Adam asked.

"I'm going to capture them," Taber said matter-of-factly. "*The Raven* is equipped with sixteen six-pounders."

"Great," Adam exclaimed. "We should be able to blow them out of the water."

"We could," Taber agreed, "but that's not what we're going to do."

"Patrick, tell the men to stand ready. It's time to attract some attention."

At Taber's order, the six-pounders were shot purposely short of their mark. One of the British cruisers turned in the close quarters of the harbor and pursued *The Raven*.

Taber made the British ship think he was trying to escape, and just as planned, he came in swift pursuit. In a brilliant maneuver, he swung *The Raven* hard port just as he reached the shoals. The British ship caught unaware ran aground and stuck hard and fast.

"We'll come back for her," Taber laughed. "The other one is already in pursuit."

Adam watched in nervous excitement as the enemy ship drew closer and closer. This time they weren't heading for shallow water, and Adam was becoming concerned. "Taber, I hope the hell you know what you're doing." He could see Taber smile in the darkness, but he said nothing.

"Execute my next order by the rule of contrary," he quietly told Patrick.

"Aye, aye, Captain," Patrick smiled.

They were both crazy, Adam thought. The British ship was so close he could count the buttons on the sailors' jackets. My God, what was he doing? Adam wondered. He was letting them get too close.

As the ship drew alongside, Taber sang out loud and clear. "Hard a-port your helm. Do you want him to run aboard of us?"

As Taber had intended, the British captain overheard his command and at once responded with an order to his helmsman that normally would have been appropriate, but when *The Raven* swung hard starboard instead of port, the British captain watched in disbelief as his jib boom was run through by the privateer's fore-rigging, and then lashed to the privateer's ship.

With the British ship thus trapped, Taber and his crew demanded immediate surrender, which the British captain did.

Taber boarded his prize ship in a flash and found that her signal flags and code book had not been destroyed. He immediately ordered a signal sent to the largest of the British ships waiting about a mile off shore, announcing, "All is well. The enemy is captured."

Leaving a boarding crew on the British ship, Taber and his crew waited silently, hoping the other ship would enter the harbor to celebrate their victory.

"Do you think he's going to fall for it?" Patrick asked.

Taber stared out into the darkness. "They've extinguished all lights on board, and I canna' see a thing. Damn, I think he's slipped away. One of the other British ships must have warned them off."

"My God, man, do you realize you've captured two of them, and a third is sinking in the harbor," Adam said, slapping Taber on his back. "I've never seen anything like it. Damn I'm glad I was here. This was the most exciting thing I've ever witnessed," he exclaimed.

"Maybe you'd like to join our crew," Patrick suggested. "We can always use good men."

Taber laughed. "Adam is one of the richest men in Maryland, Patrick. I dinna' think he wants to give that up for privateering."

"From what I hear, you'll be one of the richest men in the state before long," Adam said.

"For the good it's done me," Taber laughed bitterly.

"Taber, what happened between you and Raven today?" Adam asked.

"She still turned me down, my friend. I'm not surprised. It's what I deserved."

Taber turned to his crew. "Let's take our prizes home," he shouted to the cheers of the men.

Crowds of people met Taber's ship, everyone congratulating the crew as they tied up at the dock.

409

Adam caught sight of Elayne and Raven running toward the ship. "I have another plan, Taber. I don't have a lot of time to answer questions, so just do as I ask. Go below and lie in your bunk. When Raven comes aboard, I'm going to tell her that you were injured. If her true feelings don't come out now, they never will."

"I dinna' know, Adam. I think we've had enough deception between us."

"I think you should do it," Patrick encouraged, "and you better hurry. She's almost here."

"Adam Lawrence, if I weren't so glad to see you safe and sound, I'd be furious with you," Elayne laughed as she hugged him. "When Charles told me that you had gone out on Taber's ship . . ."

Raven noticed the long faces of Patrick and Adam, and a knot formed in her stomach. "Patrick, where is Taber?"

"I'm afraid he's been hurt, Raven. We're waiting for a doctor . . ."

"Where is he?" she asked, her voice rising hysterically.

"He's in the cabin below," Adam said, "but I don't know if you should—"

Raven ran across the deck and down the

hatch. She threw open the cabin door and rushed to the bunk, kneeling on the floor beside Taber. His eyes were closed, and in the darkness of the cabin he looked pale to her. "Please don't die, Taber," she said, laying her head against his shoulder. "I want us to have a chance," she sobbed. "It can't end like this."

"Do you love me?"

Raven's head snapped up and she stared into his smiling blue eyes. "Taber," she lashed out at him.

"No more anger, love. Just now you said you wanted us to have another chance. That's what I want more than anything."

"You are not hurt?"

He stared at her, an agonizing expression on his face. "It's not a physical thing, Raven, but if you turn me away again, I shall surely die."

She stared at him, trying to decide whether to be angry or happy. "Oh Taber," she laughed. "How did I ever get mixed up with an Irishman?"

A slow smile replaced the anxious look on his face. "You're just lucky, I suppose. Do you love me?" he asked again.

Her gaze was warm with promise. "Aye, Taber O'Flynn," she sighed. "I love you more than life itself."

Taber pulled her down on top of him. "I need you, Raven my love. God, how I need you," he swore, placing kisses all over her face.

"Since this was a conspiracy between you and those rascals on deck, they wouldn't dare interrupt us, would they?" she asked, running her hand inside his shirt.

"They wouldn't dare," he whispered, capturing her mouth.

TANTALIZING ROMANCE
From Zebra Books

CAPTIVE CARESS (1923, $3.95)
by Sonya T. Pelton

Denied her freedom, despairing of rescue, the last thing on Willow's mind was desire. But before she could say no, she became her captor's prisoner of passion.

LOUISIANA LADY (1891, $3.95)
by Myra Rowe

Left an orphan, Leander Ondine was forced to live in a house of ill-repute. She was able to maintain her virtue until the night Justine stumbled upon her by mistake. Although she knew it was wrong, all she wanted was to be his hot-blooded *Louisiana Lady*.

SEA JEWEL (1888, $3.95)
by Penelope Neri

Hot-tempered Alaric had long planned the humiliation of his hated foe's daughter. But he never suspected she would become the mistress of his heart, his treasured, beloved *Sea Jewel*.

SEPTEMBER MOON (1838, $3.95)
by Constance O'Banyon

Ever since she was a little girl, Cameron had dreamed of getting even with the Kingstons. But the extremely handsome Hunter Kingston caught her off guard, and all she could think of was his lips crushing hers in a feverish rapture beneath the *September Moon*.

VELVET CHAINS (1640, $3.95)
by Constance O'Banyon

Desperate for money, beautiful Valentina Barrett worked as the veiled dancer, Jordanna. Then she fell in love with handsome, wealthy Marquis Vincente and became entangled in a web of her own making.

Available wherever paperbacks are sold, or order direct from the Publisher. Send cover price plus 50¢ per copy for mailing and handling to Zebra Books, Dept. 2115, 475 Park Avenue South, New York, N.Y. 10016. Residents of New York, New Jersey and Pennsylvania must include sales tax. DO NOT SEND CASH.